YOU
Right Now
Is the
BEST

Contents

Epigraph

"Everywhere is somewhere to someone."
—Zach Bryan

Dedication

for those who need a reminder
to live life a little slower

Playlist

1. *Matilda - Harry Styles*

2. *You're Gonna Go Far - Noah Kahan, Brandi Carlile*

3. *Ghost Town - Sam Barber*

4. *The Archer - Taylor Swift*

5. *There Was This Girl - Riley Green*

6. *CWJBHN - Jake Scott*

7. *Ride The Wave - Russell Dickerson*

8. *Mine for the Summer - Jameson Rodgers*

9. *Electric Touch (feat. Fall Out Boy) - Taylor Swift*

10. *Everybody Loves Her - Vincent Mason*

11. *Maybe We Do - Zach Seabaugh*

12. *Summertime Blues - Zach Bryan*

13. *I Have Questions - Camila Cabello*

Sensitive Content Warning

<u>this book includes:</u>
the mention of the death of a loved one (before the story starts)
substance use (alcohol use)
age gap relationship (12 years)
explicit language
sexually explicit scenes

***

should you choose to make this a closed-door read,
feel free to skip over **chapter 24** and **chapter 32**
but please note you may miss some of the plot by doing so.

Chapter 1

Lucy

I always believed the act of tossing graduation caps at the end of a commencement ceremony only occurred in the movies. If that was the case, then I was the main character in my own blockbuster film and I never wanted the credits to roll.

Every single person in the auditorium screeched and yelped as the announcer declared us The Class of 2023.

Throughout the auditorium, a medley of caps were launched above while rainbow confetti trickled on down. Some chucked theirs up so high you'd think they were trying to hit the light beams on the ceiling. Others didn't go higher than a foot above their head.

But I slowly removed my cap and held it out in front of me.

I skimmed my fingertips over the finest black velvet, then gathered the silk tassel in the palm of my hand. Every fiber of my body burned, and for a moment, I was lost in my own line of thinking. It was as if I was falling into the pile of quicksand known as reality and I was being swallowed whole. My future was in the palm of my hands—*literally*.

"My Lucy! How do you feel?" I was brought back down to earth as my best friend, Gracie, shouted at me over the roars. I picked my head up and searched for her voice in the row behind me.

I gave her a faint smile as I gripped my diploma tight to my chest. What was I to say? I was thrilled, of course. I was relieved, tired, scared, but one thing for certain, I was ready. I had never felt more ready and motivated over something in my life.

My words were scrambled like the thoughts inside my brain, so much so that I mumbled a concoction of strangled noises and gave Gracie two awkward thumbs up.

I wove through the displaced chairs and briskly hugged those in passing, commemorating our solidarity. There was the guy with the Buddy Holly glasses that I often saw at the bookstore and the group of girls who played with a bunsen burner in the back of chem lab one year of undergrad. Whether I truly knew them or not, we were all in the same boat and we were the group that didn't sink. We swam. And now we are going to swim straight into a much larger body of water.

Working towards my medical school degree was the longest, most rewarding time of my life. Even after countless nights of having my hand glued to a coffee pot, and welcoming the sunrise before I had even fallen asleep, I never once regretted choosing this life.

The array of feelings was paralyzing.

I wish I could bask in it for a sliver of a moment. But like clockwork, I immediately began thinking about what was next. *There's no rest for the wicked.* I had a residency program that was starting up in the fall and I cannot lose my touch now.

Just because the summer left room for a break, didn't mean I would take one.

"Love to hear it!" Gracie shrieked as I reached her.

Her golden hair swept over her shoulders as she skipped away through the crowd. Her enthusiasm was contagious. It was almost powerful enough to break the mask made of stress that I'd been sporting. *Almost.*

There was a natural, gravitational pull towards Gracie when we first met.

It was the first week of classes in my second year of med school. Everyone scrambled around the room, trying out the different corners with the best view of our professor or finding the airflow from the air conditioner. I had thought I was going to drop the class altogether when I found myself next to a guy who had never heard of deodorant...or closed-toe shoes.

By the third day—and what felt like the millionth shift around—she and I were bonding over stickers of Joey and Chandler that I had on the back of my laptop. We never went through the awkward stage of smiling in passing or wondering if we should say 'hi' or not. We just knew we were going to be best friends from the start.

And despite being on separate ends of the social butterfly spectrum, we found out that we mesh well. Instantaneously, she became—and forever will be—the Rachel Green to my Monica Geller. Anatomy was the only class that was able to fly by or seem manageable. And I had our friendship to thank for that.

We shared notes, brought each other heaps of caffeine, and eventually, we started hanging out on the weekends and making plans outside our study sessions. Wherever there was one of us, the other wasn't too far behind. We have been inseparable since the beginning.

Trailing a few steps behind, I watched Gracie mingle with her girlfriends. They were all tall, tan, and blonde—they resembled angels on Earth and were essentially clones of one another. These girls could hypnotize anyone with their sweet laugh. Any time spent around them, you found yourself feeling a little lighter and brighter.

"Are we ready to get going? Our ride is on the other side of the parking lot," I say, holding my phone screen up to them.

All six of us piled in an Uber XL and drove toward Gracie's childhood home. After a short ten-minute drive, we arrived outside of a house that has become one of my stomping grounds over the last couple of years. A tunnel of clapping and congratulatory praises welcomed us. I nodded their way and even mouthed out my *thank you*'s, but I quickly became overwhelmed.

I made a beeline for the sliding glass door where I could steer clear of the commotion. It was my first chance to finally breathe today. Only seconds later, Gracie's mom, Fran, approached me with sparkles in her eyes. Her dad joined us with tears in his.

"My little girl. It feels like only yesterday I was pushing her on the swing in this very backyard," Sam said while looking over at their tire swing covered in spiderwebs, held together by a disintegrating rope.

It was as if he replayed the memories of her adolescent years as he watched her move through the backyard, telling party guests about her summer plans before her intern year was set to start. Fran gave him a sympathetic look while rubbing his arm and now holding back tears of her own.

It made sense that they were the people I was surrounded by on this momentous occasion. The Evans family, their household in its entirety, always welcomed me with open arms. I never expected to share this day with my mother. No matter what I did, I couldn't seem to make her proud of me while growing up.

I learned quickly to be my own cheerleader. Along the way, I found people who were more than excited to be on the sidelines for me. That mattered most—not the person who birthed me and hasn't spoken much to me in almost twenty years. But I'm sure she'll find out about today through tagged photos on social media and pretend like she found out straight from the source.

Gracie waved me over and I swiftly maneuvered away from spending my night with her parents. I love them to pieces, but I would have been trapped in an endless conversation that resulted in taking out photo albums—ones that I've already seen—at one point or another.

Gracie's boyfriend, Asher, standing on the other side of her, took a swig of his beer and swiftly slapped her ass before letting his hand rest there. He never once looked in my direction, and I didn't blame him. I gave him a noticeable side-eye once as I approached the group.

They have been together for almost six years, though I don't think he ever deserved six *minutes* of her time. Gracie Evans was the girl that deserved everything and more, she just needed to realize it herself. And being with a guy who aspired to be a "finance bro" was not going to help matters.

"So, what's the plan for tonight?" Gracie turned to face me, moving us to the drink table.

"I thought this was the plan?"

Asher scoffed at my question and motioned to the bartender for another beer.

"You're silly, L.C... I love my parents and all, and this is a great party that they put together..." She looked around at the Pinterest-worthy table with food labels that somehow relate to the medical field. "But I want to do something with just you guys."

I groaned in all of my antisocial glory as I picked up one of the little sample cups titled *Vitamins* and popped a couple of gummy bears in my mouth.

The distinct chatter and giggles from the girls behind us rang in my ears while they all took videos clinking their drinks together. I leaned in towards Gracie where only she could hear me. "Alright, but when you say *you guys,* is *he* included in this outing?" I cocked my head in Asher's direction.

She clicked her tongue with a teasing nudge at my arm to follow. "Come on, it will be fun. I promise. You gotta do something for yourself every once in a while!"

"What are you talking about? My trip back home is something for myself."

Granted, I was heading back to roll up my sleeves and get my childhood home ready to be put on the market. Nonetheless, it's still something I wouldn't normally do. It's far from my usual extracurriculars.

Reading books, textbooks, and reference books was more my speed. Studying and being hired to help others study was more my speed. Getting sweaty and coming face to face with a life I've put off too long was *not* my speed.

She scoffed. "That is *not* the same thing. We're doctors now! *You* are a doctor now, Little Lucy Lou...That deserves to be celebrated. Come on, let's celebrate together!"

How her words somehow made me feel like an adult and a child simultaneously was almost alarming. "Little Lucy Lou" was seemingly a doctor, at least that's what's printed on an eight-and-a-half by eleven piece of cardstock. And that's when a terrifying thought washed over me: Was I nothing more than a little girl playing pretend doctor?

"Sorry, guys, but I don't know. I think I am going to turn in early. We will celebrate another time, another way. You guys have fun whatever you end up doing!" I gave Gracie a quick parting kiss on the cheek and waved to the girls. "I have a six a.m. flight, and you know me... I like to get to the airport three hours early."

Alright, maybe not literally, but I sure as hell was never going to be the person who rushed through TSA or shouted at the gate attendant to hold the plane.

Gracie flashed me a pout, but nodded softly, accepting the inevitable. This was a fight she knew she was not going to win. She turned back to the group while I snuck out the back gate, deliberately avoiding any more conversations. I've never been one to add to an already busy mind, so I opted for a self-care type of night with eye patches and fuzzy socks to celebrate.

Within a few blocks, I was already walking up the front porch to the townhouse that Gracie and I shared, and I practically scurried into my room the second the door shut behind me. I kicked off my heels in opposite directions, let my dress pool at my feet, and climbed under the covers.

Right as I found the best position, Gracie's cat, Paul Varjak, pushed his way into my room. His long, white fur shed from his coat as he jumped onto my bed and pushed his head beneath my hand to pet him. While he is *technically* her cat, I've convinced myself he prefers "Aunt Lucy" a tad more, being that he and I are the homebodies of this household.

Instead of hitting the sack, I naturally reached for one of the many books stacked on my nightstand. I contemplated between my pick from last week's bookstore trip and the Jane Austen novel I've read a million times over but landed on the book that's been sitting on my e-reader for months.

My new read and I had a long night ahead of us.

Chapter 2

Lucy

It was 5:34 a.m. and I considered ordering yet another triple espresso.

Just when I thought I'd become immune to an excessive amount of caffeine, I started to fight with the growing urge to shake my leg or fidget with the lid of my coffee. There wasn't a lot of angst building up to this trip, not until I drove to the airport this morning.

Then it hit me like a ton of bricks.

I mindlessly scrolled through tagged photos on social media from the night before to distract from my racing thoughts. But then the overhead announcement system called out my boarding group and brought me back to reality within a matter of minutes.

I gathered up my duffle bag and backpack and submerged myself into the herd of other scrambling passengers. Standing behind a woman not too much older than me, she started a conversation with the people beside her.

"Is your final destination Connecticut?" the woman asked so naturally as she pulled the strap of her carry-on over her shoulder.

"Oh, no," the others responded. A grin was plastered on their faces as they began to speak. "Just a layover, we are spending our summer abroad."

I didn't make it a habit to eavesdrop, but I'd be lying if I said I didn't sometimes pretend to have music playing through my headphones so I could hear peoples' side conversations—ya, know...naturally.

But right now, they're right in front of me, talking at a normal volume, and my headphones are at the bottom of my backpack. Was I not supposed to listen in?

"Wow, that's exciting!" The first lady sounded genuinely intrigued, so much so that they all grew closer in distance to carry on their conversation. Eventually, they pulled out their phones and shared their social media.

I had no issue talking with others, really I didn't. My entire academic career, and soon-to-be professional career, required me to fall right into conversation with people I'd never met.

But out in the wild, in places like the grocery store or this case the airport, I could never strike up a conversation so easily.

As the line got shorter and the plane boarded, I found my seat in the third row of First Class—a little graduation gift to myself—and settled in. It's quieter as opposed to Economy. Comfier, too.

I snapped a photo wearing my neck pillow and sent it off to Gracie with the caption, "told you I know how to have fun."

Already unpacking the contents of my carry-on, I took out a miniature notebook and a book that's been lodged smack dab in the middle of my bedside stack since freshman year of undergrad. I clicked my pen a couple of times, tested it by drawing squiggly lines in the upper right-hand corner, and got to work on my summer to-do list.

The idea of going into the summer blindly frightened me. I had to familiarize myself with taking each day as it came, a foreign concept to say the least. Every day—every week—was planned out on the first of every month. Now, it was the end of

May, and I had no idea what I was walking into. I was destined to fly by the seat of my pants this summer, and "disaster" was the first word that came to my mind.

I'm excited, terrified, eager—but I don't know if I can say that I'm ready. At least not for this. How is anyone ever ready to face uncertainty?

"Excuse me," an older gentleman said, nodding at the seat beside me. I shifted my legs off to the side so he could squeeze by. He had countless creases in the corners of his eyes and plenty of freckles that made it clear he'd been kissed by the sun more than once. "Have you read that before?" he asked, pointing to my book with his free hand. The other started to pour out a miniature-sized bottle of vodka into a short cup of orange juice.

"Oh, uh," I coughed out, then adjusted my belongings on the tray in front of me. I shifted them straight, lining them up perfectly with one another. As if I was making a mess when I knew that I wasn't. "No, I haven't. But here's hoping the next five hours give me enough time to make a dent."

I fidgeted with the rips in the spine and the bent-up corners of the cover.

I had bought it second-hand at a used bookstore in my early years of college. I was fresh off the plane from Connecticut, with no money to my name, and all of my books took up residency in boxes and bins inside my childhood home. That wasn't going to deter me, all I wanted was to find a book I could escape into.

The man held his plastic cup up for a distant cheers. "Here's to hoping," he repeated after me, and said, "That's one of my favorite reads of all time."

I smiled into my lap, then slipped the notebook back into my bag. I flipped open to the first chapter and got straight to reading. We were both silent for the remainder of our flight, except for the quick grumbles in passing for bathroom trips or when we went our separate ways at the end. There was a sense of comfortability that he brought to me and I didn't even catch his name.

Something about literature being able to bring people together was comforting. It was familiar.

***

I stepped out of the airport and made my way down to the rental car port. All of the stress and worry that ran through my body was relieved once the scents of Connecticut hit my bloodstream.

A summer in New England was exactly what I needed. I drove further into that daunting uncertainty, I drove further into Rider.

Suddenly, I was seventeen again in a town I couldn't wait to get out of. I rolled down my window and let the smell of beach roses and salt air from the seaport dance throughout the car. I passed by the storefronts and traveled the main road. People filtered in and out of the shops and sat at the small tables out front of the coffeehouse. Muscle memory kicked in, and out of instinct, I turned down a long dirt road.

An invisible string pulled me toward Hummingbird Lake, a place I'm forever tied to.

There was no question about it—coming here was as natural as breathing. I spent more time here than I ever did at home.

The lake water and the summer breeze hit my face as I climbed out of the Mini Cooper I managed to rent for the summer. I walked in the front door of the grill that looked out over the lake, and the entryway bell rang like it always had before.

Just like that, the echoic memories all flooded back. Except, this was *not* the place that I remembered.

The two-top tables were replaced with light brown leather booths with metal plate-top tables, the lighting was certainly warmer, and all of the quirky knick-knacks and family photos that once lined the walls were simply gone.

The real kicker was there's now a nameplate above the entrance outside.

The Hideout: Bar and Grill.

This was more of a place I wanted to hide from.

An old-school jukebox was positioned near the door, and a fireplace was centered on the back wall.

This was *not* Gus Dennings' restaurant with the weirdly named sandwiches and fluorescent lights—the place he never bothered to name. The charm of the place was that you'd get a headache immediately upon walking in, but you didn't care because you felt welcomed—you felt at home.

No, now it had a name; there was an identity beyond whatever you wanted it to be.

I walked over to the bakery case. Thankfully, it's the one thing that hasn't changed. Pies and pastries, cakes, and cookies were stacked in neat rows.

I searched behind the counter and peeked through the kitchen window, but nothing. A brown dog perked themselves up from their curled position by the register while the cook on the line gave a quick smirk before returning to his job.

A cook? Someone who wasn't Gus. There was no way I'd get used to that.

Gus took care of the cooking, while his wife, Leanne, was in charge of the baking. They are the heart and soul here, the best duo I ever knew. Even with her confections right in front of me, and the smell of Gus' potato salad wafting through the vents, nothing felt the same.

There was no sight of them at all.

I turned on the balls of my feet, knowing I'd catch either of them during my time here. I had the whole summer, after all. In an instant, I smacked right into the jukebox. The beginning instrumentals of Alan Jackson's *Don't Rock the Jukebox* started to play.

How fucking fitting.

Steam filled my cheeks as I slammed my palms down on all sorts of buttons in a frenzy. I realized there was no way to stop it. I either chose another song or waited for this one to end. Numerous songs from Chris Stapleton's discography flipped through, each only a second long before the jammed buttons played the first few chords of *Man, I Feel Like a Woman* by Shania Twain.

I didn't know if I wanted to start line dancing, or if I wanted to run and never show my face again.

I chose the latter.

I booked it for the front door but was intercepted with a hard chest to the face.

He swung a white bar towel over his shoulder, then stepped around me. He gave the jukebox one swift kick to the side accompanied by a low groan that escaped his mouth. The music stopped immediately, and the dog whimpered as the racket died down.

I pressed the palm of my hand to my forehead as I turned to face him.

He had kind eyes and a nice-looking jawline. I know I'd been gone for a while, but Rider didn't tend to produce men who looked like *that*.

"That happens sometimes." He snickered, then the corner of his mouth lifted only slightly as he held back a smile.

I couldn't believe that he found amusement in this fiasco... While I couldn't do anything besides shrink into myself. He ran his fingers through his tousled sandy hair and flashed me a grin as he moved us off to the side and out of the main walkway. The few customers that have been seated since I first got here were stealing glances in my direction in between bites of their food.

"Sit anywhere, guys," he shouted over my head as a family of four walked in. They guided themselves past us to an empty table.

"I am so sorry about that," I spoke into the ground and began fidgeting with my chipped nail polish. My legs started to tremble from pure embarrassment, I couldn't control it. And I sure as hell couldn't bother to make eye contact.

He looked down at my hands, then back at me. He placed his hand on the tip of my shoulder. "Listen, it's okay," he said, then covered my hand with his, stopping my restless movement.

He pulled his hand away like he had just grabbed for a cast iron skillet and huffed out a shaky breath. I shot my eyes up at him and that's when I noticed his cheeks had turned a light pink tinge.

"Sorry, er," he stammered out. "Like I said, that happens. No need to feel bad about it." He coughed over his shoulder. A little tit-for-tat moment, I didn't feel *as* terrible knowing that he felt equally—or at least close to—embarrassed as I did right now.

I slowly nodded then headed for the door once more. Determined to make it out without a scratch this time.

"Was there something I can help you with?" he called out after me.

"No, nope," I quickly explained with my hand on the doorknob but kept my sights on the lake. "Think I got the wrong place." *That's putting it lightly.*

I fumbled my way out the door but promptly stopped at the edge of the wrap-around porch. Waiting for my blood pressure to regulate and to kick the top ten country hits of the nineties out of my head, I looked back through the windows. I had hoped I'd find Gus, Leanne—or someone or something of familiarity—in there.

I hoped that maybe the last five minutes were all a big, terrible dream.

But I didn't. And it wasn't.

Life was always meant to move on after I left, and I didn't expect it not to, but the idea of Rider being a place I no longer knew frightened me. What if I've been gone for too long, that there was nothing familiar anymore?

Chapter 3

Sawyer

My eyes were stuck on the front door where the scent of gardenia and citrus lingered. She had a slight skip in her step as she made her way down the porch. The copper shade of strands of hair that framed her face flew off to the side, moving with the ways of the wind.

"Wow," I muttered so low that I thought only I could hear.

"She's a looker, ain't she?" Gus said as he emerged cautiously from the back office.

"Who?" I coughed out. But I knew exactly who he was talking about. I've never seen her in here before. Or anyone that looked like her, for that matter. The faint mole that sat above her permanent pout, her sea-glass green eyes... They were a form of art.

Gus nodded in the direction of the door, "Don't play those games with me, boy. You know 'who' I'm talking about. She's been out in Arizona for the last eight years. That would be Lucy Collins. One of the sweetest souls that has ever walked along Hummingbird Lake." There was a gleam in his eyes. He handed me a stack of opened envelopes. "Here are the RSVPs for this weekend's opening. My bad, I mean the *Re-Opening*. You know, it's going to get a little confusing if you keep me around here doing all of your dirty work."

I let out the breath I seemed to be holding in since she walked in here and wiped the thin layer of sweat that formed on the palm of my hands on my jeans. Without a doubt, I blacked out the second she caught my eye.

I fanned through the pile of mail Gus passed off to me, hoping to see a certain return address, and snickered to myself when I didn't. I knew that I wouldn't. But that didn't stop my heart from sinking to the furthest parts of my body, convinced that maybe, just maybe, I'd be proven wrong.

"Yup, that's me, never letting you leave," I said dryly. "This will always be your place to some extent, you know that," I continued, but he shrugged nonchalantly.

Almost two years to the day, I bought the no-named restaurant from Gus and Leanne, and dove head-first into the re-modeling process. Trying to keep the recognizable atmosphere was important to me, but so was creating a place where people would associate with *me*.

Doing that, though, and hoping that it'd take well, was tricky.

With every paint swatch, down to the crown molding and baseboards, I was thinking about whether my choices would be questioned. Whether I'd be questioned.

I spent my summer vacations in high school at the family house across the lake. When we weren't boating around or doing flips off the dock, I was running over here to Gus' with my friends and cousins to rummage through his ice cream freezer. A bunch of teenagers, sweaty and soaked in lake water, tumbled in here and Gus never gave us a hard time.

He sat back, laughed, and more times than not, let us go without paying. Gus was probably the only one who welcomed—at least tolerated—our out-of-town antics. While we headed back to New Haven as we turned the calendar over to September, the memories and magic that happened here planted roots.

Life was simple, it was meaningful here.

Everyone knew everyone, and everyone cared about those in their path. Not a lot of borrowing sugar and town get-togethers down in the city.

While I was off at college, they had removed the ice cream freezer and that's when I realized it had all changed. My life, that is. Something so simple as an ice cream freezer from the seventies in a slow town held all of my innocence. Once it was gone, so was the ability to hide behind my younger years.

"Besides," I continued, "after this weekend, I think it will be evident that you no longer run things around here."

He rolled up a nearby newspaper and swiped it through the air as if he were going to swat it at me. We let out a hoarse laugh in unison as I grabbed it from him, throwing it on the counter in front of us. I scanned the floor, admiring the blood, sweat, and tears I put into this place.

Gus and Leanne had tried to keep up with the changing times. Updated appliances, the minimalist look; the whole nine yards. But it started to look more like an old shack in a ghost town by the end of it all.

The place I remembered was disappearing more and more, and I felt myself hurting and aching as if it were a loss.

I stripped the dingy carpet, replaced the booths, and knocked down a wall that revealed a covered-up fireplace. Why a pioneer stone fireplace was covered up was beyond me. But I promised to keep Leanne's dessert case, which it kept stocked with her delicious creations daily. They are a delicacy in this town and I wanted expectations to remain the same for the most part.

The joy that Gus and Leanne were able to bring into people's lives for over forty years was admirable. And I was certain to be intentional with my updates.

I felt safe here, I felt at home here. Everyone did and they made sure of that, and the name change is an ode to just that.

This is the place we all went to hide and where we found shelter. It's a place for starting over and a place of escapism. It was The Hideout long before I made the name change.

The small-town business hours were an adjustment in itself when I moved here. I had never known of a restaurant closing before 10 p.m. And that's calling it—places only stayed open that late if it was the night of a football game down at the high school or the drama department had a production running and wanted to give people a place to go afterward.

Other than that, nothing was open past eight.

We extended hours and shifted over to a bar-only atmosphere after sunset; we became the only spot in Rider to stay open late enough to see the moon at its peak. The infamous desserts go back in the walk-in and the tables are cleared of the breakfast and lunch menus. Instead, a simple, short menu of appetizers and mixed drinks was in its place.

The switch-up initially received some side-eyes from locals, but there were no bars in the heart of Rider. A nightlife was nonexistent unless you drove down to the seaport or into the city.

This gave bikers or singles on their first date a place to hang out, a place to belong. The ones that didn't necessarily feel like they fit in anywhere else in town.

"I have to step out and call Beau, gotta make sure he has the influx of alcohol added to our usual order. Can't have a charcuterie and cocktail night without cocktails."

"How involved is this going to be that you need to call an alcohol distributor for an extra order?" Gus cocked an eyebrow.

"Nothing major, and nothing extra. It's what I usually order, except maybe a couple more cases. I just want it to be a great turnout. Mel has put in a lot of work."

"She sure has. She's taken over the kitchen counters and dining table. But she likes this sort of thing."

Gus' granddaughter moved in with him once she graduated from college, right around the time that I made the move to Rider permanently. She started working at The Hideout and is now the best manager and friend I have ever known. I owed her my life... and my sanity.

"Let's go, Billy." I patted the side of my leg, motioning for the pup asleep at my feet to follow. His whole body started to wag before he galloped out the front door.

He chased after a flock of ducks waddling around the lake while I made the call. Just as I was walking down the front steps, a cherry red k10 rolled into the driveway blaring pop punk music—my cherry red k10.

"You need gas," Mel hollered out the window.

Killing the ignition, the music cut out, and she climbed out of the truck. She traveled around to the other side to retrieve many flower bouquets from Bird's Nest, the farmers market down the street. She tossed the keys towards me at the speed of light, I barely caught them in the webs of my fingers.

She approached me, adjusting the box in her hand. "Who ya calling?"

"Don't worry about it." I paused for a beat while she glared up at me through her blunt bangs. I let out a sigh, I could never actually lie to Mel. I finally said, "I'm calling Beau."

"Oh, no need. I talked to him this morning. We're all set. I even ordered an extra case of bourbon just for you, big guy." She patted the center of my chest.

I hung up before the call connected.

"Need help with that?"

"It's the twenty-first century, I got it," she said with a wink as she walked up onto the porch.

Instead of placing my phone back in my pocket, I dialed up another number in my contacts. One... Two... Three rings... *Annnd, straight to voicemail.* Just as I figured.

"Hey, it's me. Uh, I mean, it's Sawyer. Look, there's this small event I have going on this weekend at the lake. I'd love for you guys to stop by even if it's a short trip to check out the place. I know it's been a while since you've been up here." I paused. I didn't want to hang up, but there wasn't much left to say. It's been some time since I last spoke with my grandfather. "Anyway, call me back when you get the chance."

I didn't expect him to answer, and maybe I didn't even want him to, but part of me still hoped that he would have.

When I graduated from college, it was straight to the lion's den with my grandfather and his mayoral staff. From dusk to dawn, my tie was taut against my neck. Suffocating me, restraining me from using my voice. I did all the usual intern and assistant work. I thrived in it. And I did it all while wearing a smile. Never once complaining.

At the time, I didn't think there was anything to complain about.

I had helped him prepare for retirement and even assisted my dad in getting ready to campaign for a term of his own. But before the night we were going to announce my father's run, my parents booked a one-way ticket to Europe and gave my grandfather a big *fuck you*, leaving him high and dry.

Instead of passing the baton to someone outside of the Banks family name, my grandfather decided to re-campaign for mayor. He said he didn't trust anyone else to run things.

I felt bad considering the circumstances, so I stepped in and was willing to step up. I opened my big mouth and said I would campaign for the next term. The color had returned to my grandfather's face and all was right in the world again—until it wasn't.

I had a front-row seat to seeing just how corrupt and vindictive he truly was, and how much it tore up genuine relationships. On the day I turned thirty, I had an existential crisis. It meant I was of legal age to actually run. It was all words before. Promising to become the next elected mayor of New Haven was something that seemed so far off. *Until it wasn't.*

Now, it could become a reality. And I didn't know if I wanted it to be *my* reality anymore. The pressure was on more than it ever was before. Heck, I didn't even know if the city wanted me. They worshiped the ground my grandfather walked on, believing he could do no wrong.

But I have never been the type to fall in line with the other sheep.

I shuffled my feet through the dirt, making my way up the porch as Mel slapped down one of the remaining boxes on the patio seating.

"Do you plan on leaving anything for me to do?"

She hummed as she tapped the tip of her chin. "Probably not. Just show up and look pretty."

I grumbled and rolled my eyes. "Fine. So, what do I owe you for all of this?"

She waved me off.

"Get over yourself. Seriously, give me a number."

She cocked her hand on her hip. "You're not the only one excited to make something new out of this place, ya know. I told him he should have sold, remodeled, *something*, back when I was sixteen. That was like…" she started counting out on her fingers, "twelve years ago. And nothing. Not until you marched in here, that is. Then all of a sudden he was signing away his most prized possession."

"I did not *march*. These boots are heavy. I walk heavy, that's all." I reached behind myself and pulled out my wallet. "Now give me the invoice or something."

A smirk scribbled across her face as she, too, pulled out her wallet. She waved my business credit card in front of my face. "No need," she said with a devilish grin before slithering inside.

"First my truck, then my card. I'm taking all of the keys away from you!" I shouted out after her.

Chapter 4

Lucy

I passed by Gus' cottage which was two down from mine and had every urge to pull over and bang on his door. To talk to him, to hug him. Almost like I was programmed to do so. Instead, I drove down the road that led to the very last cottage.

The unevenness of the pathway was not going to give the Mini Cooper an easy time this summer. The scratching from small pebbles and dirt beneath was loud enough that I'd believe it was shooting up through the floorboard.

All of the cottages were close enough in distance that only a couple of rows of hedges and narrow side yards separated us from our neighbors. But from the main road, we each had a long driveway that convinced us that we were pushed back into our own secret world.

Oh, to be back at the Hillside Cottages.

Each cottage was practically the same, and the landscaping was predictable. Vibrant green grass in the front and back yards, and flower bushes lined the walkways and bordered the house. I loved the sense of knowing what to expect from the Hillside Cottages.

They sat back on the other side of the woods and were adjacent to the creek that wraps around and leads into Hummingbird Lake. White-washed shiplap runs throughout every main room accentuated with low-hanging natural wood beams and floorboards.

And I got to call the fourth one on the left my home, or the *Collins Cottage* as my grandmother Tiffany and I liked to refer to it. At least I did. I haven't considered any of this to be home for a while now.

In a few short months, I guess it won't be.

I didn't create any expectations when planning my return home. But knowing an instant feeling of calmness had not crossed my mind. It was almost as if being back in Rider was enough and everything else in my life would work itself out.

The same way it used to.

There was a time when my mother lived here with us. It was when I was young and she was focusing on the early days of becoming a lawyer. But once her bank account reflected her new success, we moved out.

I had gone with her initially, but you wouldn't have guessed it. She dropped me off here enough on the weekends that the cottage was more of a home to me than anywhere else. Soon enough, it became weeks at a time because it was easier. Whatever that meant.

My mother found herself in the city more times than she was in Rider for her cases. Sometimes she decided to stay down there because it was more convenient. *Being away from her home and her daughter was more convenient.* Where her career was concerned, nothing else mattered to her.

I got tired of never knowing where I was going to stay, or for how long, so at the ripe age of nine years old, I told her that I was moving into the cottages full-time. My grandmother was beyond excited to have me while my mom didn't even bat an eye or look up from her laptop to acknowledge her child—I had a backpack filled to the brim slung over my shoulder that housed the only clothes I bothered to keep at my mom's for the spare time I was there.

Even when she was back checking on her condo every so often in later years, she never bothered to visit. She hated the slow life that Rider provided and tried to leave just as fast as she would arrive.

I was more than content with calling the cottages home for as long as I lived. But when my grandmother passed away, only a week after my high school graduation, I promised myself I would go off to college like she wanted for me. And I promised myself that I'd never come back. I couldn't. My send-off into the real world, my closure, was knowing that she was with my grandpa Tuck again and I was going to make her proud. That's all that mattered to me.

By the skin of my teeth, I made the deadline of accepting the offer for the fall semester within hours. I packed everything that I could into my two suitcases, bought a one-way ticket, and never looked back.

Until now.

I stood at the front door like I had many times before, but the air between me and the house's foundation suddenly felt eerie. The ghost of a life that was no more was waiting in line, waiting to enter uncertainty alongside me. The shutters and the door frame were painted the same white dove color they'd always been. Except now they were chipping away at the joints. I picked away at an already empty spot beside the doorbell. I lodged the key into the lock, the one I kept on my key ring after all these years, and opened the door.

A gust of cold wind brushed along my skin. Straightaway, goosebumps formed on my forearms. The tapping of the suitcase wheels on the flooring competed with the thoughts inside my head.

Visions of being curled up in the corner breakfast nook on Sunday mornings with my grandmother flooded my brain. The smell of bear claws and coffee cake seeped through the crown molding and she and I were arguing over me drinking coffee at such a young age. All of it danced around me on re-play. Hypnotized by memories of another life, I barely noticed that my eyes were swelling up until I felt the warmth of a tear trickle down my cheek.

I pulled at the back door. The dampened door jam gave me resistance, I had to yank it towards me a couple of times before it finally budged. The patio boards creaked beneath my feet when I walked along it. But if you were careful, you could walk along the third board as if it were a balance beam and no one would hear a thing.

After she had gone to bed, I'd sometimes sneak out here and sit along the creek. Not to meet someone in secret, or leave for the night, but I'd sit at the end of the porch and listen to the rustling of the water and the chirping of the crickets. It was white noise while I delved into another book.

I extended my arms out on either side of me and balanced along the third floorboard. One foot in front of the other, I walked slowly down to her chair. It was in an angled position, and the tip of the armrest ever so slightly kissed the edge of the chair that used to belong to Tuck.

He and Gus went to high school together and were on the same wrestling team. Despite an initial rivalry about who was the better wrestler, they became quick friends. Not until after they had an amateur wrestling match after practice one day to "settle it once and for all" as I've heard many times over. No one won, and it ended up with them laughing and going to get burgers afterward. That moment sparked a timeless friend-ship.

When Tuck passed, Gus promised him that he would look after Tiffany. I could recite the stories about how they were practically the three musketeers back in the day.

I had never met him, he passed away before I was even born, but the stories that I was told made it feel like he spent many nights out here with us in that very chair. Sometimes she would sit out here and *talk* with him about her day. Eventually, I started to, too. If the walls behind their appointed seats could talk, I'd know enough stories and secrets to last a lifetime.

I ran my fingers along both of their armrests before settling into Tuck's seat to experience the feeling of sitting beside Tiffany once more. I shut my eyes, letting the midday sun kiss my face for the entirety of this moment. Her laugh, her humming of familiar songs—I heard it all.

Fully expecting a neglected landscape, I was thrown off by the maintained yard when I slowly opened my eyes back up. Either we had faux grass all these years, or...

I stood to examine the rest of the backyard.

The hedges were trimmed, and the tree branches were cut back. Her rose bushes were thriving better than they ever were. But one thing in particular stood out—the hydrangeas. They were fuller than ever, a soft shade of sky blue.

We had planted them within my first year living here, sans my mother. My grandmother could sense the sadness that came with not hearing from her much and wanted to distract me. It gave me something to focus on rather than waiting by the phone or checking every car that came into our driveway.

It might have been *our* project, but I took the reins. I watered them and trimmed them. I maintained the whole bush and it had become my favorite part of the weekends.

The hydrangeas smelled like Memorial Day. They smelled like the start of summer.

When they were finally in full bloom, we would pluck a few and place them on the entry table, in the nook, and out here on the patio. It was rare to find a surface in the house that didn't have a handmade bouquet complimenting it.

It's how we knew summer had arrived.

I ran inside to check the rest of the house. It was untouched, furniture covers and mismatched throw blankets were still draped over everything. Upstairs and into my grandmother's room, her gingham quilt was taut against the mattress and the bear that my grandfather won for her at the state fair sat in the center of the throw pillows. I left her blouses in the closet next to her coats which were neatly packaged away and hung up in garment bags. All else was loosely organized or exactly the way that I left it, the way she left it.

Next door was my room.

I sucked in a deep breath, one that tasted both recognizable and murky.

"Here goes nothing," I spoke under my breath.

Framed pictures, awards, and certificates that were once hung above my desk are now stacked on top of my dresser. The outlines of where they used to be were still faint on the walls. The tassel from my high school graduation cap hung on the edge of my vanity mirror. The thin fringe was so tiny, a small decorative and insignificant piece, yet I felt it suffocate me from four feet away.

The homework, the tests, the extracurricular activities... I kept myself busy for those four years. And the standards and expectations of what I *should* be doing during my teen years never caught up to me. I never felt left out by not going to parties, and losing my virginity was so far off my radar.

My high school years were simple, they were predictable. I was gone for most of the day, came home to do homework, and then spent the rest of the night preparing to do it all over again. I never moaned and groaned like many other kids my age did over school—I enjoyed it.

But that was another lifetime. I thought I had it all figured out at eighteen. I don't remember feeling exhausted or stressed, and I never felt the pressure that soon appeared in my college years.

I knew it came with the territory, but I believed that my "pre-requisite" known as being an "obsessive scholar since middle school" would have prepared me enough. I realized it was a completely different ball game. And I was persistent to never falter.

I picked myself up from an inevitable spiral where I thought of all of my academic habits and decisions, and walked over to the door frame. Zipping by it when I entered the room, I had completely missed the etches that remained in the paneling. You could still see the original paint color under the pen marks, but the rest was the violet shade I had since I was ten.

My grandmother had avoided the markings, afraid to paint over all of the years of my growth. Four years old, five years old, six...all until the age of thirteen; she had measured my height every fall before the school year started. At that point, I had inherited the "short-stack" title from Gus for good once the numbers were stagnant.

I looked back at the room as a whole. My entire childhood lived in the confines of these four walls, under this roof. And while a good portion of the house was packed up, I still had a long way to go. I was unsure if I'd ever be ready to pack up our rooms.

Here goes nothing.

Chapter 5

Sawyer

I followed Mel back into The Hideout. If this opening was going to turn out how I'd imagine it to, I was going to need some lunch for fuel. Granted, it didn't seem like much was left for me to do, but I had to at least pretend like I had some say in what went down this weekend. The invites did have *my* name on them, after all.

She pushed one of the boxes filled with the smaller vases underneath the counter and exchanged it for an apron. Hopefully, customers didn't mind the smell of daylilies wafting over their soup and salad combos.

"Do you ever stop to, uh, I don't know... breathe?" I asked as she got straight to work on orders.

"Someone has gotta do the work around here." She pursed her lips and tapped ferociously away at the tablet system.

"Hey! What about me?!" my daytime server, Cherry, chimed in as she walked in for her shift.

"We're kidding!" Mel and I said in unison.

I snuck behind the counter and started to pack up my takeout. My routine turkey club with a side of Old Bay macaroni salad. And of course, I couldn't forget Billy's puppy patty—though it's nothing more than an unsalted burger patty with a clever name.

Cherry and Mel whipped back and forth behind me while their ponytails swayed as they sprinted through the back bar.

"There is no way this is humane. They're trying to eat us alive!" Cherry exclaimed as she gestured her free hand over the crowd of people swarming in. "Everyone is coming out of the woodwork and it's not even summer yet. And I just got here!" Her voice raised in pitch. She adjusted the teetering serving tray balancing in her hand and blew out an exasperated breath.

Cherry always had a flare for the dramatics and communicated in fluent sarcasm. She kept us on our toes around here. It was always that she was "burning in hell" on a day that was over eighty degrees, or in this case, our customers were "eating us alive" all because it was a busier day than we have had in a while.

"Girl." Mel stopped in her tracks in the midst of writing out tonight's specials on the chalkboard menu. "You say that every year. How long have you lived here?"

"My whole life..." Cherry deadpanned.

She clicked the cap back on the chalk pen and sauntered to Cherry. "Exactly, your whole life. You *know* that summer starts right after Memorial Day here." Mel gave Cherry a pat on the butt, "Now get going! There are hungry people out there! We don't want a bunch of hangry Sawyer-like zombies walking around here."

Cherry perked up with a laugh before scurrying off to tend to her tables.

"What's that supposed to mean?" I cocked my head to the side as I swiped a fry off of one of the plates in the kitchen window.

"What, you can become unpleasant if you haven't had your allotted meals and snacks..." Mel shrugged, smirked, then joined Cherry on the floor.

She acted as if I was a toddler who needed a constant flow of food. She likes to be the "bigger sister" despite being way shorter than I am, and ten years younger. But I had to give it to her—there have been countless times I've needed to be reminded to eat a solid meal in a day.

You'd think spending most of my time around food that could be made within minutes, I'd have no trouble. But the habit from my interning years of thinking "I'll eat when my work is done or else I'll never finish" still lives on.

I scanned the floor as I blindly threw napkins and utensils in my to-go bag.

That's when I caught a glimpse of her fiery red hair that was now pulled on top of her head. Loose strands hung on either side, framing her face. Cherry guided Lucy over to an open booth, and immediately, she burrowed herself inside of it.

She pulled her leg up, bending it against her chest. She opened her laptop up and started typing away. Her attention bounced back and forth between a notebook, a slew of papers, and her laptop screen. I could hear the swipe of her pen scribbling away aggressively across the pages from over here.

Whenever the bell above the front door rang as someone new entered, her head shot up.

When a family of seven with young children flew by her table, getting a little too close for comfort, she followed them with her eyes until they were long gone.

In the midst of whatever was stealing her attention, she watched it all. *And I watched her.*

"I think you're good there, bud," Mel said from behind me.

Thirteen forks, seven napkins, and somehow a stray pen ended up inside my bag during my Lucy-induced haze. Cherry started to giggle as she walked over and took a peek in the bag.

They both hovered their heads over the opening. I swear, they looked like little kids on Halloween above a candy bowl.

"What exactly did you have planned for this?" Cherry asked as she wiggled the pen in front of my face.

I swiped it out of her hand and clicked it an obnoxious amount of times before chucking it at the register. I started to pull out the excess, avoiding all eye contact with either of them. I've never felt this pulled in to know someone before. Just when I thought that I was getting familiar and comfortable with everyone in town, she walked in.

"Pfft, d-don't worry about what I'm doing."

"Alright, I have never seen you so spacey before. What's up?" Mel asked, speaking out the side of her mouth.

"I bet it has to do with the redhead that I just sat at table twenty," Cherry said lightly as she got to work on cutting drink garnishes.

Mel and I both snapped our heads by looking in her direction. My eyes sunk into the back of my head, while Mel's practically bulged out of hers. Cherry's remained on the lime slices on the cutting board.

"Oh, my god. You're *totally* right!" Mel slapped her hand down on the bar while half of the place almost broke their neck, turning their attention to us. "Sorry," she winced with a whisper.

Cherry let out another giggle, and her chopping of fruit quickened. "It's adorable really," she says with a shrug. "You think I haven't noticed you checking over there every other second, but I have. I have a sixth sense for these types of things. I think you should go talk to her. And when you guys fall madly, deeply in love, please let me be the flower girl at your wedding."

"You two do know I can fire you, right?" I say, completely ignoring her nonsense.

Mel scowled at me. "Good luck with that."

"If you won't talk to her, I will," Cherry teased.

I stole a glance in Lucy's direction as Cherry paraded her insane need to play matchmaker over that way. Lucy had her fingers interlocked, her chin was perched in the dip of the palm of her hand as she focused on her computer screen.

Once Cherry reached her table, a larger-than-life smile appeared on her face as she sat up against the booth. Cherry pointed back towards the bar and I made myself busy by fanning through credit card receipts, attempting to look busy.

After a quick chat, Cherry was already heading back. I felt like a preteen girl in the middle of a gossiping hour, I inherited sweaty palms while waiting for some intel.

"What did you talk about?"

She slapped the order pad down on the bar beside her. "Uh... Food?" A thick valley girl accent spilled out of her mouth. "I went to take her order."

"But you pointed over here. At me."

She points off to the side, keeping her attention on the tablet as she types away. "*Nooo*, I simply pointed to the chalkboard. I told her about the beer on tap. Ya know, pushing the alcohol sales like *somebody* keeps telling me to do. That was all," she pursed her lips.

I clutched my chest from the instant feeling of relief.

I don't get nervous, I don't hide like a scared puppy with their tail between their legs. Especially not when it came to girls. But my nerves were just as strong as they were when I was in middle school. I talked to her before, so what the hell was my issue now?

Maybe it's because she's there, and she's real. And even after our encounter earlier, she still came back here. I had hoped I'd see her around again, but I didn't think it would be twice in one day. It's my lucky day, right? I couldn't let this opportunity pass.

She looked busy and probably couldn't care less about a guy—especially this guy—coming up and bothering her. But if it *was* my lucky day, then she would be the type of girl who was fine with me saying a quick hello.

As a buffer, I cut up a slice of pie from the dessert case before I made my way over to her.

"Key lime pie?" Her eyes went wide when she locked them with mine and drew on a smile.

"Always," she said, wiggling in her seat.

I slid the plate of dessert topped with a lime garnish in front of her, only slightly crumpling the edges of her papers that were spread out. She picked them up and moved her laptop off to the side.

I took this opportunity to sit across from her, hesitantly. I watched as she ate a couple of forkfuls of the pie, the last bite left a speck of whipped cream on her upper lip. She bashfully wiped it away with her napkin.

"I wanted to apologize again for earlier," she expressed with a rosy shade forming on her cheeks.

"I promise you're okay." I flashed her a quick smile and her face returned to its fair state. I extended my arm across the table. "I'm Sawyer Banks, by the way."

"How formal of you. I'm Lucy *Collins*," she enunciated her last name in a mocking way as she shook my hand.

"I know. I mean... I—" I started to stammer like a fool. "So..." I leaned back into my seat with my arms crossed over my chest, acting cool, calm, and collected as ever. "I don't mean to intrude on your lunch, I won't stay here long, but I wanted to know, did you find what you were looking for this morning?"

She scraped the thinnest layer of pie off the side, but let it sit on the edge of her fork. "What makes you think I was looking for anything?"

"Just a hunch."

She grazed her teeth over her fork, slowly eating the bite of pie. Her eyes went soft, and her face was unreadable. "Well, I was looking for someone," she said, setting her fork back down. "Gus, actually. I was hoping to catch him. I am surprised he didn't come running at the mini concert I had put on." She nudged her head in the direction of the jukebox.

Moments before she walked in, I was exiting my office the same time he had run off into the walk-in freezer with a heaving chest and flushed cheeks. I had never seen that man so avoidant before. Said he swore he saw a ghost. He looked like a guilt-ridden child. An emotional, scared, guilt-ridden child.

Cherry brought over a half sandwich and fries at the same time that her laptop dinged with a new notification. She snapped her neck so fast at the noise and pushed all else away from her. The clacking of the keys that started under her fingers was as loud as the conversations behind me. I fidgeted with the napkins and straightened out the unused utensils that were in front of me.

A moment had passed, "Everything okay over there?"

"Yeah, sorry, it's—" she stammered, and crinkled her nose in the cutest way as she strained her eyes trying to read her screen. "I have spent my morning contacting realtors and contractors and yup," she slammed her laptop shut, "just as I figured. None of them are available."

Lucy released a loud grunt and folded her arms against her chest. She had zoned out in a way that made me think she forgot I was sitting across from her.

"Are you looking to buy here?"

"Selling, actually. I had a feeling I was getting on top of this too late. It's my fault."

She blew out a breath in defeat, making the loose strands of hair that hung fly all which ways. I don't know why, but her childlike frown crushed me and I only met her hours ago.

"Let me see what I can do," I said firmly.

"No, you really don't have to—"

"I might know somebody."

I had a Rolodex of realtors forever on standby waiting to work with the Banks family. For once, I could use my family name and not be filled with shame. The corners of Lucy's mouth lifted for a split second. Immediately, I found myself taking in each crease that formed upon her face.

She reached for a fry and nibbled off the end. "Thank you," she said endearingly.

I looked over at Mel who was giving me a smile of her own, one that was more mischievous than I would have liked. I mouthed an exaggerated *fuck off* her way. I could see her chest move with laughter as she moved to punch things into the register.

Before I could restart my conversation with Lucy, I was quickly drawn to the buzzing that started to stir at the bar. A little early for a brawl considering it's one-thirty in the afternoon on a Wednesday... But what do I know?

"What? You can't smile for me, townie?" A scrawny, good-for-nothing asshole taunted Mel, swiping his fingers underneath her chin.

She whipped her head away so fast, I thought her next step was going to be biting his head—or dick—off. "I don't smile at people who disappoint their parents. How *is* your influencer presence going, anyway?" Mel snapped back without missing a beat.

Aaron Nelson was the kid who always said he would make it big but never did.

His family was just one of the ones who joined us at the lake house for our Fourth of July parties. People in town were rarely invited, it was more so an evasion of city folk coming up for the holidays, making a whole bunch of unwanted noise, and leaving the place worse than they found it. Assuming the town would clean up after them like their maids and servants do back home.

I remember Aaron's dad being the type to one-up everyone in crowded conversations, though their reality back home in the city was far from what they projected. Massive debt, never promoting at work like he alluded. But they'd never tell a soul the truth. The apple doesn't fall far from the douche—I mean tree.

Aaron is now in his thirties, living in his grandparent's estate which he inherited, and talks about powdered drinks on social media. He'd never admit that he's a "townie" along with the rest of us.

The way he sees it is that since he isn't from here and doesn't plan on staying, he is on an indefinite vacation. Somehow, our families believe if we don't *reside* here, then it's okay and we can keep our status. For whatever that's worth.

For all my grandfather thinks, I became a hermit who is so far off the grid.

I stood from the table and immediately stiffened my stance between the two of them once I reached the bar. "Alright," I turned to Cherry behind the bar and whispered to her, "maybe no day drinking for him anymore."

"Oh, that's right. I forgot that Sawyer Banks controls all of his bitches," he slurred his words. Mel pounced hard against my back, trying to tackle the bag of bones standing in front of us. Those around us roared with distaste. But all I could hear was the clenching of a jaw from one worked-up Mel behind me.

"I will tear that L.L. Bean catalog shirt right off of your scrawny body, Nelson!" Mel shrieked, trying to claw her way around me.

I gritted my teeth together—and bit my tongue. Entertaining Aaron Nelson wasn't worth it, it never was. He believed we were in some sort of competition with one another since primary school.

When he learned that I spent my sixteenth birthday in New York City, he had to book the penthouse at the Ritz a few months later on *his* birthday. Just to prove that he could.

"I don't think you realize that I don't control anyone here," I said, pressing a firm finger against his chest. "Mel here could snap your twig ass in half. And after the stupid comment that you just made, I would let her. But I don't feel like cleaning your blood off my bar stools. They're new. I like them. So how about you turn around, leave my restaurant, and go kick some rocks before *I* kick the aforementioned twig ass of yours."

He threw his hands up in surrender with a sly grin drawn across his face, then he looked around. Everyone was staring in his direction, unimpressed. He dropped his hands and his face went blank before leaving.

"Sorry about that, everyone," I shouted out. "A round of Bloody Mary's on the house."

Everyone cheered.

On days that become harder than the rest, I found myself in a place of regret for leaving the life I once lived. Everything was laid out for me, even my freshly shined shoes and dry-cleaned socks that my assistant would pick up for me.

But then I saw people like Aaron Nelson, and how that life has literally torn him apart. As it had many people I grew up around. This very moment confirmed that I am far from regret.

"Are you okay?" I said softly to Mel, who was cornered against the prep counter by Cherry.

"What? Me? Of course!" Her lips said one thing, while her eyes said another.

Mel can hold her own. That is something I am sure of. But once the clouds of dust settle and the adrenaline rush from puffing out her chest dies off, she becomes shaken up. Regardless of the confrontation's magnitude, her pupils dilate and her focus wanders.

I knew this, and that's why I'd never buy her *of course* bull-shit.

"Go home."

"But—"

"Mel."

"*Sawyer.*"

We had a staring match so intense that Cherry walked backward away from us.

"Okay," she sucked in a breath, then untied her apron and threw it under the counter.

As I headed back to Lucy, who was wide-eyed off in her corner, I got distracted by the barking coming from outside.

I turned my head to see Billy chasing bunnies up the hill, then turned my head back at her. Her head was buried back into her keyboard. The dog, the girl. The dog, *the girl.* I could get whiplash from flipping my head back and forth so much right now.

I shot my arm up over the seated crowd and waved it around like an absolute maniac. "Lucy!" Her head shot up. "I gotta go, but I'll see you around!"

Her eyes widened before they went soft. She waved me off before throwing up a thumbs-up. I flashed her a wink, then rushed out the front and went after the mutt.

Chapter 6

Lucy

I gathered up my papers and computer and headed towards the front. Stumbling out from behind my table, my heart struggled to regulate itself from that wink of his.

Sawyer Banks.

I had always known of the Banks family and their lake house to be the house filled with people who had deep pockets and shallow hearts. They brought their mess and mayhem from the city and left when they got bored. They're the kind that had loud parties in the summer months and then left their place vacant for the remainder of the year. The town as a collective would have to spend a week or two after the fact recuperating from the headache they inflicted.

The family was nothing more than the kind we created stories about because we knew nothing of them. Cleaning ladies and landscapers were at the property more than the actual family was. We conspired about how many kids they truly had, or how many wives. Seriously, there was nothing to know about them beyond a simple Google search.

After a few passing seconds, the dark-haired server snuck back in after just leaving and retied her apron around her waist. I slid my ticket and credit card along the countertop. "Hey, are you okay?"

My server Cherry was rubbing the shoulder of the one who was being harassed, though she shrugged her off. "I'm fine. That's sort of his thing? If his thing is being a complete tool." She said it nonchalantly as if that happens regularly.

"Which it is!" Cherry chimed in.

"Is he an ex-boyfriend or just not your type?"

"The latter. I don't date bigots, blockheads, or boys. But enough of that..." She let out a humorous scoff and then reached her hand out towards me. "I'm Mel. Thanks for checking on me. Truly, I appreciate it."

"Of course. I'm Lucy," I said, shamefully disengaged. I couldn't help but look out the windows and through the trees trying to find Sawyer as she closed out my tab.

"I'm sorry about Sawyer," Mel said pointing in the direction that he stormed off in. "He's not usually so... awkward."

I waved my hand over her comment.

Awkward was not the first thought that came to mind, though I don't know what did. Charming, outgoing, and dare I say good-looking? But definitely not awkward. I wasn't used to that level of confidence without it being repulsive in return.

I had fallen immune to arrogance from people thinking their pending medical degree was enough for me to fall head over heels for them. In retrospect, it only drove me away.

But Sawyer wasn't driving me away. I was infatuated, almost. And infatuation was *not* on the to-do list I had written up at the airport. And here I am obsessing, replaying yet another encounter with him over in my head.

Did I seem too open to talking to him? Maybe I should have played hard to get, make him work for my attention. But that's not me. Or possibly it's the complete opposite, and he thought I was too reserved, too standoffish. That's not me, either. Eh, whatever. I could not start obsessing over this. Instead, I distracted myself by zeroing in on Gus' grill and all of the evident changes surrounding me.

If the outside didn't look relatively the same, I would have thought I was in a completely new establishment. The changes were polarizing, to say the least. I dragged my hand along my opposite arm from the chill that traveled through my body—the blanket of warmth of Gus' now felt flimsy and worn through. I felt like a stranger in a place I called my second home for so long.

They had ripped up the carpeting, revealing natural concrete flooring. And instead of the larger-than-life strips of overhead lighting, there were low strands with large bulbs that hung above the bar, and old, industrial sconces were drilled into the walls. It was overall dimly lit and grungy. But the natural light from the windows still gave it that cozy feel I was thankfully familiar with.

"I gotta get to cleaning up the remnants of the lunch rush, but hey," Mel gives me a single nod before walking away, "I hope to see you around this summer."

She placed a receipt on top of my card even though she never once picked it up. Stamped across the top it read **PAID IN FULL**. When I turned to correct the mistake, she was lost in the crowd, and Cherry was back to slinging drinks and taking orders.

I tucked the receipt between the pages of my notebook and reached into my bag for loose change. I pulled out the only cash I seemed to have on me and stuck it under the stapler beside the register. I knew it wasn't the whole bill, but at least it covered the pie and a tip.

I pushed through the front door, letting the rattling of the overhead bell ring through my body. I watched as Sawyer and his dog sped through the water toward their white dock on the other side of the lake. His pup jumped out before the motor even shut off.

Instead of heading through the hillside and back to the cottage, I perched myself on the weathered picnic table that I spent many hours on before. A pair of blue jays intertwined with each other, chirping away excitedly.

"It's like no time has passed." I heard a deep mumble approaching behind me. I was met with icy blue eyes when I craned my head around. I found comfort in them; the way he could look at me and I'd feel safe instantaneously. "Hi, darlin', how have you been?"

I stood up to meet him with a hug. "Hi, Gus," I said over his shoulder.

Hugging Gus, I knew that I was officially home.

"Let me be honest with ya right off the bat, I did see you in here earlier. Didn't know if that was really you, still can't believe that it is. It spooked me so bad I didn't know what I could've said. Still don't, I suppose..." Silence filled the space between us as we pulled away from our hug.

He didn't know what to say?! *I* didn't know what to say. I left. I never called, I never wrote. Nothing. Do I say that I am sorry for never visiting? Because I am.

We sat down side by side, looking out over the water. The ripples on the top surface of the lake and the rustling of the trees from the early summer breeze were centering, and boy did I need to be centered right about now.

"What are you doing here, kid?" He stared at me like he was trying to find the answers behind my eyes.

"Thought I'd take a little vacation," I nervously chuckled.

He looked at me in a way that let me know he wasn't buying my bullshit. He never has.

I let out a deep sigh, then blurted out, "I'm here to sell the cottage," as if keeping anything from Gus was impossible. Maybe because it was. When I had finally made the decision, the first person I wanted to run it by was him. Half of the wear and tear on the cottage's floorboards was put there from his heavy work boots.

There were many times I wanted to call him up, but couldn't, because I didn't want to hear his voice crack from hurt or the silence grow louder out of anger. I knew I'd change my mind in an instant if he gave me any inkling that I shouldn't sell.

Gus rolled his shoulders back, sitting straight as an arrow. I felt the pads of my fingertips break out in a sweat. He placed his hand on top of mine that was resting between us on the table and gave it a squeeze. The floodgates opened and tears sprinted down my cheeks.

Sitting beside him made everything feel real. Everything that I had left behind and had tried to forget for almost a decade was still there, it still existed, and leaving never erased it as I had hoped.

He exhaled. "I figured that would happen eventually."

His comfort and presence brought me back to the early mornings and late afternoons when we'd sit at this very table. And on the weekends, he would come over and play card games with me and my grandmother and somehow became the board game champion of 2012.

I must've been struck with the flu that weekend, or something like that. A rare kind. I swear it's the only reason. I'm sure of it. Otherwise, I would have been crowned.

He and Leanne sat at our dining room table every Sunday night for family dinners and we'd take staycations by the harbor. It was rare if my spare time wasn't spent with at least one of them. I asked him why they never spent time with their kids or grandkids. You know, their *real* family. They laughed it off and simply said, "You guys are our real family," and left it at that. It made enough sense to me.

"You're not mad?" I finally asked.

"You will always do what you think is best, bud," he rubbed the center of my back.

I wiped away a straggling tear and collected myself.

"I figured there was no better time than now. Close one chapter to start a new one, and all of that." Deflecting as I do best, I let out a strangled laugh. "It's not a big deal, really. It will be fun, I bet."

Yeah, if *fun* meant not being able to find a realtor and having no game plan for the first time in my life. His face was filled with sorrow.

"I have noticed there have been some magic landscaping fairies at the cottage, though. You wouldn't know anything about that, would you?" I continued, nudging my elbow into his side playfully to lighten the mood.

"That garden wasn't just hers. It *was* her. When I saw the flowers wilt, the memory of her started to wilt, too. And I wasn't going to let that happen."

Fuck, how poetic. There goes the waterworks again.

"She and Tuck were my best friends. But they were family. You're family, you know that."

"Look, I'm sor—"

"Don't." He angled himself toward me and pointed a finger in my face. "Tiff would've haunted you if you didn't go off to college and just sulked around Rider. Besides, how was your graduation, kid?"

"You remembered."

He remembered. Of course, he did.

He shrugged. "Stop by this weekend, I have a little gift waiting for you."

I wiped away a straggling tear and repositioned myself on the tabletop. "Okay, enough about me. Let's talk about The Hideout, shall we?" I raised an eyebrow at him. "What's with all the changes? It has a name?! I never thought I'd see the day."

He shook his head, letting out a shallow snort. He shifted his attention to Sawyer throwing the ball to his dog across the lake. He nodded his head in their direction. "It's all him. A good kid, that one. He's really making something out of what was almost nothing." When I didn't respond, he continued, "Sawyer bought it a couple of years back."

"That was your whole heart."

"It still is, always will be. I'm still schlepping around those tables when I feel like it. I just couldn't do the business side of things anymore. You know that Leanne and I started it all up back in the late seventies. She liked all the logistics, the bossing of people around before she got bored of it." He let out a chuckle. "She stayed home, baked her little heart away, while I came here to work. She was ready to slow down a lot sooner than I was. But not even Hummingbird Lake could come between me and my lady."

A true testament to his love for her, because I know that Hummingbird Lake is pretty high up there.

"What did he do? Pay you a million bucks? Blackmail you? What would a guy like him want with a place like that." My voice got quieter with the last question. I trailed my finger around in circles, tracing a knot in one of the wood panels. Key lime pie and a polite conversation with Sawyer didn't change the fact that this place, The Hideout or whatever, was Gus'.

He looked at me blankly.

"No offense," I winced and bowed my head.

"He isn't like the rest of 'em at all."

Even from this side of the lake, I had a clear shot. I followed the way that he moved, the way that he smiled. His short sleeves were cuffed at the hem, hugging his biceps tight but his shirt moved loosely around him. He is definitely not stiff and stone-faced like the rest of his family. I suppose I had to give credit where credit was due. If Gus opened his heart, and his crowning achievement, to him, then maybe he wasn't half bad.

I don't remember him around much when I was younger. I guess they're not memorable when they all look the same. They had chiseled bodies covered in tanning oil and their hair was styled perfectly, despite being out by the water all day.

He looked nothing like that.

His hair was messy, and his jeans were ripped at the knee.

There was a ruggedness about him.

So much had changed since I last stood along this lake. Now I worry that I don't know it, or the people, like I used to.

Chapter 7

Sawyer

Every summer on our drive up from the city, we would drive past the hillside and through the main road. To get to the lake house, we'd have to loop around the storefronts and up the road to the private estates. I didn't focus much on any other focal points, or houses—or people for that matter. Except when we'd zip by the houses that lined the hillside in our Escalade—my grandfather talked about how they were nothing more than eye sores. He said anything less than a two-story house was not a real home.

The lake houses were sparse from one another, but we still knew the other summer residents. Of course, we did. They had status and savings, and those were the type of things my grandfather appreciated about someone. To my understanding, we socialized with our inner circle and whoever sold us our seafood broil or steaks to throw on the grill.

I never understood why there was such an upturned-nose attitude over Rider, maybe that's not something for me to understand. But either way, I knew that the Banks family was all about the hustle and bustle. Anything else, anyone else, simply didn't exist.

I was taught to believe Rider was a place for nobodies.

The Hillside Cottages housed the people whom he called nobodies.

And to my surprise, they housed the people who ended up feeling most like home to me. And the one at the end along the riverbend belonged to Lucy. And Lucy was definitely not a *nobody.* She was somebody that I wanted to know. Beneath her flustered disposition, I felt her welcoming glow. There was a cloud of serenity that radiated off of her.

With my hand curled into a ball, I was knocking at Lucy's front door.

"Sawyer." Her eyes widened as she hunched over, pulling at the bottom hem of her shirt. "What are you doing here?" She tried to stretch her shirt over her thighs, trying to hide the fact that she was wearing nothing but an oversized, faded 90210 Beverly Hills tee.

Not oversized enough, when she walked away from the door for a split second, her ass played peek-a-boo beneath the hem of her shirt. She returned to the door wrapped up in a throw blanket.

"I am sorry to have stopped by like this."

"No, it's okay. Just thrown off, that's all."

"I told you I was going to find you someone."

"Uh, yeah." She peered her head out the front door and looked around then scratched the side of her head. "You're going to have to use more words."

It took me a second before my brain caught up with her words. "Right!" I quickly reached into my back pocket and held up three business cards. I spread them out like playing cards. "I come bearing gifts," I said waving them in the air.

She let out a curt laugh, then stepped off to the side. "Come on in." She led us down the hall and into the kitchen. It was small but had a lot of personality from what I could tell. Ceramics and vintage dishware were on display on the shelving. "Coffee?" she asked.

"Yes, please."

She tugged at her blanket, making it tighter around her body before bending over into the opened box on the floor. "Sorry it's such a mess," she said as she pulled out two mugs, unwrapping packing paper from around them.

The house was bare for the most part, but it was far from a mess. There were boxes and a lot of them, but everything seemed to still have a place. It was an organized mess if anything.

"Creamer?"

"Black is fine." The coffee machine roared in completion, filling the awkward silence in the room. I leaned up against the fridge and watched as she stirred her coffee. "It's nice to be able to put a face to the owner of the house. And to see where Gus spends the better half of his Sundays."

She had let me into her space so effortlessly, willingly. And I sat here strung out, worried that I'd say something stupid. With both mugs in hand, she slid into the breakfast nook underneath the window. I moved across the room and sat in the spot across from her as she pushed mine across the table. Hers had a cardinal on it, and mine had Tweety Bird with a surface-level chip on the beak.

"So," she dragged out the single word.

"Right, yes." I slid the cards across the table. "There's a real estate agent in there that's the best I have ever known, but he's in New Haven. That one," I pointed as she filtered through, "she's efficient but she's a little harsh. Okay, a lot harsh and I may have wanted to cry when I met her, but we will not be talking about that." Then she got to the last one. "That's Kai. They also work down at Jitters when it's a slow season for them, but they're my buddy from growing up."

She held Kai Bellair's card up in front of her for a beat before throwing the other two across the kitchen, both flying in different directions. "Bellair, huh? I think we have a winner," she said with a twinkle in her eye, then walked the business card over to the fridge, securing it beneath a magnet. When she returned to the table, she dropped the blanket off to the side as she climbed back into the booth.

"Again, I'm sorry to have just come by unannounced like this."

"No, no. You're all good. I appreciate it, seriously. This makes my life easier, so thank you," she smiled into her coffee before taking a sip.

"I'm glad that I was able to help. You know, right when I thought that I had won everyone over, and knew the ins and outs of the town, you showed up."

"What are you talking about? It's not like you've never been here before." She knitted her brows. "You all came in like a hurricane every summer, acting like you owned the place. Surely you tried to know *someone's* name at some point. Right?" She pursed her lips and narrowed her eyes.

The flawless sweet facade that masked some sort of hidden spicy attitude started to slip away. She extended out her claws and latched them right into my ego.

Normally, I'd despise having conclusions drawn out about me from the outside looking in. Knowing she knew who I was meant she already had preconceived notions that didn't seem too positive.

Regardless, though, it almost felt like there was hope, even a chance, that she would try to think a little bit more of me when she didn't tell me to kick rocks as she saw me standing at her door. Even more when she asked me how I took my coffee.

Sitting in her kitchen, across the table from her, I was naive to believe I had a chance.

God, what was wrong with me? All of a sudden I cared about what people thought?

"A hurricane, huh?" I leaned forward, across the table. She sunk back into her seat and started to twist the charm on her necklace. "You were paying attention?" I asked, a little more cocky than I would've liked.

"No. I just meant that... Yeah, actually, I don't know what I was thinking." She slid her coffee out in front of her. "You never gave us townspeople the time of day. But what do I know, I stopped seeing you around as years went by." She drew her mouth into a thin line and closed into herself, a little more closed off than she'd been.

I pushed my coffee away into the center of the table and leaned back against the bench, mimicking her movements. I studied her, trying to find what her words were really saying. I could've rebutted, defended myself. Find the exact thing she needed to hear to change her mind. But I didn't blame her.

"You know, I'm not like the rest of them," I finally said. I wasn't going to pretend to act hard. There was no point.

"So I'm told," she said in a whisper.

"I don't blame you for thinking whatever you do, though. I never ventured out from behind my confines, never really let anyone get to know the real me beyond the family name."

"You make it seem like you were held captive."

Sometimes I felt like I was.

I ran my fingers through my hair. "I mean, I was in the city more than I was here. I never saw the point of getting to know people or their names."

"And now?" She ran her thumb over the handle. The claws had retracted themselves.

"Now, I figured if I was going to live here full time, I might as well make a community for myself."

She dropped her shoulders, and her face went soft. "Can I ask you something?" she asked cautiously.

"Always."

"What was it that made you get Gus to sell? I just can't wrap my head around it. I don't mean it in a bad way or anything, it's just... What exactly did you say?" There was a sadness about her as she gnawed at her bottom lip.

"I don't think it was any one thing in particular. I honestly threw it out there as a joke one day, but as you can see, he did not take it as one. He almost jumped out of his skin at the idea."

"Interesting," she said with a disturbed tone as she stood from the table. She clutched the bottom of her shirt keeping it in place as much as possible. She placed her mug in the sink, and I followed after. We were a foot apart. Inches, really.

Her perfume hit me like the first day back at The Hideout and I lost all train of thought. She spun on her heels to face me, her arms crossed against her chest. "Well, you better do his place justice," she demanded, pointing a stiff finger at me with a scowl. Her hip was cocked out. Lucy might be small but she stood strong.

I moved her hand down and out of my face and held it in mine. Except I wasn't the one who pulled away first this time. She brought her hand to her collarbone and fidgeted with her necklace again.

"I couldn't imagine doing it any other way," I said breathy between the two of us.

"Uh, anyway," she coughed out. "Look, so, I have so much I have to take care of, but I appreciate you bringing those cards over."

"I completely understand." I took a step back.

Her energy shifted and she turned on a serious voice. As if she was saying *it was nice doing business with ya, I'll see you around.*

I didn't want this to just be a business deal with Lucy. I wasn't going to sit back and whimper like I had the other day. I had a feeling that Lucy wasn't the person that you let time pass and wait around for. She was the girl—the *woman*—that you make first moves for and be forward with.

She pointed over to the business card on the fridge. "And I will make sure to give Kai a call later this week."

I walked over to Kai's card and pulled it out from under its magnet. I found a stray pen near a notepad that sat on her counter and clicked it. "If you find yourself free tonight, and I know that it's last minute, The Hideout is having a little re-opening. Nothing major. But I'd like to see you there. And if not," I wrote my number down on the back of the card, "give me a call if you need any help. I am a great baseboard cleaner."

I clicked the pen into itself and returned it to its place on the counter before sticking the card back on the fridge. I looked over at Lucy, a deer caught in the headlights.

She nudged out her hip again and a playful grin danced on her face. "Are you saying my baseboards need cleaning?"

I took my keys out of my pocket and twirled them around my finger. "I'll see you around, Lucy," I said before walking out, leaving her standing against the kitchen sink.

I was not going to be playing it safe with Lucy, especially not when she looks and smells and talks as exceptionally as she does.

Chapter 8

Lucy

I trailed a few steps behind Sawyer as he left the cottage. I hid behind the makeshift curtains I nailed up along the living room windows, shielding me from Sawyer's view as he walked down to his truck. I could smell the year's worth of mothballs all over them with my face pressed up against them. I made a mental note to find the box with all the candles packed away to get rid of the stench.

Afraid he'd see my silhouette in the window as he pulled out of the drive, I crouched down and army crawled to the center of the living room. I hadn't moved since, and six hours had passed. Give or take.

I managed to get sidetracked and sorted through two boxes in the meantime. And by sort through, I mean I dumped everything out in front of me, looked at it all, and then slowly placed it back in.

Nothing caught my attention enough to decide whether to "keep" or "toss" so I saved it for the "deal with later" pile. As I've been doing with most of my responsibilities the past few days.

How was I to decipher what deserved a place in my life when it felt as though everything here had some sort of value?

Anytime I considered tackling the never-ending to-do list, I wanted to crumble inside of myself. Having a structured plan has always assisted me in how to go about things. But now, I found myself having to pencil in time to process my emotions.

I had always taken pride in being mature when it came to my feelings, I never let much get under my skin. There's no point in dwelling on the happenings of life when they're out of my control. With that being said, I think I fell headfirst into handling life alone after my grandmother passed, and I was never given the time to mourn her the way I felt like I needed to.

Did I cry? Of course. Do I miss her? I can't imagine a day that I won't. But I didn't give myself *time*. Now? Now...all I have is time.

Her favorite spoon which she used to stir her coffee stares at me in the kitchen drawer. And the boxes that hold all of the memories from her life are stacked around, taking glances of me in passing. The little nothings that I refused to touch eight years ago hounded me in every crevice and crook of this house. Wondering where they'll be placed in the selection process, all asking questions I didn't have answers to.

I didn't know why I could pack some things but not others. I didn't know why some things were harder to look at than others. I didn't know much of anything anymore and it felt like it was eating me alive.

Inside one of the boxes in front of me were some punch needle coasters and knitted throw blankets. I took out the fuchsia chunky knit and wrapped it around me. It molded around my shoulders like a much needed hug. The other box was filled to the rim with vinyl records. I filtered through and tugged out the *Rubber Soul* album by The Beatles. I dragged the needle over eleven tracks, *In My Life* started playing through the decades-old record player.

I closed my eyes and let the floor absorb me while I cried there. Soon enough, I fell asleep.

The stained glass window panel that hung above the front windows left a blue, purple, and yellow kaleidoscope-type pattern on the wall. The colors danced with the golden hue that started to enter the room from the sun setting. They so much as trailed all the way to the side of the grandfather clock that sat in the corner by the entrance. I couldn't ignore the loud striking sound it made when it hit seven and jolted up from my spot.

It was minutes, thirty to be exact, before Sawyer's opening was going to begin.

I had hoped he hadn't seen how ghostly my face became as he scribbled out his information. I stopped at the fridge to read the card because I needed to see it with my own eyes. *Tonight, 7:30*, the card read, with his number right beneath it.

It was simple, really. Common, even. He gave me his number—it was no big deal. But it was the *way* he did it. So confident, yet so relaxed. Very suave in the way he leaned against the counter, talked calmly, and then walked out after flashing me a crooked smile.

But there's no way I could go. I don't care if Gus willingly sold it to the guy. I don't even know him. I don't care that he is nice, or that he has a comforting smile and a strong jaw to accompany it. I know nothing about him. He just moves his way in and starts buying businesses with his big-boy bucks.

That's not what Rider is about. Rider is for the people who grew up here, not those who decide to gentrify it. I liked Rider exactly how it was.

The time ticked with twenty-nine minutes to go. I folded the blanket back up and placed it beside the box. I stopped the vinyl from mindlessly spinning and covered it back up with the dust cover lid. But still, the intrigue was there.

I'm not like the rest of them. Sawyer made it a point to mention.

He's not like the rest of them. Gus sounded so sure with his statement.

Their declarations sounded so clear, so definite. Like I would be a fool to not believe either of them.

Fuck.

I scurried upstairs and busted into my room. I was going to make him keep his word. I owed it to Gus, it was the least I could do to see what he was all about.

I rustled through my closet, but nothing screamed out at me. Nothing said, "You should wear this to an event put on by a hot businessman that you don't even know because it will look like you tried, but didn't try too hard."

I flipped through the hangers faster, as if going back and forth was going to make new items appear. News flash, it wasn't. I opted for a fitted white tank and cut-off jean shorts and squirmed into pointed-toe booties.

I blew out a breath of relief. Just like that, I was dressed and presentable with five minutes to spare. Except that didn't matter when I could not make myself move for the life of me. My eyes were glued to my reflection in the mirror.

My breathing was shallow. *This is stupid*, I thought.

The three times that I have seen Sawyer, my heart skipped more than it ever had. My stomach ended up in knots. I was getting butterflies for a guy that I didn't even know—one that I wasn't too sure I *wanted* to know.

But then he just showed up with his fitted tee shirt and five o'clock shadow from the night before. And he asked me to come to his opening—last minute, might I add—right before leaving. It's bullshit. It's even worse that I wanted to go.

I am here for the summer and the summer only. I was not going to fall for the nice, neighborhood boy—er, man—act. It was an act, it had to be.

Going tonight means absolutely nothing.

I brushed my hair by running my fingers through it and stood up straight. I marched downstairs, lightly pushed everything into the "deal with later" pile, and grabbed my phone.

"Going tonight means absolutely nothing," I repeated out loud to myself as I walked out the door and got in the car.

I buckled myself up before flipping down the sun visor. I looked in the mirror and gave my eyelashes a lift with my finger. I took a couple of deep breaths and smiled back at myself.

Tonight means absolutely nothing.

Chapter 9

Lucy

It was the perfect summer night in Rider. The early parts of June were always my favorite time. It was warm during the day, but by sunset, it had cooled down to a perfect seventy-degree temperature. And the humidity was barely noticeable at that point.

I could hear Leanne's laugh before I fully exited the car. There was a magnetic pull almost enticing me to run over to her and Gus. I knew they'd be the only way I'd make it through the night, but instead, I became a fly on the wall. I was far enough from the stirs of the evening, but close enough to my car so I could leave in a moment's notice if it felt too weird.

And boy, did it feel weird.

A few small children were running down by the lake, screeching and smiling as they took turns chasing after one another. There were some familiar faces, some of whom I had never seen before, but they all mingled and chatted and clinked their drinks together.

A few tall tables were scattered about, covered in sheer muslin throws. Flowers, each a different arrangement from the next, sat in the center of each one. A combination of blues and folk music played over loudspeakers. I truly felt like I had walked into another world, another dimension of sorts, one that I had yet to acclimate myself with.

The whole town showed up, though I don't think there's a get-together these people would turn down. This town supported its people. This town rallied around its people. And from the looks of it, Sawyer Banks was now one of their people.

He stood against the porch railing with an ear-to-ear grin plastered on his face. Mel stood beside him as they chatted it up with one of the owners of Jitters. But I made sure to prop myself up behind one of the wider trees. I hadn't figured out if I wanted to be seen just yet.

He had a way with those he spoke with. He gave his undivided attention, made sure to hold eye contact—even if they were rambling on for too long. He genuinely cared to listen to people and what they had to say.

He stood there tall, confident, and secure with his chin angled up ever so slightly. Not in a pretentious way by any means either—but in a proud way. Satisfaction beamed off of him and I didn't feel so icky about him making a name for himself in Rider. At least not at this very moment. Sawyer genuinely fit in here, and that was an odd concept to wrap my head around.

But then the strangest thing occurred—the newest rotation of party guests that approached him with their praises must've shared the greatest joke of all time. The loudest laughter I had ever heard was plucked from the depths of his chest. I became attuned to the crinkles in the corner of his eyes or how his cheeks blushed the longer he laughed.

Tonight's turnout and the acceptance from a town that hates outsiders helped chip away at the biased pain. It pained me to see so many alterations to a place I had considered my safe haven for so long. But I know if this happened to any other establishment, it would have already received a five-star Yelp review from me.

I grabbed champagne from Cherry in passing. Instead of continuing through the crowd, she stopped when she realized it was me. "Lucy, right?" She grinned, then leaned in for a hug, balancing the tray with a few more drinks in her other hand. "It's so great to see you here!"

"Oh, uh—" I returned her hug. She steadied the tray as she pulled away. "Yeah, hey. How have you been? This place turned out—"

She cut me off. "I know, right? Sawyer and Mel are masterminds."

I brought the champagne flute to my lips and smiled awkwardly into my next sip.

"Well, anyway, I'll see you around," she continued before walking off, handing off the last bit of drinks.

I stepped back and away from it all.

I could see myself walking up the refurbished porch and letting the bell above the door ring as I walked inside The Hideout for lunch. I'd order some of Leanne's pies, and Sawyer and Mel and Cherry would take orders from the tables around me. If I felt up for it, I'd walk over to the new-to-me jukebox and intentionally play a song, and with wishful thinking, it's stocked with at least one of my favorites.

And through my copious amount of doubt, I would feel at home again.

Well, that was a new thing I had to add, and then tick off of my to-do list: find the little pieces of home within The Hideout.

Chapter 10

Sawyer

I liked that no one here believed in the egotistical practices of being fashionably late. Right at seven-thirty, everyone that I had invited had shown up. Almost everyone.

I was able to notice when Mel gave herself mental high fives over the success of tonight. She'd wiggle her eyebrows as she appreciated her work. My name was on the invite, but it wouldn't have been possible without her.

I had Jet, my night worker, secured inside all by himself—the way he preferred it. I told him he could set up the appetizers and organize the music for when it was time to shift the party indoors. I thought I saw a smile form on his face when I finished my proposal, but it was probably just the way the shadows cast on his face.

Jet liked his space, and for it to be exactly how he wanted it. He's a one-man show and that's why I leave the night shifts to him.

"Hey'a Sawyer," Mel broke off from her conversations. "Ready to make a speech?"

"You're joking. That wasn't talked about. We didn't talk about a speech." There was no way I was going to make a speech. I'll give a couple of *thank you's* in passing, a head nod of gratitude even, but I will not be making any sort of speech.

She started to hysterically laugh. "I'm kidding, bud." She nudged her hip into me. "You really did something, ya know that?"

I studied the group moving about the dirt lot. They pointed to their friends, admiring the new paint job and hanging lights I had around outside.

I had gained a sense of accomplishment for something so mundane to some, yet so miraculous to myself. I did it. And without my family's name attached to it.

"I hope so," I finally responded.

Clink, clink, clink...

Ringing from a glass flute stopped everybody in their tracks. Mel and I nipped our conversation and descended from the porch steps. Gus had managed to huddle everyone out front, gathering their full attention.

"I guess they beat ya to the speech, after all," Mel whispered over her shoulder.

"Hi, everybody," Leanne started. "It is so great to see how many of you showed up tonight." The crowd whistled and cheered with excitement.

"As you know, this shack of a restaurant here is mine and Lee's firstborn," Gus chimed in, looking at their children and grandchildren who were clustered in the back of the store. Some nodded, others rolled their eyes. It was a rarity that they came down here, so I knew how much it meant to Gus and Leanne that they showed up.

Mel couldn't help but snort out a quiet laugh. She knew how much this place meant to her grandparents, and she just might be the only family member who ever accepted it for just that.

"But over the last couple of years, we haven't been as hands-on as we once were." He started to walk over, stopping an arm's length away from me. He extended out his arm and let his hand rest on my shoulder. He looked dead straight into my eyes. "This man right here has turned this place into something I could have never imagined it being. It feels like a home away from home, the way it was always meant to be."

I looked down at him, as he is easily a foot shorter than I am, and saw that he was fighting back tears. I patted his back, gave him a single nod, and then gave Leanne a wink. I felt my eyes swell up too. And unlike my previous habits of never showing my emotions around people, I let a tear trickle down my face right there in front of everyone. I wasn't going to hold back any of my feelings. These were feelings that deserved to see the light of day, and I cherished the fact that they held me on a pedestal.

It made me want to work that much harder.

Gus continued, "This is his night. This is all his now." He turned his attention back to the crowd. "And we are so pleased to see you all welcome him and The Hideout with open minds and big hearts."

And just like that, I couldn't ignore the petite redhead that peeked out behind my produce guy. She bobbed back and forth behind the burly man's shoulders, trying to follow Gus and Leanne as they wrapped up their speech. There was a calmness that she exuded even in chaos.

"...to Sawyer," Gus and Leanne said in unison and the crowd repeated after them. "We pass the torch, *officially*, to you." Gus handed me his glass of sparkling cider.

I downed the drink and everyone went back to chatting among themselves as they moved inside. I placed the glass down on the railing and wove my way towards her while the crowd passed by me.

"You came." I stopped in front of her right before she reached the bottom step.

Her head shot up, her eyes went wide with shock. Once she realized it was me, her face sort of lightened up. "That's what she said," she chuckled, then moved past me.

Alright, so she's pretty *and* funny.

"I don't think I have ever seen this place this packed before," she continued as we met the threshold. I stopped beside her. "Except for one time when there was a bad storm that came out of nowhere and everyone huddled in here to take cover. We were squeezed in here like packed sardines, but I didn't care. I wanted warm fries and vanilla ice cream."

"You wanted ice cream while it was cold out?"

She enthusiastically nodded her head and let out a small snort, one she thought she could hide, but I unavoidably heard. She blushed and covered her face.

"That is so gross, I'm sorry."

"I don't think gross was the word I would use," I said. She removed her hands from her cheeks. "What *is* gross is that god-awful combination. What would compel someone to mix those two things?"

She scoffed. "You're telling me you've never heard of anyone doing that before?"

"My cousin Holland does it. That doesn't mean that I support it."

"You have to have some sort of weird food concoction," she said, crossing her arms.

I dramatically tapped my chin and looked up at the sky, displaying my thinking face. I laughed at the first thing that came to mind. I knew that I had no place to judge... "Chocolate-covered bacon," I said definitively.

As she made a theatrical gagging noise, pointing her finger at her tongue sticking out of her mouth, I felt a firm hand grasp my shoulder.

It can't be. Because it wasn't. Of course my grandfather wouldn't show up.

It seemed I twisted the knife when I headed off to Europe to join my parents in all my angst years ago. I was tired of being controlled by the puppet master known as my grandfather. I thought he would respect me a little bit more, for I had at least given him notice, unlike my dad. But it made no difference whatsoever.

It was clear that he was furious with all of us at this point. So much so that he couldn't even show up tonight when he only lives an hour away.

I'll never regret Europe, though. I'll only ever reminisce over it. My parents and I drank our wine and ate the best food there ever was. They got to relive their adventures all over again by showing me the special crooks and crevices.

I had the chance to watch them smile and love life immensely, something I hadn't seen much of growing up thanks to the long nights in office buildings.

An indefinite vacation of bouncing around England, Ireland, Greece, and everything in between sounded like the perfect "unplanned" plan I had in ages. If I no longer had to follow the one laid out for me, I had endless opportunities to create one of my own.

There were even a couple of weeks that summer when I sent the family jet back to the States so my buddies could pile on in and meet me in Prague. We tore up the nightlife scene there. I didn't have to monitor how many drinks I was taking in, or who I kept as company. I wasn't being watched. For the first time in my life, I didn't have eyes, or camera lenses, on me.

Once I learned that my parents were actively making a life of their own there, I decided to head back to Connecticut. To Rider. It was more than a vacation for them, more than a break from the Banks Business. They were truly living the life they were meant to, the life they deserved.

Now I'm living the life I believed I deserved, too. *I deserve this.* Even if he didn't agree.

"Hey'a, you bothering our girl over here?" Gus interrupts us, Leanne goes to Lucy with a bear hug of an embrace. Think I heard a couple of her bones break with how hard she hugged her.

"He's being a very polite host by coming over here to greet me," she said over Leanne's shoulder, staring at me.

The way she is looking at me, playfully. Maybe there's hope to win her over after all.

"That's good to hear," Gus says with a raise of both his brows, followed by a teasing grin.

"I was just about to show Lucy the lake," I cut the conversation short.

"You're going to show *the lake* to the girl who knows this lake like the back of her hand?" Gus said disgruntled.

I chewed on the inside of my cheek, waiting for him to call bullshit. Instead, he clicked his tongue at me but nodded at us to go ahead. *How generous of him to permit us.*

Jet's biker friends were the majority of those who mobbed the patio tables outside and filtered in and out of The Hideout in between their drags of cigarettes. They stuck to the late-night crowd for the most part, but I always appreciated when the regulars could all be together. Cherry was already bringing out a second tray of appetizers to their tables.

Lucy and I passed by, and I exchanged the go-to nod with them. You know, the kind that says, "Hey, good to see you.

How are you doing? Oh, that's great. Alright, let me get that shot of whiskey and a tall boy for you right away." They weren't men of many words. It was a change of pace from what I am used to with the girls—I appreciated the vast difference.

"Ah, yes," Lucy twirled, her boots kicking dirt up underneath her feet. "Hummingbird Lake. Oh, yup," she cupped her hands over her eyes like makeshift glasses and squinted. "Still there. Lookin' the same!" she teased.

"Oh, come on," I started ahead, unbuttoning the top two buttons of my dress shirt. Right on cue, Billy galloped behind us emerging from wherever he was, and trekked alongside me. Lucy swiftly joined, skipping behind.

"Hi, doggy!" Her eyes lit up.

"That's Billy," I said, pulling the hem of my shirt from my denim waistband.

"Billy, you might just be my new best friend. How does that sound? Are we new besties, Billy?" Lucy crouched to give him neck scratches. Right on cue, he started kicking his back left leg, rustling up the dirt beneath him.

The willow tree lights that hung along the lake loop were bright tonight. And the cicadas were emerging, competing with the chirps from crickets while the partygoers socialized, enjoying the evening in its entirety. The humming of distant chatter became further as I decided to take a step away from it all.

When I was a child, at mandatory Christmas parties with a majority of people I hadn't known, I found unused rooms often occupied with coats and purses of whatever family member's house I was at and hid away for the night. The difference is that I knew everyone here tonight, loved their company even—but I guess old habits die hard.

I wanted to avoid any commentary, even if it's been posi-tive so far. I don't think I'm ready to see my place filled with opinions and standards. At least not yet. It was different than before. I know that some were aware of the changes being made, but it was all gradual. Now it was *BOOM!* All mine. Just like Gus said it was in his speech.

And the definiteness of it all scared me.

I had the power to mess up and had no one to pass it off on.

The whole town had their eyes on me.

I am well aware that a night walk wasn't on Mel's itinerary for me, but I was writing it in. *Time to loosen up.*

"Maybe it's time to see Hummingbird through a new shade of colored glasses," I said, leading us on the walking trail.

Chapter 11

Lucy

A twilight walk in the woods wasn't mentioned in Sawyer's invitation for tonight, but here we are. Had I known, I definitely wouldn't have worn these shoes.

"Hurry up, slowpoke," Sawyer yelled back. Billy and I both jog toward him—I use the word *jog* lightly. Having not been worn since my Junior year of high school, the pull strap of my booties dug into the side of my calf.

The first couple of buttons were undone from Sawyer's shirt, and I'd be a fool not to take a couple of glances at his exposed chest. It was firm with the perfect amount of chest hair. I was certain that a small puddle of drool was collecting in the corner of my mouth, so I concentrated only on putting one foot in front of the other.

"You're not going to murder me out here, are you?"

He shot me a look, his brows were furrowed.

"Sorry, I've listened to a lot of true crime podcasts not to ask," I continued.

He combed his fingers through his hair, ruffling up his slicked-back look. Thin strands doused in gel fell out of place and hung loosely in front of his face. He almost felt like a real person, not one that was as *on* as he seemed to be before. He's been flirtatious and forward with me. It was nice, but it was nothing that would sweep me off my feet.

"So, are you thinking about sticking around for a while?"

"I guess that depends on what you consider *a while*. I'm here just for the summer. Gotta get back to Arizona," I admitted.

He kept his sights on the ground in front of us. A large pause grew between us before he finally said, "What's back in Arizona?"

"Work. I start my residency program in the fall."

"No, shit?" he pulled his head back, utterly shocked. I nodded. "That's pretty badass," he continued. "A doctor, hmm… What kind?"

"I plan to be a neonatologist," I said, choked up.

My skin began to crawl and I felt hives form along my arms the moment I mentioned myself or any of my interests. Talking about myself makes me nauseous. I try not to talk to many who aren't also joining the medical field. It never held anyone's attention. People tend to ask to be polite, but then zone off in the middle of my excitement once they realize I could go on and on. And I could.

"What made you choose that?"

I shrugged his question off, but the heat from the hole Sawyer was burning into the side of my head told me he wasn't going to leave it. He was waiting for his answer and he made it known. That didn't matter. Reality sunk in and I stuck with my programmed, generic answers.

"Guess I've always had an interest in it."

"Hmm."

Then, crickets. And I'm not just talking about the ones that followed us on our trail.

I hated that our conversation went dull and that I was the reason for it. I can't make myself share little bits and pieces of who I am, regardless if it's harmless or not. Regardless if *he's* harmless or not.

I couldn't get to know him the way that he wanted to get to know me. Knowing that he took his coffee black and always wore leather boots, even in the summer heat, was the extent to which I was willing to know about him.

I didn't care that he found salvation in the same people I have. Or that he cared for them as deeply as I did. That was all disposable knowledge once the leaves started to change in the fall.

It had to be.

"So, you're *not* heading back to a boyfriend?"

"Don't have one."

"Hmm," he said once more, this time with a smirk.

"*Hmm* nothing."

Absolutely nothing.

That was not at all valuable information to him whatsoever. I was really regretting showing up to this shindig after all. I thought I was going to have a couple of drinks and mingle with people I haven't seen in quite some time. At no point did I think I was going to have a Dr. Phil moment in the fricken woods.

"If you must know," *and it seemed like he did,* "I haven't had one of *those* for quite some time now."

"That's a very relative concept if you think about it." He raised both of his eyebrows, scrunching up his forehead. "What does that mean, exactly?"

"Uh…" I scratched the side of my head, inquisitively, dramatically to buy myself time. "Seven years?" I said as a question, though there was no question about it. I am very in tune with that knowledge.

He's giving me that shocked look again. And I didn't like it as much as before. It doesn't feel as validating this time around, but more so that he thought something was wrong with me.

"There's no way. Seven years? You haven't had a boyfriend in seven years?"

"Thanks for rubbing it in, jerk," I pushed into his arm. "I mean I have dated people casually since then. But if we are talking seriously, then yeah. I haven't been with anyone since my freshman year of college. If you really want something to tease me for, just know that they were my first, and only real relationship, too."

My ex-boyfriend David and I dated for our entire first year of college. We had met at freshmen orientation and spent every waking second together when we weren't in classes or working. It was new and exciting and I was playing into the new season of life I was in.

There was a short time that I thought David was going to be there for the long haul, I thought I was lucky enough to have found my soulmate so early on in the game. But I was tired of dulling myself down.

Soon, I learned that I was hiding myself and my feelings through the relationship that I had with him. He was sweet and caring, and the perfect first boyfriend. But he was still a distraction.

I learned that a soulmate didn't need to be romantic. The idea of a soulmate had every possibility of being whatever I wanted it to be. It wasn't until I met Gracie that I realized relationships weren't meant to be scapegoats—platonic, or romantic. They're not meant to be used as a shield to hide behind.

I put off relationships after David, afraid that I was going to lose myself in a relationship again. The friendships that I made along the way that let me shine are what I prioritized. I focused on school work and staying busy, it made the most sense.

Putting time in what mattered most to me is what made the most sense.

Sawyer was giving me that look again, and I was growing really tired of it.

"Was that a personal choice, or—"

"Personal choice, professional choice…"

I wasn't too sure how I felt about his determination to ask such invasive questions.

Anytime someone tried to get to know me, it was never really to *get to know me*. It was just a lame attempt to get me in the bedroom, hoping it was my idea of foreplay if they paid enough attention to me. Spoiler alert: talking about myself is *not* my idea of foreplay.

I swore it would never work, yet I fell for it each time.

Once I picked up on the tactics, that's when I started applying a direct approach to answering questions. A simple "yes" or "no" and the occasional "sometimes" did the trick.

I found a mask to wear and put it on when necessary. Eventually, I played it safe and applied it more times than not. Nothing more than five words, each one no more than two syllables long. It worked.

At least it did.

"I swore to myself that I wouldn't get into a serious relationship again. At least not until I knew that person was going to add to my life, rather than be my whole life. If that makes sense."

But now I realized Sawyer wasn't being invasive at all. He kept his attention on me the whole time and his eyes didn't grow heavy once. He was genuinely interested.

That scared me so much more.

I became unsettled with the consciousness that I could be so open about one part of my life, but not another. I like to believe it's because my career is something I cherish so deeply. Talking about relationships, or the lack thereof, was as meaningless to me as talking about the weather or asking if anyone caught the game last week.

"That makes perfect sense," he smiled down at me, then pulled me into him. He wrapped his arm around my side and we fell into a synchronized step as we finished our walk. Being held by him felt a lot nicer than I anticipated. Almost natural, too. "And I wouldn't tease you, you know."

I looked up at him, confused for a moment.

"You said I could tease you about that being your only real relationship. I want you to know that I wouldn't tease you for that."

"Really?" He just might be the first.

"Never. You're just waiting for that perfect addition."

My heart, stomach, knees—they all turned to mush like a domino effect down my body.

"The stars are bright tonight," I said to change the mood of the evening, my voice a little higher pitched than I would like. As someone who hates talking about themselves, I sure found a way to share one of the biggest parts about who I am tonight.

"You think so?"

"Yeah... I've spent too much time away, I forgot that you can see every star out here. The sky is deeper, darker. And the stars, they're—"

"Brighter," he interjected.

"They're brighter," I repeated back to him.

Before I knew it, we'd made it back to The Hideout where the crowd population had been cut in half and the music became louder. A string of bulb lights hung from the roof to the large trees across the way.

Cherry and Mel were perched up on the porch railing while the bartender and his buddies were leaning against their bikes grumbling and groaning about who knows what. Gus and Leanne were in lawn chairs in front of the patio, looking out over the lake. And stragglers were grouped, sprawled on top of picnic blankets.

Here I was, surrounded by a group of *almost* all new people in the town that I thought would never change. It was impossible to think that it would.

Hell, even Hillside High down the road had forever been painted a depressing, dark gray color. And all of a sudden it's a nice, new rich blue shade. The streets were freshly paved and they had more than two stop signs outside the storefronts.

"Lucy!" Gus waved me over.

I looked over at Sawyer, and he gave me a nod. "I'll see you around, Lucy."

Gus reached for his jacket pocket as he rose from his seat. Shoving his hand into his limp jacket draped over his arms, "It's in here somewhere," he said, before shifting to the other pocket. "Ah, ha!"

I looked down at Leanne who had a sneaky but proud grin as she observed the exchange. She winked up at me as Gus handed over a wrapped gift.

"What is this?"

"Well, go on and open it."

I scrambled my way through tearing off the neatly folded paper, nervous to fully rip it off.

"Oh, just give me that!" Gus ripped the gift out of my hand in excitement and started to tear off the wrapping paper.

A Moveable Feast by Ernest Hemingway was shoved back in my hands. I let out the largest, loudest girlish squeal of my life.

"You did not?!"

"He did!" Leanne jumped up from her seat and hugged me. "He's looked everywhere for it and *that*," she viciously taps her fingers on the cover, "is the first edition. It was Hemingway's original copy with his notes all in the margins."

"Happy Graduation, kiddo."

I flipped through the pages. Scribbles of ink—some legible, some not—were all throughout the book. I thought I was going to throw up from pure love and excitement. Instead, I said, "Thank you," and threw myself into Gus' arms.

"You're the best, you know that?" I said over his shoulder.

He said nothing except sniffled into my ear.

Gus was the person who got me into reading in the first place. Fitzgerald, Orwell, Dickens... Hemingway. Weekly, we'd meet at the picnic table right down here by the lake and he'd bring me a new book to escape between. I was eleven years old with classic novels as my best friend. Of course, as I got older, I discovered more contemporary selections. But no matter what, my love for reading started with one little book titled *The Old Man and the Sea* and I have never looked back since.

This moment felt wonderful, otherworldly. Even with all of the changes in town, this right here felt like nothing had changed at all.

It almost felt like this moment alone was enough to feel that magic of Rider again. Hummingbird Lake still looked the same, I'd be damned if it didn't. And it still held the power to push my boundaries and force me to open my heart more than I'd like, that's for sure.

But here I was, standing in the same spot I have many times before, exchanging literature with Gus.

I'll enjoy the walks down memory lane, but still, I fear that one good night, one good-looking man, wasn't going to change the fact that I felt so out of place. When I shut my eyes at night, I couldn't help but feel so out of place.

All I knew now was I had to give it a proper send-off this time around. A final goodbye to Rider.

Chapter 12

Sawyer

I had coffee sitting at my fingertips at any hour of the day, but there's something about coffee made by someone who wasn't trying to give people a heart attack before eight in the morning.

Mel can mix up a cocktail better than anyone I know, even better than Jet—and that's saying something considering he taught her how to bartend. But her coffee-making skills are where the mixology expertise stops.

I think she's too immune to her caffeine intake that having a potency any lower than lethal is considered water for her. For that reason alone, I was willing to walk ten minutes down the road for a sane person's cup of coffee.

Jitters, the quaint coffee house at the end of the main road, had mahogany plank countertops with mismatched chairs and tables. A couple of chess boards lived at the tables in the back, and stacks of books were scattered around on mismatched shelves throughout. If there was an open seat, you sat down and would strike up a conversation with whoever was near. Jitters wasn't necessarily a grab-and-go type of place. It was a place where you'd grab your coffee and want to stay awhile. It was a community here.

There was more of an eclectic look to it than the coffee shops I was used to going to growing up. I was familiar with all white and marble surfaces with menus that had four things listed as options. And you better hope you liked it as is because there was no way they tolerated any substitutions. The workers were as stone-cold as their cemented flooring, leaving you feeling judged no matter if you ordered whole or almond milk.

"Hey, Sawyer," the barista on the shorter side and a *Florence and the Machine* button on their apron sang as I walked through the front door.

I walked up to the counter, "Hey, how's it going, Kai? I'll have my usual."

"I don't think a straight, black coffee can be classified as someone's usual, but okay."

"Isn't that what I *usually* get?" I tease, they nod. "Exactly, so pour me my caffeine. You don't want to piss off an un-caffeinated customer, do you?"

They throw loose sugar packets at me with a laugh. "You're a pain in my ass."

"Hey, I think you should be nicer to the person who is possibly conjuring up some business for you. A new girl in town. Well, semi-new. She's here and she is looking to sell one of the Hillside Cottages."

They look up at the ceiling, "That doesn't make any sense. Because the only people that live over there would be—"

"Lucy Collins," I completed their sentence as I grabbed my drink.

"Man, she is not new whatsoever, you idiot. She and my siblings were in the same grade in high school."

I shrugged my shoulders, "Okay, whatever. She's new to me."

Kai let out a snort and rolled their eyes. "I appreciate it, nonetheless. But I wonder why she is selling. Pretty sure the

Collins family has had that cottage since the eighteenth century." They walked away to tend to a new order.

The shop was on the slower end for a summer morning. A group of teenagers were huddled in a corner couch, pelting each other with crumpled-up straw wrappers. At the table opposite them, people were typing away on their laptops, having hushed phone calls, or reading books thicker than sandwiches I'd eaten before.

"Sorry I had to miss your opening a couple of weeks ago, I was swamped," Kai admitted.

"I just hope to see you down at the lake sometime this summer. Get you on one of the pedal boats."

"Not for a million bucks will you see me on one of those again," they said with a straight face.

"How about *two* million?"

"Oh, he's got jokes now?"

Kai has never been one to enjoy large group settings.

On one of our last summers, before we all went off to college, Kai was kicked back, idling in the middle of the lake. After my cousins and I snuck a few too many beers, more than what our parents *allowed under their supervision,* we thought it was a good idea to practice interpretive dances on the side of the speed boats. Granted, none of us danced a lick in our life. But that didn't matter once the Budweiser hit our adolescent bloodstreams.

We were speeding by Kai, already annoying them with the waves we were creating. We upped the ante when my cousin Holland backflipped mid-pirouette off the edge. What we thought was harmless fun, Kai classifies as trauma.

For the rest of that summer, Kai sat on the dock or in the lawn chairs between our family's houses with a glare in their eyes and a book in their hands. I felt bad for a while after, but now it's something to reminisce on.

Kai always followed the rules and called people out when they were complete tools. Sometimes, I was the said tool. Back then, I hated how it killed the vibe. They had always been that way, though. Quiet, stand-offish. I was surprised we even became friends.

It wasn't until I realized we weren't too different after all.

I was quick to learn that they just might be the only other person that I could keep an intellectual conversation with. Anyone I went to school with was either too uptight, with their righteous stick up their ass preparing to be the future president, or they were off partaking in extracurriculars that weren't really my scene and started snorting blow in the bathrooms. Neither of those crowds appealed to me.

I never had to wonder about Kai, though. I knew they'd never fall down the path of stuffy ties and pressed slacks. Maybe the fact that they lived here in Rider full-time with their mom kept them grounded deeper than the rest of us.

"Look, I gotta get going. Don't work too hard," I yelled as I walked away from the coffee bar while new customers flocked to order at once.

Even beneath a worn-in baseball cap that had the Hillside High logo on it and behind towering college students home for the summer, I was still able to spot Lucy in a room of crowded people. She's the type of person you could feel in a room if you were blind. The space felt brighter, warmer.

Her head was hung low, her face covered.

"Well, I can tell you right now that Gus isn't here, so who are we looking for this time?" I lowered my head near her ear. Her body rattled with shock, though she kept her eyes on her feet.

"Sawyer," she whispered into the ground.

"You knew it was me just by the sound of my voice, how sweet."

She lifted her head and looked at me out of the corner of her eyes, then shifted her whole body to face me.

"You haven't seen anyone come from upstairs, have you?"

"No?" I questioned her, peering over the slew of people.

Her voice was lower than before. She bobbed her head around the teen boy rivaling the height of a giraffe in front of us, swaying back and forth as she scanned the long line in front of her. "Wow. Super long line today. I don't need coffee that bad. Are you heading out? Yeah, okay, I'll head out with you."

With a perfect imitation of a roadrunner, she turned on her heels and sped out the front door. I am positive she left track marks on the small pooch hiding under the legs of its owner. Once we crossed the street and reached the sidewalk, she took her cap off and slicked down the stray hairs.

"Lucy, what's up? Are you okay?" I looked back over my shoulder and then back down at her. I noticed that the color had returned to her face.

"Yup. Fine," she said sharply. "Sorry. I've just been busy the last couple of weeks. Ran out of coffee and haven't made it to the store to get said coffee, so I thought I'd stop in here, but on second thought, I think I'll drink some tea today. Too crowded in there."

"*Okay...*"

"So, how have you been? I've been busy. Oh, I already said that. Sorry... So, yeah. How are you?" her voice got higher and higher with each sentence, her lips moving almost as fast as her feet. I was struggling to keep up with her.

"*I'm going to ask you again... Are you good?*"

She let out an exasperated breath, stopping in her tracks. Perching her hands on her hips, she slowly nodded. "Yeah.

God, I haven't had a moment to breathe in days. I wouldn't have known it was Tuesday unless my friend hadn't called me and said something. I have been nonstop cleaning and yet I feel like I haven't even made a dent."

"Is there anything I could help you with?"

She looked around and lets out another large breath, this time a little more relaxed. "You know what? Yes. I would love some help."

Wow. And I didn't even need to insult her crown molding.

"But first, we are going to get you that coffee. We can stop at The Hideout on the way. I have a feeling you might like the way Mel makes her coffee."

Her eyes widened and a smile filled her face. She twirled around, her workout skirt spun around against her body, and she started ahead of me.

I have seen Lucy smile before, but I'd do anything for her to smile that way again. There was something special about it, an ease in her mind I had yet to see. And it was brought on by something as simple as coffee. Whatever the reason, knowing that I played even a small part was enough for me.

Chapter 13

Sawyer

We walked in as Mel and Cherry were finishing up morning prep.

"You're here before nine." Mel stopped mid-rolling the silverware in her hands.

"I'm here before nine."

"You're never here before nine."

"Well, today, I am."

"Hi, Lucy!" Cherry said cheerfully, rounding the counter to hug her.

Once they released themselves from their hug, I led Lucy over to the bar. One hand on the small of her back, I pulled out the stool with the other. "You sit here, I'll get you some coffee."

"I heard you make the best coffee around."

Mel swung a bar towel over one shoulder and playfully swiped the imaginary dust off the other. Lucy was doing exactly what Mel loved—someone was telling her how amazing and perfect she is at everything she does. "Yeah, well... *Some* people would like to disagree with that statement."

"I'm sorry that I don't want to go into cardiac arrest by the time that I'm forty," I teased as I poured coffee in a to-go cup.

I slid it across the bar towards Lucy. I crouched down, under the counter and pulled out every option I had to offer from the fridge. I hugged five different milk options in my arms and dropped them between us. "I don't know what you like, so here's all of them."

But when I looked up from the cartons, Lucy's eyes were lined red.

"Fuck. What did I say?"

She stopped a tear from falling before it even left her eye socket and sat up straight. She let out a faint, broken snicker. "Nothing, I'm okay." She grabbed the oat milk and mixed it into her coffee. She snapped the lid on. "Do you have a pen and paper? We are going to have to write down our objectives for today."

All at once, Cherry, Mel, and I swiped out ordering pads from beside the register or underneath the bar. We tossed them out in front of her, with an array of pens to follow. We had *plenty* of pens and paper here.

"Perfect," she perked up.

After she completed noting something down, she would strike a strong line beneath it. Some even received three lines with stars doodled on the side. She wrote like she was running out of time. After only a quick minute, she hopped up off the stool. Swiping her hat off the bar, she threw it back on top of her head.

"All done." She turned to me. "Ready to go?"

I pulled the pad from her hand and looked over today's agenda. "Looks doable," I said as I tucked it into my back pocket. "Let's get going."

Lucy walked out ahead of me, giving both Mel and Cherry a wave in passing. "Thanks for the coffee!" she said cheerfully.

Before I reached the door, Mel interjected by pushing a firm hand on my chest.

If a scowl from a raven-haired girl could kill, I'd be dead.

"Do me a favor?"

"Okay," I stood at attention, mocking her authoritative tone.

"Don't say anything dumb, don't do anything dumb. Don't. Be. Dumb."

I pulled her head inwards and kissed the top of her head. "I don't plan on it."

Mel, my voice of reason.

I met Lucy outside on the porch where she was leaning against the railing, both elbows propped up as she looked out over the lake. She took a sip of coffee before facing me. "This might be my favorite coffee ever."

Chapter 14

Lucy

My hands might have been shaking, but I needed Mel's coffee more than anything. I took another sip as I walked up the front steps. Sawyer trailing behind me only a few steps back, I rattled the keys out of my purse.

"I apologize in advance for the mess. It's a lot more... It's different from when you saw it last."

I slowly pushed the door open, delaying the reveal of the utter mess we were about to walk into. I slid boxes out of the walkway and kicked at loose packing paper scattered across the floor.

I was officially drowning in the "deal with later" pile, and it was *way* past later.

"I thought you needed to pack this place up?" Sawyer let out a joking snort.

I scoffed. "Every time I think I'm making headway, I find three more things I need to take care of. There's no way I can bring even half of this back home with me. I live with someone who owns more handbags than I do clothes. I started unpacking to sort through everything and now," I waved my hands over the mess, "this sort of just happened and I couldn't stop it."

He rubbed his hands together. "Put me in, coach." He clapped his hands together, then rolled up his nonexistent sleeves. He reached for his back pocket and held up my list. "It's a good thing a super duper smart person decided to make a game plan."

I started down the hall, trying to hide the warmth I felt building on my cheeks. "We can take these downstairs," I said, pointing to the pile of boxes near the entryway. "It will help clear out the main area."

"I'm sorry, there's a *downstairs?*"

I opened up the hidden door and made my way down. He followed after.

"Wow, I guess I didn't expect these places to have a basement. They're so…"

"I like to think of it as a Mary Poppins house."

Sawyer said nothing.

I turned to look at him, adjusting the box in my hand. "Please tell me you know Mary Poppins?"

We reached the bottom of the stairs, I flicked the lights on. The musty smell of mothballs and dryer sheets lingered in the air, it was the signature scent down here.

He sat his box down at his feet. "Is that the same lady in the Princess Diaries?"

"You know the Princess Diaries, but not Mary Poppins?!" I planted my hand on my hip.

He shrugged his shoulders and looked around. "Guess that means we'll have to watch it together," he said, inching closer.

I took a step back, almost stumbling over the stacked boxes behind me. I was certain my face turned a crimson red. I felt it more than anything and I thanked my lucky stars that even with the light on, it was too dull and dungeon-like down here. Sawyer caught me quickly before I fell. His hands wrapped behind my waist, stabilizing me.

"Thanks," I whispered out.

He pulled himself back and walked towards the stairwell again. He coughed out. "I wonder why Gus' doesn't have a basement."

I moved myself over beside the washing machine. Allowing my heart rate to return to its normal state. "He does. All four of the cottages do. You know that gaudy coat rack that he has by his stairwell?" I asked, and he nodded. "Behind it is their basement door. They never use it. Leanne is terrified of it. Out of sight, out of mind."

Gus would do anything for Leanne, as long as it made her happy. Something as small as using a coat rack as a cloak for the basement that houses so-called monsters, or something as big as selling the grill so he could spend more time at home. He would do any and every thing under the sun, moon, and all of its stars for that woman.

I don't ever want a love if it isn't like the one that they have.

I blew out a breath as I studied the space. "Okay, I don't think a list, a pamphlet, or a book is going to help in this case... I have no idea how I want to go about this."

"I'll follow your lead and try not to break anything as much as possible."

I widened my stance. I was paralyzed with the heaps of boxes. "I guess I'll deal with this over here, and you can head over there. Sound good?"

He gave me a thumbs-up. Crouching down to lift some boxes, he quickly became frozen by the creak of the stairs.

"Don't worry about that, that's our ghost friend Tony."

He squirmed, shaking out his entire body. "That is so not funny," he winced.

I giggled before tackling my headache of a pile. Photo albums, painted pictures, sad excuses of mugs that I made in pottery class that my grandmother refused to get rid of... I pushed them all off to the side to add to the rest of the mayhem upstairs.

The other boxes consisted of winter coats and boots and they were stacked high up to the ceiling. Those, I knew, could go straight to the donation pile. I can't remember the last time I wore anything heavier than a light sweatshirt in Arizona. I pulled them down only to reveal behind it all was Tuck's folded-up flag displayed on the wall. Framed awards and medals hung on either side of it.

I mourn a person I have never even met. I knew of a laugh that belonged to someone I had never even met. The home videos and memorabilia kept him close, though. I traced my fingers over the photo of him that sat in the center of the award plaque.

Sawyer shuffled his way up behind me. I felt him without him even laying a finger on me.

"Can I ask you something?"

I sucked in a shallow breath and nodded. "Always."

"Why sell? It's not like it's going anywhere," he asked. *How bold of him.* He asked a question I hadn't wanted to ask myself. I slowly pulled my hand off the photo of Tuck before turning around.

"There's nothing left for me here."

He tried to find the answers behind my eyes as he jumped his attention back and forth between them. Answers that I desperately needed, too. But nothing escaped his mouth.

I never expected to leave Rider. Rider was going to be the place that I always came back to. I was going to go to school, get my degree, and come back to start my life here.

Within my first year of med school, I was convinced I wouldn't make it to see my last. After the first semester was over and I had finished my finals, I had booked a flight home ready to accept defeat and return a failure. I swore I had tanked all of my exams, something that had never happened before. I felt like all of my dreams and everything I thought I knew about myself was coming to an end.

As I arrived at the airport, the first report rolled through in my email. I moved like a zombie through the TSA check-in line. I scrolled and scrolled, and hit refresh about a million times. The airport Wi-Fi was absolute trash. But as I was about to hand them my passport and ticket, it loaded. Every score for every class was right there at the tips of my fingers. And every single one read that I passed. I passed with flying colors.

I ranked incredibly low, but I passed nonetheless. A fire was lit inside of me. And I made a promise to myself to keep at it, even on the hardest and longest days.

I stuck around and made sure never to let it get to that point again. I studied any free chance I had. Woke up early, stayed up late. I never got lower than a ninety-two for the rest of med school.

"It's not the same anymore," I continued.

Sawyer lifts his hand and runs his fingers through my hair, pushing it behind my ear. He stopped at my jaw and my heart skipped a beat—or two. I rested my face in his palm.

"I get it," he said. "The place you thought would never change, did."

I nodded and closed my eyes. The warmth of his hand comforted me.

"I need to be honest with you."

I saw all of the color of his face disappear with that statement.

"Earlier. With the coffee. It wasn't about the coffee."

"I had a feeling it wasn't."

"Coronary Heart Disease. My grandmother, I mean. That's what she passed away from."

I hated that even the slightest mention relating to her passing, the cause of it, turned me into a mess. It didn't make sense, I don't think that it ever will. The person with the greatest, biggest heart I'd ever known lost her life to it. Sawyer's comment had no ill intention behind it, that I am sure of, but still, I let it shake me up.

"And I was making jokes about having heart issues," he dropped his hand from my face and pulled me in for a hug.

I could feel his heart beating against my cheek. *Thump, thump, thump.* I could hear it throughout my entire body. But then I couldn't decipher if it was his or mine anymore.

I pulled away from him. "You didn't know." I wiped away a tear I didn't even realize had formed.

"She was sick for a few months, which seems like a long time. But it happened really fast. And it being so close to the time I was planning on leaving for college... I didn't think I was going to accept my offer."

"But you did."

"You asked me why I chose neonatology." He nodded, then pulled at my hand, directing us to a makeshift seat made of some of the firmer boxes. He never once let go of his hold on me. The palms of my hands became clammy, but I couldn't bring myself to pull away. I liked feeling him hold me, even if it was just my fingertips. "When I was waiting around at the hospital, I spent a lot of my time up at the nursery. I thought being around newborns would cheer me up. I was staring death in the face so much that I wanted to focus on all of the little, adorable lives that were just beginning. Until all of the alarms went off on one of the monitors for this little girl. All of these nurses rushed in, their coats flew in the wind after them.

They looked like they had on capes," I let out a chuckle, "and I guess in a way, they did. They were real-life superheroes.

"My heart dropped and I didn't even know this little girl. But a couple of days later when I went to visit my grandmother, Tiffany, that's her name... Well, anyway, that little girl was back in the nursery looking better than ever. I had always known I liked the idea of taking care of people, I thought I was going to go to school to become an English teacher. I hadn't always had an interest in it. I said I did. Honestly, blood spooks me and the smell of Isopropyl Alcohol makes me sick. It wasn't until that moment that I decided I'd focus on medicine. When I decided to leave, I went to college for that little girl, for Tiffany... For me."

"Either way, you left to save the world, Lucy Collins."

I took a step back. "Sometimes it's hard to believe it for myself."

His brows threaded with a sense of anger, and annoyance. "How could you think that? You're doing amazing things."

"I was supposed to become an English teacher. The plan was to teach at Hillside High just like she did. I never even got to tell her about my career change."

"And you don't think she knows regardless? That love, that connection? I am positive that she is with you always. She knows, and she's proud."

I looked up at him. Sawyer's jaw was clenched and his chest heaved as our faces were inches away from each other now. I reached my hand up the bottom of his face, the scruff scratched under my palm and he covered mine with his.

"Lucy..."

I quickly pulled my hand out from underneath his, "I'm sorry." I stood and stepped off to the side. "D-do you want to grab some food? I can clean another day." I patted my fingers along the frame of my face, dabbing away the sudden layer of sweat that grew in a matter of seconds.

My cheeks were warm, but the moment I no longer felt him, the coldness grew exponentially.

"Yeah… Let's go."

We scooted past the boxes and headed for the stairs. "Watch your step for Tony."

The silence as Sawyer followed me up behind the stairs was deafening.

You left to save the world, Lucy Collins.

I felt unworthy to receive such words. And I dismissed it like I do everything, talking about how what I was doing wasn't good enough. That I'm not good enough. All because I didn't stick to a plan.

Life hasn't gone according to plan for as long as I can remember. Whether it was in my control or not. Yet, I felt responsible all the same. I have always had this insistent need to make sure people were proud of me. It was my mission to never stop until they were. Though, when I received the praise I so desperately wanted, it still wasn't good enough.

I still wasn't good enough.

Chapter 15

Sawyer

The screen door slammed shut. Instantly, we were swallowed by the horde of out-of-towners as we entered The Hideout. Lucy beelined it to the counter, and we pushed our way through the crowd.

"What in the world—"

"I know," Mel cut me off.

"Is she okay?" Lucy pointed at Cherry zoned out in the corner, staring off into nothingness.

"She asked someone how they were doing and instead of responding, they just shouted 'table for 4' at her, and she has yet to recover from it," Mel explained as she rustled through order tickets.

"Where do you need me?" I shouted out over the roaring chatter.

"Me, too!"

"You know how to serve?" Mel and I asked Lucy in unison.

"Mmhm," she nodded, we stared at her for a beat until she continued. "Okay, actually, no... *but* I did play pretend restaurant when I was a kid and never had a complaint."

Mel shrugged, I laughed. "Good enough for me," Mel said. "These drinks need to go to table seven. And table four needs two Bloody Mary's."

"I got the drinks covered," I said. "Think you can get those folks over there seated?" I pointed to the front porch.

"And I'll take care of this one over here," Mel motioned to Cherry who was on the verge of tears at the end of the bar.

Lucy headed up to the front, with a huge smile sprawled across her face. Her warmth hit the customers just like I knew it would. The people who once had a cold demeanor, with their arms folded across their chests, instantly relaxed as she approached them. You would have never guessed she just came from crying in her basement.

It pained me to see how easy it was for her to flip the switch. As if it was such a routined thing to do.

Two mimosas, a mule, and a Shirley temple—I slid them onto a tray and made my way to table seven. Seeing faces I'm not used to once the summer months hit is something I'll never get used to. I liked knowing the regulars' orders or being able to gauge what time of the day certain people were going to come in and how long they would stay. But in the summer months, I feel as clueless as I did when I initially took over.

I remember when the talks about buying from Gus began. I had never worked a day in the industry in my life, and he fully expected me to take over smoothly. I admired the trust that man had in me, but shit... I was terrified. He eased the stress by asking me to work a couple of days a week, to see if this was even something I liked.

I started with hosting duties, and I didn't get such easy smiles from people. They grumbled the moment they saw me. Eventually, I moved over to serving and dropped every plate that day. By the next day, I had only dropped two. I took that progress and ran with it—I became cocky.

He reassured me when he told me it was okay if I didn't know what I was doing, that that's what a staff was for. That instantly hit a nerve. Hiring staff to do all my dirty work while I cashed the check—I would be no better than my grandfather. From then on, I was determined to be as hands-on as I could. I learned all of the ins and the outs, and by the third week, I was already imagining plans for the place.

"What is there to do around here?" A bold and rather annoyed-with-everything teenager interjected as I greeted the family.

"Harry, you could start by saying hello first?" The father nudged his shoulder before looking up at me. "Sorry, we don't take him out enough."

The whole table laughed.

A poor joke about children being like animals...I groaned over my shoulder.

I gave a strained smile and a curt laugh as I placed their drinks on the table. The mom snatched one of the mimosas and the mule for herself, and immediately started alternating between the two.

"*Sorry*," Harry rolled his eyes and dramatically adjusted himself in his seat. "My parents dragged me along to this good-for-nothing town and I am depressingly bored. What can I do here that isn't strictly for old people."

His father clicked his tongue and gave Harry a look.

"Ha, well—"

"I am not old," his mother chimed in, slurring her words holding an already empty glass, the other one halfway gone.

"We're on vacation," the father spoke out eagerly. "We are from Michigan, visiting family for a few weeks."

I turned to the kid, tucking the empty tray under my arm. "There's lots to do, it's up to you to decide if it's something you would enjoy."

He threw himself back into his seat and rolled his eyes again before taking a sip from his Shirley Temple.

"We are hoping to tour some colleges while we are here, too!" his dad said gleefully.

"I'm not going to college. Especially not here."

The dad waved the kid off dismissively.

The restaurant gradually grew in noise and population. "Look, I am sorry I can't be too much help. But I promise this is a special place. Make the most of the summer here. And as for colleges," I look at the dad, "look closer into the city. We have a community college here and that's about it. Nothing he will like, I don't think. Look over those menus and one of us will be right back to take your order." I split off from the table.

I started to make Bloody Mary's, though I never took my eyes off Lucy once. She strutted through the place with the utmost grace. I fumbled my hands through the prepared garnishes. Bacon, olives, a single lime—I fed them through a pick and placed them on top of the mixed drink. Purely relied on muscle memory.

"Wow," Cherry said as she came up beside me. "I can't even do that."

I came out of the Lucy trance and looked down at the counter. I repeated the same pattern with the next one.

"You doing good, bud?" I pulled her in for a side hug with one hand, sprinkling salt and pepper on the drinks with the other. I finished them off by sticking a piece of celery into each glass.

She blows out a deep breath, "Yeah, I'm fine. Ugh, you know how I get."

Cherry was a little ball of energy, friendly with everyone she came in contact with. Most of the time, people took it well. Sometimes, not so much. But then again, these were all people who didn't know and love her for her, so I understood it being "too much" at times.

When I first met Cherry, I desperately needed a drink afterward. I never did well with people who could speak faster than I could think. But then I soon learned that she would do anything for anyone and every other stupid excuse of why I didn't want to be around her vanished. Cherry was the light that I needed in my life. That, and Mel basically adopted her. Some might say I didn't have a choice, I say that she grew on me.

I couldn't imagine it any other way.

I slid the drinks in front of her. "You think you can bring these to table four? If they bite your head off, too, you send them my way." She grabbed both of them with shaky hands and walked them on over.

I kept myself preoccupied behind the bar for as long as I could, wiping up the countertop, and organizing the plates in the order they needed to be picked up. I didn't want to move and risk obscuring my view of Lucy.

"Hey, hey, you're messing up my system!" Zander yelled out from the kitchen window and rearranged the plates back to how they were.

I recognized the childlike laughter coming from the back of the restaurant. It was as if I developed a spidey sense of some sort when it came to Lucy. I moved down the bar to get a closer listen but faced the opposite way to pretend otherwise.

"...lime pie is my favorite. But everything here is so good! What do you typically go for?"

"Anything sweet," one of them said.

"You're looking pretty sweet," another voice chimed in.

I spun around at the rapid boiling of my blood.

She rolled her eyes and started to pull herself further from the table, but he continued to inch closer to her.

"Lucy!" I yelled out, louder than expected. The whole restaurant fell silent and turned their attention toward me. "Sorry. Hey, Lucy, can you come here for a second," I said at a lower volume.

With flushed cheeks, she looked down at the table, then back at me. Everyone else returned to their eating and drinking.

She quickly shuffled her way over to me. "What's up? Did I mess something up?" she whispered out.

"No, no, of course not. You okay over there?"

She looked over her shoulder at the table, they're all refusing to look this way, except the one who got handsy took glances out of the corner of his eyes.

"That? Oh, that's nothing compared to a night out in Downtown Phoenix." She placed a hand on my upper arm, "I promise I'm fine. But thank you for caring." She gave it a squeeze.

"Do you want to take a break? I know this isn't what you had planned for the day." I took one more look at the table, which moved on to the girl sitting beside them. I see that the piranhas were out today and they weren't leaving until they had prey under their thumb. "What do you say?"

Lucy said nothing. Instead, she grabbed a menu and started to flip through it. She wiggled in place, doing a little happy dance. "I am starved!" She rounded the counter and took a seat at the bar.

I opened a menu as well, for no other reason than to keep myself from staring at her. I don't think my blood pressure is ever at a normal resting point when I am around Lucy.

Chapter 16

Sawyer

Jet trekked in, heavy-footed in his leather Doc Martens and all, as I was sending Mel and Cherry home for the day. "You guys can get out of here early if you want, I'll take care of the closing side work."

They shifted their shock between each other, then back at me.

"What's the catch?" Mel asked suspiciously.

"No catch. Enjoy your Thursday night," I said, gathering the stack of tickets for the day from Cherry's grip. They didn't give it another thought.

As Jet emerged from the kitchen, the girls almost knocked into him and his fresh crate of glasses. He didn't hold back from groaning as the girls passed him.

"Please never let them work my shifts," Jet grumbled into his workstation, starting in on his opening side work. "Uh, hey. I'm Jet," he said with his focus kept down in front of him.

Lucy looked around and then at me, evidently unsure if Jet was speaking to her or not. "Oh, yeah. Hey, I saw you here at the opening. I'm Lucy."

Jet didn't utter another word. Instead, he wiped the pint glasses. Holding them inches away from his face, he made sure not to miss a single dry spot.

We were in our afternoon lull where the late-lunch patrons had cleared out. The in-between time of now and bar hours was blocked off as Jet's time to give prep work his full attention. So, he wasn't going to allow the two seconds it took to greet someone to throw him off. Jet took his work seriously and was particular about the way he handled his responsibilities. It was my favorite trait about him.

But I wasn't going to lie, the unmistakable neglect to acknowledge Lucy irked me. Sure, he wasn't the most sociable person. But he was one of the nicest that I knew. So I guess for that alone, I wasn't going to hold it against him.

The three of us were the only ones here now, so the uncomfortable silence poured over the bar rapidly. Lucy angled herself towards me as she pushed her empty plate across the bar. She and I had been picking at a shared portion of fries for almost two hours. The sun started to set, It seemed as though we spent the better part of our day here.

"Well," I waved the fanned-out tickets in the air, "I'm going to take these to the office, I'll be back in a bit."

I reached my hand out and Lucy softly placed her hand in mine as she jumped down out of the stool. We busted through the kitchen doors, the slapping sound against the opposite walls echoed down the hallway.

And the pitter-patter tapping and occasional scuff of her shoes on the ground behind me drowned out the sound of my heart, which was now beating inside of my head.

I was really about to let her into my sanctuary.

We poked our heads into the walk-in. Stacked cases of produce and poultry were suddenly the most interesting thing between two adults pretending not to be nervous around each other. She and I have been alone together before, so tell me why knees were about to buckle out from under themselves.

The backstock of inventory was stored away in the closet on the other side. We skimmed right over that. Next, we reached our last stop on our short-lived tour. My office.

I stepped off to the side, letting her walk in before me. She immediately dragged her attention over to the photos up on the wall.

"Gus is in some of those," I said, tossing the lunch tickets on the desk. I threw myself into my desk chair and logged on to the computer.

She strolled along the few feet that the wall would allow her and gawked at the collage hanging up. "I remember when he had them out on the walls out front."

The way her head tilted back, her neck extended, I found myself thinking about the way it tasted. She started twirling a long strand of hair as she was fixated on each frame.

"Why aren't there any of you or your family up here?" she said pointing up.

I pushed away from the desk and stood up. I walked up beside her, taking a closer look at the photos for what I think is really the first time since moving them in here.

Gus and Leanne were smiling in all of them. Their kids looked as though they genuinely enjoyed being around their family. Only a few small babies were pictured at the time, one being Mel who was running around the front yard of their cottage with nothing but a diaper on and a water hose in her hands.

Had I wanted photos of my own up there, I don't think I'd have any that I'd be proud to display. The only ones that I own were taken because my grandfather bribed my parents and me to be there. I don't know what's worse. That he made the offer, or that we took him up on it. The second one I knew of was disgustingly photoshopped. Only my grandfather, Holland,

and my uncle showed up. The rest of us were edited to appear as though we were there.

That's Lewis Banks for you. He didn't want to tarnish the family-man image he held with the voters.

"Eh, you know... We aren't a very photogenic group of people."

"I beg to differ," she said, moving her attention over to me. I kept my sights straight ahead. The corner of my mouth on the opposite side started to lift, though. "I keep up with the Connecticut news. Your grandfather has a new headshot every six months it seems." And then my face returned flat.

Lucy took my place in the office chair making it sway back and forth. I sat on the edge of the desk and faced her. I tugged at the chair, pulling her in closer, and made the wheels stop as she rolled between my legs. I tilted her face up at me and took her chin in between my finger and thumb, "Thanks for helping out today. You keep proving to be good company." I dropped my hand from her face.

"Yeah. A-anytime," her lips wavered with a stutter.

"I know this wasn't what you signed up for. I volunteered my help, and then all of a sudden you're the one helping me. I owe you, I promise."

"I might hold you to that," she wagged a playful finger at me. "But no, I promise, it's no big deal. I had fun."

"You mean it?"

"I needed this," she spoke softly as she quickly rested her hand on my knee.

But as quickly as it appeared, it was gone and she pulled her hands into her lap. She started to pick at the polish on her nails and the trembling of her fingers occurred the same way it did the first time we met. I wanted to take her hand back in mine, this time I wouldn't pull away like I had before. I'd calm her down the best that I could and tell her that I was there to help or vent to or...I don't know. But I couldn't. So I sat there and watched her be at war with the leg that tried with all its might to start shaking, too.

"This whole selling thing is more involved than I expected. And as you've seen, the cleaning process isn't going too well. But Kai is a mastermind and is taking care of all of the real hard tasks. I appreciate them. And you, for giving me their card."

"Hmm, I wonder if this means they'll give me a cut of their commission," I said, tapping my finger to my temple.

"Oh, if only!" she mocked as she pushed away from the desk.

As she stood, her eyes leveled out with my chin and she sucked in a breath, one deep enough that convinced me she got a handle on her nerves. She slowly tilted her head back to meet my gaze, they shifted between one another.

I was now familiarizing myself with every inch of her innocent face. Hesitantly, but instinctively, I allowed myself to inch closer toward her. I glided my thumb over the inch-long scar that sat at the top of her forehead.

"Where'd this come from?" I muttered in a broken whisper.

"Oh," she ran her finger over it as if she was unaware of its existence. "A reenactment of *Risky Business* in the living room, I was twelve. No one told me that sliding across a hardwood floor was actually that slippery."

I traced the indentation once more. Then my hand trailed down the frame of her face. Her whole body shuddered at my touch as I cupped my hand beneath her ear. Her breath got caught on the way I skimmed the nape of her neck as my fingers fed themselves through her hair.

Her anxious breathing had subsided, but now it had grown into a heavier—hotter—tempo. And my eyes... They've grown heavier—softer—as I stared deeper into her sea-green irises. "I really want to kiss you," I said following from her eyes down to her lips.

"Then do it," she said firmly.

I was less than an inch away—mere centimeters—from knowing what she tasted like. Our lips moved closer, only to be interrupted by the door flying open.

She stumbled away from me.

"Oh, shit. I—" Jet stuttered. "It doesn't matter, I'll talk to you about it later." Even thrown off guard, Jet remained monotone.

"No, it's okay," I lied. "What is it?"

Jet had already turned away at the door. "It was about scheduling. Nothing important." He shut the door behind him, but it didn't matter—my serendipitous moment was officially over.

She neared me again and we let out a sigh of distraught into one another, her forehead pressing into the center of my chest as she let out a giggle.

"I-I-I, I'm sorry. I—"

"It's okay."

"I really should get out there and help close up so he has less to worry about for bartending tonight."

"Sheesh, that's right, I forgot. Guess I gotta get used to that. I don't really think of this place and then think of *alcohol*," she said.

I huffed out a quick laugh, then gave her a quick kiss on the top of her head.

"I'll talk to you soon, yeah?"

"Yes."

A confident *yes*. No hesitation on her end whatsoever. That almost made up for the interruption. *Almost.*

I was less than an inch away, mere centimeters, from knowing what it felt like to feel as though Lucy was mine.

Even if it lasted a fraction of a second, I would pack up my bags and travel to that state of delusion if it meant I got to have any part of her.

Chapter 17

Lucy

As I woke up, I was met with the memory of Sawyer's subtle touches. They sent a shiver down my spine all over again as my eyes adjusted to the sunlight.

He knew I was only here for the summer, I knew I was only here for the summer, and there he was asking to kiss me. And there I was saying yes to a kiss faster than I ever had to anyone before. I don't think I ever wanted to be kissed so badly as I did at that moment. And by Sawyer Banks.

I swiped my phone from my side table and pulled up the phone keypad. When I reached out to Kai, I may have added Sawyer's number that he left on the back of the business card into my contacts. You know, just in case.

> i had a nice time with you yesterday.

> x.o. lucy

I wiped the sleep from my eyes and sat up straight against the headboard. It was barely six in the morning, there was no way I would expect a response back so quickly, but sure enough, text bubbles popped up almost instantly.

> **Meet me in fifteen? I want to see you.**

> **not at all cryptic. but i'm intrigued…**

> **i'm in. where?**

> **See you soon!**

Those damn butterflies—they were more like a swarm of wasps—were getting harder and harder to flush out of my system, and avoiding getting stung was getting harder and harder to do. I was immobilized with infatuation. Rushing to his beck and call with stars in my eyes was not going to help my case, either.

But fuck, those eyes. They visited me in my sleep last night. The dark, gold halo surrounding the pool of amber-green stared back at me more times than I could count. His eyes are ingrained into my brain forever.

I could handle going back to Arizona with a couple of weeks in great company under my belt, it didn't mean I was going to have a boyfriend in tow. And I definitely wasn't going to return with a broken heart. The way I see it is that a little party never killed anybody.

I roll out of bed, throwing every bit of energy I could muster up this early in the morning to make sure I didn't look like a literal sewer rat for this impromptu, not at all mysterious meeting I was about to have with a man I almost kissed.

I opted out of a short car drive and made my way through the backyard into the hillside. The early morning lake haze still lingered, it lifted about halfway up the trees. But maybe my wardrobe choice of wearing a crewneck wasn't ideal because the incessant humidity of late June followed me through the woods.

"White sneaks on a dirt path? Brave." Sawyer's voice rang through my bones. Fifty feet away from the picnic table, he started to walk toward me holding our text thread up on his phone. "Anyway, clearly I wasn't *that* cryptic. You found me with no problem at all." Sawyer pulled me in for a warm hug as we reached each other. "Morning, Pretty Girl," he whispered right above my ear, into my tangled-up mess of a bun.

I swallowed his words, looking down at my feet. "They're my favorite," I said with a crack in my voice. "Besides, I figured this is the only common stomping ground. When you wouldn't give me any other information, I knew this was my safest bet."

"Such a smart girl."

He stalked his way up the steps and over to the side of The Hideout. The storage closet creaked at the hinges. Rustling through the inside, he pulled out a large, sharp axe. He slammed it down beside him, barely missing his feet when he locked up the door.

"Ready?"

"For *what* exactly?!"

His boots shuffled through the dirt and then walked off ahead of me. He looked back over his shoulder with a sly grin.

"I don't like this one bit!" I cried out, frozen in my spot.

"Are you coming, or what?"

We had made it only a few hundred feet down the trail when he led us up an open slope. It was hard to keep up with his strides. But eventually, I caught up with him. My white slip-ons were no longer holding up.

Today's outfit-1, Me-0.

At the very top of the hill, there were stacked stumps in which he sliced the blade of the axe into the top one.

"So—"

He cut me off. "Sit down," he commanded, gesturing to the empty makeshift tree stump seat off to the side.

It was a longer log with dull, sunken spots like it was made to be used for intentional seating. A few straggled cigarette butts on the ground to the side confirmed just that.

Besides a *watch out for that branch*, trees blowing in the wind in passing and our footsteps were the only sounds exchanged between us. That, and the far back hoots of the owl that followed above us.

Sawyer rooted his stance and began lifting his shirt out from his waistband. With both hands crossed on either side of his torso, he pulled his shirt off in one fell swoop. The sheen of the morning sun bled through the trees and ricocheted off of his exposed chest.

He slanted his head down ever so slightly, giving me one of his infamous winks—the kind that stole my breath away and made my toes curl.

He picked up one of the tree stumps beside him and threw it to the ground, the muffled thump of wood hitting the dirt brings me out of the clouds and back down to earth. Wiggling the axe out of the log, he threw the rod over his shoulder before he slammed it back down.

Over and over, the thwacking sound would ring through my body, making me jump at every hit. With every strike, he let out a low grunt. His arm muscles twitched a millisecond before his back muscles did.

Watching him felt illegal. I knew I should turn away, but I was glued to him. Watching him was all I wanted to do.

"So," I started again, this time with a jagged breath.

He struck the blade into an untouched, idling log and let it rest there. "Am I boring you, Pretty Girl?" he questioned.

Pretty Girl.

He needed to stop calling me that.

Maybe it's a knee-jerk reaction, maybe that's his thing. I had no clue. But he continued to repeat it, and my heart continued to skip a beat.

I wiped away at the nonexistent dirt in my lap, "N-no. Actually I was going to say it's been nice to see you like this."

He raised a brow and huffed a breath out his nose.

"I don't mean like *this*," I waved my arms around frantically over his body. "Sure, this is nice, but what I mean is..." I shot up from my seat, attempting to gather my words, myself. "Oh, my god. What I mean is I like seeing you live in the moment. Yup, that's what I am trying to say," I managed to express.

"I could say the same about you." Sawyer picked his bunched-up shirt off the ground and wiped away the sweat from his temple. "But please, you go first."

"Have you ever seen Spongebob?"

"What does that have to do with anything?"

"Just answer the question," I shot out.

He let out a chuckle, then nodded. "I would love to see where this is going. Yes, I have seen Spongebob." A man of multitasking abilities, he gripped the canvas straps of the log carrier rolled up in his back pocket and whips it open. He placed it on the ground and began loading them inside. But there was a sly grin plastered on his face, anticipating whatever foolishness I was about to spew out.

"When he's so on edge, talking to himself and spaced out... you have given me those vibes whenever I've seen you."

His mouth fell open, he tossed his head back. The loudest laugh I have ever heard escaped his mouth and he clutched the side of his stomach.

"I don't even know what that even means."

"It means that you seem so focused on your work, and how you present yourself. I like watching you enjoy yourself. It's been nice," I stammered out while fumbling with the charm on my necklace. "Also, did you know that when you're concentrating on something, you furrow your brows but when they are stuck like that for a little too long, you wiggle them loose? I noticed it yesterday at The Hideout when you were rolling silverware for what felt like forever."

"You like watching me, huh?" he moved in closer to me, grabbing the side of my waist.

"That's what you got out of it?" I locked my eyes on him. Sawyer dropped the tote, the collection of wood made a single *thump* sound. My skin jumped at the rippling vibration that traveled under us.

He wiped away at the dirt debris on the side of his neck, elongating his throat as he dragged his hand downwards. He brushed his hand on the side of his jeans before running his fingers through his hair, evening out the misplaced strands.

"No, of course not," he finally said. "But you haven't been so carefree yourself, ya know."

My heart rate returned to skyrocketing numbers. I wasn't sure if it was from his close proximity or my not wanting to know his answer. Easily, it was both.

He continued, "I know it's a lot to sell a house, trust me. I was in my early twenties when I sold my condo. It was a pain in the ass, and I didn't even have that much of an emotional connection to it. That's beside the point, I promise I am not trying to flex."

"Could have fooled me," I said with a head tilt.

"I promise. What I'm saying is, I haven't seen, what I believe to be, a genuine smile on that," he gulped before continuing, "perfect face of yours since you got here."

I needed to stop looking into his eyes immediately. Or who knows what would happen... I brought my attention up to the top of his head. There, I saw a small stem sticking out at his hairline.

"You, uh," I said with a crack in my words. I reached up to pluck it from his hair and I could feel him watching me, though I kept my sights locked on the leaf. *Don't make eye contact with him.*

He grabbed my wrist in a tight hold as my hand moved back down. I gasped, and a broken whimper escaped my mouth. It was almost embarrassing. He twisted the crumpled-up leaf out from between my fingers, his fingertips grazing over mine.

The slightest touch of his felt like—I can't even categorize it. Sawyer's touch felt electrifying.

He dragged his thumb over my cheek, bringing it down my face. He tilted my chin up before stopping. He looked at me. He *looked* at me in a way only he ever has—like he is seeing me for *me*. His exhausted smolder lightened and his eyes relaxed. Sawyer looked relaxed in every sense.

He tugged my face towards him. Firmly, possessively.

"About that kiss?"

Our lips were in sync when they parted, welcoming one another as if they had a mind of their own. The sense of relief that my body released, it was like it was waiting for this moment long before my heart knew that's what it wanted, what it craved.

Our kiss felt like coming home at the end of a long day, sitting on the front porch in the summer heat with an iced tea in hand. Necessary and refreshing.

There wasn't a lot that made sense in this god-forsaken world that we lived in. I didn't have many answers to many things in life and normally that'd kill me. Meeting Sawyer was never supposed to happen. Enjoying my time with Sawyer was never supposed to happen. I didn't have an answer for what's to come next between the two of us. All I knew was my lips were made for his.

Kissing Sawyer made sense.

My heels raised off the ground—I was defenseless. Completely, undeniably helpless. My body fused with his as our kiss grew stronger. His grip around my waist held me up, and for once, I did not have to stand on my own two feet alone. On my tallest of tiptoes, with my arms wrapped around Sawyer's neck, I never once removed my mouth from his.

I slid my hand along his jaw, his stubble scratched the palm of my hand. I couldn't help but let out a soft cry when he tugged at my bottom lip between his teeth. One that he could hear, but nothing that would scare him away. And thankfully, it didn't. It only enticed him to tighten his grip around me while moving his other hand through the back of my hair.

He broke his mouth away from mine and spoke into my neck, "I actually," his chest heaved hard against mine. "I want you to spend the weekend with me."

"What?" I said with a shaky voice.

"Oh, no, not in the way that you think," he pulled away from my body. "Okay, let me be more clear. There's something about you Lucy. I can't quite figure out what, though. But I feel lighter around you."

My mouth slightly dropped open, but nothing came out. *What was I supposed to say?* A kiss, that was all this was supposed to be. Wasn't it?

I thought there'd be a few "here and there" hangouts, the promise to not shut him down if we run into each other at The Hideout… But he's talking about definite plans. Definite plans. That's a whole other ball game.

"I know you're busy, I know you have a lot going on, but—" He ran his fingers through his hair.

"It's not just that!" I cried out. "You know that I'm leaving, you know that I'm not staying. You do know that, right?"

He had to know that, I wouldn't shut up about it.

"Yes, I am well aware of that."

"You can't get attached to me, to this." I motioned my finger between the two of us.

"I'm a big boy, Lucy."

I promised myself I'd make the most of the next couple of months here, but this would be taking it to a new level. I couldn't deny the pull that I feel towards Sawyer. He was everywhere I turned, I couldn't ignore him if I tried. It's pathetic.

But there's a huge difference between kissing a person I knew surface level information about and spending a weekend with someone that I could potentially fall for. I couldn't fall for surface level. But letting someone in, someone that I think has the power to make me fall hard… It's a risk. One that I don't know if it's worth the fallout.

"Spend the weekend with me," he repeated himself, this time with a softness in his voice. "I want to get to know you. Seriously, it will be the best forty-eight hours of our lives. Dinner date one day, a day date the next… I already have it all planned out. We will make the most of it," he said, closing the space between us more and more. "Just you," the tip of his finger lightly tapped right beneath my collarbone, "and me," he continued, pointing back to himself. "All you have to do is say that you will, say yes."

The moment the words left his lips, a bouquet of hummingbirds swam in the air around us. There was something about how still their body remained while their wings flapped vigorously keeping them afloat.

I twisted my necklace between my fingers as I watched them fly by. A thin gold chain with a quaint charm of a hummingbird sat at the center. I bought it as a Christmas gift to myself, the first one I spent alone, it acted as a reminder that home was always with me.

The last time I saw a flock this large, so intense, was when I was a young girl walking along this very trail with my grandmother and my mother. It was when life felt simple and normal. Maybe it was because I was five and life hadn't turned so complicated yet.

I ran up ahead of the two of them, following a single hummingbird. I skipped over and veered around every obstacle on the trail. I was going to catch up to the hummingbird. Once I finally did, I was met with a whole collection of them glistening under the early morning sun.

Hummingbirds will forever be associated with my adolescent years. They reminded me that love and hope will always be present if I allow it to be. I was surprised any of them were out this late in the season. Taking this as a sign is the only way I could go about this.

I dropped my necklace, letting it fall flat against my collarbones. I diverted my attention back to Sawyer as the hummingbirds continued down their path.

Meeting Sawyer had to be a sign. I just couldn't figure out what the universe was trying to tell me by putting him in my path.

Chapter 18

Sawyer

I threw on my standard, worn in jeans and a white tee with my midtown rambler boots. But my hair had become the fork in the road. It had undoubtedly been forty five minutes and I had yet to take care of this mess. I never cared much before.

On a normal day, I'd let it hang around naturally. But this wasn't a normal day. This was my first date with Lucy. I grabbed my black trucker hat and spun it around backwards as I placed it on my head.

I swiped the keys from the handmade trinket dish from Leanne that lives on top of my dresser, but I paused before walking out. The reflection staring back in the mirror hounded me, attempting to figure out how the hell Lucy agreed to spend the whole weekend with me.

There had to be better things she could do for the holiday weekend, but instead, she said yes to me. I'm the luckiest man in the world.

Billy hung his head off the end of the bed, staring back at me through the mirror with ultimate puppy dog eyes. "You're staying home, bud." I ruffled up the fur on the back of his neck and gave his head a couple of pats before leaving. He whimpered in response. "Sorry."

I rushed out of the house and made the drive around the back parts of the hillside and pulled into Lucy's cottage.

It had been ages since I last had a *first date*. It's pitiful, really. Maybe she took pity on me. Word travels fast around here, she must know that it's been a while and she felt bad. I guess when you spend so much time escaping the careless title—being the young adult that ran amuck with their trust fund—you become the full grown adult that stopped caring altogether.

I stopped caring about the dates and the parties, the clothes and the price tag on a pair of pants. But I also stopped caring about finding someone that made me laugh or feel light.

Lucy walked out the front door of her cottage with her hair in loose waves that hung over her shoulder. Her fitted, silk cream colored dress fell right before her ankles. It was no more than a shade darker than her fair complexion. It clung to all of the best parts of her petite frame.

She skipped down the steps with a wide smile as I met her with a kiss on the cheek. Any worries I had dissipated once she reached me. She made me *want* to care. Because she genuinely wanted to be here with me.

But then her energetic disposition quickly faded once I stepped out of her field of vision. So, who knows now.

"There's no way I am getting on that." Her face fell flat.

I looked between her and the tangerine-orange 1990 Harley that was positioned on its kickstand. Aside from Billy, it was my literal baby. My pride and joy.

I pulled the passenger helmet out of the saddlebag. "I came prepared."

"I don't care if you showed up with an entire roll of bubble wrap to dress me in," she took a step back, "I am not getting on that. I like my modes of transportation to have four wheels, *minimum,* with a cover on it. There's no way. Nope," she declared, crossing her arms against her chest.

I stepped in her direction. "Do you trust me?" I asked, then extended the helmet out towards her.

She stole one more glance at the bike, then back at me. Reluctantly, Lucy reached for the helmet with a look of fear, possibly disgust, on her face. She grumbled as she slid it over her head.

"That's a good girl." I patted the top of the helmet, then walked her over to the bike.

I held onto her, supporting her as she swung a leg over one side. I climbed on after, and pulling each arm of hers from behind, I wrapped them around my waist.

"Had I known, I would have worn something different," she yelled over the engine starting. Her dress was cinched all up her legs, the majority of the fabric pooled up in her lap.

"I'm glad that you didn't. You look amazing."

With my words, her grip around my waist got tighter.

I switched my hat out for a helmet of my own and I booted back the kickstand. I headed down her driveway, creating a cloud of dust underneath us.

I was insistent on getting away from everything that we already knew, hopeful that a change of scenery and pace was exactly what we needed. And tonight, we were driving away from it all. We made our way through the hecticness of Downtown Rider and headed straight for the water. Everything was better at the seaport.

Nothing else mattered beyond the trees that rustled in the wind or Lucy's hair whipping underneath her helmet as our speed increased. All I could think about were the miles passing and the time that was dwindling, bringing me closer to having a real moment with her. Any time around her before had been run-ins, a time I was lucky to be in her presence. Now, I got to have her to myself. *Intentionally.*

I turned down a narrow, cobblestone pathway that took us to a dark blue shack at the end.

"Here, let me help you with that." I turned off the engine, climbed off, and stepped around the bike. As she reached to unbuckle the chin strap, I went to lift the helmet off of her head.

The graze of her fingertips against mine sent a tingle of heat through my bones. It's insane what a simple, single touch from Lucy does to me. She brushed down her hair, taming the frizziness created by the ride.

Her legs straddled on either side of the bike... God, she looked amazing. With the fabric of her dress shifting side to side, I recognized a faint birthmark on her upper thigh trying to play a round of peek-a-boo with me. The desire to keep playing the game was tempting, but I focused on the stones beneath my feet instead.

"Thanks," she said as she slid off the back of the bike sideways, shimming quickly to avoid major exposure. She smoothed out the bottom half of her dress and interlocked her fingers with mine as she looked around, checking to see if anyone caught her.

I stroked my thumb over hers. "I am so happy to be out with you tonight."

She pulled herself into my side and clung onto my entire arm as we walked off.

Carter's was one of those spots that you only knew about by word of mouth. Or in my case, wandering the backstreets of the seaport on a drunken night.

Kai, Jet, and I had stopped at one of the seaside bars a few years back. Communication between the three of us was a shit show that night, and my phone was dead. In all of my hard headed glory that consumes me when I am plastered, and the ninety-proof bourbon that swam through my bloodstream, I was determined that I could get home all on my own.

I learned really fucking fast just how wrong I was.

The neon sign of a crab and lobster holding hands with colors of red, blue, and purple flashing on and off was enough to pull me in. When I came across Carter's, I hadn't yet decided what my next step was since returning to Rider. I was on a permanent summer break, even in the middle of January. There were no responsibilities. I had pockets lined with a disposable trust fund and all of the time in the world.

Within a week, I was considered a regular here.

Carter's is the closest thing to a proper English pub I had found in the States. I fit right into the bar stools like they were a glove. The dark leather upholstery, almost non-existent lighting, and every surface covered in something sticky tied the place together.

Lucy giggled at the sign out front. "That's so cute!" she squealed in excitement.

Lucy and I settled into a dark corner booth way in the back.

"What can I get ya?" The dark-haired waitress asked without looking up from her notepad as she rushed our table.

The smacking of her gum and *don't care* attitude was exhilarating and I expected nothing less from the staff here. Subtle surliness was all a part of the experience at Carter's. A grumbling man came up behind her before I could even open my mouth all of the way.

"Don't worry about them, Gina. This guy never orders food anyway. He slams back beer, and then dips out."

"Yeah, after giving you a hundred and ten percent tip!"

He let out a low laugh, patting the top of my shoulder.

"Hey, Carter, how have you been?" When I stood to hug him, he smelled like his usual stench of "a pack a day" cigarettes—sounded like it, too. "This is Lucy."

She let out one of her wide smiles, the kind anyone is lucky to get from her.

She reached her hand up for him to shake. He grabbed it, then kissed the top. "Lucy. Nice to meet you," Carter said with a wink. "This city boy right here can give any of these old drunkards a run for their money. What are you doing out with a guy like this?"

I grabbed the back of my neck and looked away from the table. These types of anecdotes are definitely not first-date material. I worried that she would think I was some sort of boozy bum.

Another one of Carter's rough pats hit my shoulder. "Hey, boy, I am just messing with you."

"Heh, yeah," I winced, pressing my back against the booth. *Fuck, did I wish I could retreat into...I don't know, a place anywhere else but here.* "I know."

I felt a soft grip of Lucy's hand on my leg, she rubbed her thumb over my knee, giving it a quick squeeze. She then looked over at me out of the side of her eye. This banter with Carter is the usual, it's what we do. But she didn't know that, and she was trying to reassure me, let me know that she was there. The heart of this woman. I placed my hand over hers and squeezed back.

Carter pointed and snapped his fingers, and mouths something to Gina. She pranced off, then returned with an abundance of empty pint glasses and pitchers filled to the brim with beer.

Lucy was completely enthralled, she started to wiggle with excitement in her seat without even knowing what was going on. I sat forward, with my head in my hands contemplating how this night turned into *this.*

I outdrink everyone in this establishment *one* time, and Carter is convinced it's my go-to party trick.

Maybe bringing her here wasn't the best decision after all. But I wanted to share little pieces of me, a place that has helped form me into who I am. And large parts of myself have been found here at Carter's. These booths, barstools, and large pints of beer—a lot of clarity has been found in each of them.

"They're acting like I should have gotten you a birthday present or something. What exactly is going on here?" Lucy leaned over and spoke into my ear, just loud enough.

"A stupid drinking contest," I said back to her.

She sat back up straight and joined in on the fun, let out a *whoop, whoop,* and started clapping. Everyone started to get louder, they even started to chant my name. It was ridiculous, I bowed my head and let out a low laugh. I looked over at her and mouthed *sorry,* but she shrugged my apology off.

"Show me what you got," she said with a wink.

I clutched onto the glass that Carter finished pouring. He pumped his fist in the air a couple of times, while Gina stood there with a deadpan expression.

"I will do this... under one condition."

"What is it?" Carter cuts in.

"*You* do this with me," I nodded over at Lucy.

Her already fair complexion turned ghost-white. Lucy contemplated my offer. She scanned the faces of those hovering over our table but then grabbed a glass of her own. Carter scrambled for the pitcher to fill her glass. She snarled, she squinted. Her sweet, comforting persona was no more. *She meant business.*

"You're going to be the death of me, Banks."

Banks. She's already giving me nicknames.

"On the count of three, okay?" Carter called out. "One, two.."

"GO!" She tapped the bottom of her glass on the table before she brought the glass to her lips.

With her head tilted back and her neck stretched in its entirety, the beer was already dripping down the corners of her mouth. A triple threat, that one. Hot, adaptable, and can throw back beer in a breeze. *This is so not fair!*

Carter yelled out, "Sawyer, come on boy! You're slacking!"

I lifted the glass to my mouth and chugged back as fast as I could in an attempt to catch up to her. With throats wide open, I could hear the guzzling and gulping that alternated between the both of us. Those around drunkenly cheered us on. Some even joined in on the friendly competition. But this was my race to win against Lucy and Lucy alone.

She never stopped. Glass number two... three... four, they slammed into the table after slurping them down, moving to the next one like they were on a conveyor belt.

Beer number seven was the lucky number.

Lucy smacked her hands down on either side of her empty glass, then threw her arms up in victory. The crowd cheered and chanted her name.

I have never met a more perfect woman.

"How did you...There's no way."

She flashed me a playful grin and a wink. One powerful enough to make me think not public-friendly thoughts. *She's going to be the death of me.*

"Do you do this a lot?" I wiped away the leftover beer foam from my three day old stubble.

She was living on a high, barely able to hear me as everyone continued with their loud praise. She leaned in quickly, kissing me for only a moment. I could taste the second-hand buzz that fell off her lips onto mine.

She whispered into my ear, "Actually never. Guess this makes you my first." She spun around and faced the crowd, feeding more into the drunken attention.

But eventually, the adrenaline died down and everyone vacated our vicinity. It was finally just the two of us—we were left alone with our flushed cheeks and slurred words.

I started to stack the dishes, moving them away from us, but she scooted in closer to me, bringing all other movements to a halt. I moved her legs to drape over my lap.

"Thank you for this," she said softly, kissing the peak of my shoulder.

"I promise this wasn't the plan. *This* was," I said into the crown of her head. "Just us, sitting. Alone, close. So close that I wish there was a way to make us even closer."

She let out a hazy hum as she nuzzled into me.

"Contrary to Carter's statement, I did plan on ordering food here. Their lobster rolls are the best. Nothing you've ever had before."

"Next time," she said.

Next time.

I gave her thigh a squeeze in response. But the next thing I knew, she was resting her head on me as she began to uncontrollably giggle.

I removed my hand from her. "I'm sorry. Should I not have?"

The giggling progressed. Lucy was almost delirious before it all came to an abrupt halt.

"No, no, sorry," she pulled at my hand and placed it back on her leg, tracing her fingertips over the couple of rings that I wore.

Both of which used to belong to my dad back in the nineties. He never thought much of them, he was ready to get rid of them. Until I swiped them because they reminded me of him, reminded me of how "cool" they made him.

Lucy started to spin them around my fingers before she laced her hand with mine.

"I like the way that I feel when you touch me."

I began rubbing my free hand up and down her leg. Suddenly, the roars of the bar had disappeared—she had the power to make it feel as if we were the only ones here. She softly scratched my forearm with the very tips of her fingernails.

I had contracted full body goosebumps.

I closed my eyes, allowing myself to feel every bit of her touch.

Every swipe, every slither.

Her touch was divine ecstasy.

She moved her hand back down my arm, sliding onto my thigh. We mirrored each other's motions. Even over the rough denim of my jeans, I felt *everything*. I glided my hand up her side and grasped it behind her neck, moving it softly around her throat, pulling her in for a kiss.

With the lightest of pressure, she let out a soft moan into my mouth. I'd let that sound fill my ears forever if I could.

Chapter 19

Lucy

I could kiss Sawyer forever. As long as "forever" was the new equivalent of seven weeks.

We had spent the better part of our night in the booth of Carter's kissing, talking, ordering drinks, and kissing some more. We never did get around to ordering those lobster rolls. I was too enthralled with the man in front of me.

I had fallen down the rabbit hole. Whenever his cheeks tinged out of sheer embarrassment whenever he forgot his next train of thought, I found myself taking mental pictures of his face.

His face.

Boy, that is a face I'd never grow tired of. And in between sharing anecdotes from his college years, he'd pause every so often to give me a peck before carrying on.

I had officially entered Wonderland and was fully prepared to get lost in it this weekend.

After our additional drinks, ones we probably shouldn't have had, I ended up straddling him on the leather seat.

Somewhere along the line, I had pulled the hem of his shirt up his torso. I tapped my fingers up and down his could-not-miss abs. I started playing an imaginary piano.

We were borderline indecent—and I didn't hate it.

I did, however, become intolerant to the snickers and whispers from the other stragglers. It was an instant mood killer, and I could tell that Sawyer felt the same.

"Wanna walk this off?" I asked.

I slithered off from his lap and we stumbled out front. We passed his bike and walked across the street lined with other shacks turned into ice cream shops or gift stores towards the drawbridge.

The moonlight danced on the water and the boats down the way rocked rhythmically. And while we didn't make a peep, I felt content beside Sawyer as we walked arm in arm.

I zoned in on the faint humming of the lampposts in passing, slightly letting my eyes shut.

"You good, Pretty Girl?"

The nickname that has led to heightened blood pressure in the past suddenly made me feel calm. Maybe it was the drunken cloud I was floating inside, I was unsure, but I basked in it. I was going to wear it as a badge of honor and take it for all that it was worth. And right now, it was worth everything.

"I am *so* good. Perfect, even."

On the other side of the bridge, a short, two-story lighthouse lived near a kayak rental spot. A small pier was attached to the shop, one I had spent a couple of summers dangling my feet off the end of. I'd watch as Leanne and my grandmother went out around the river as I sat with the shop owner. Ruby. She was a sweet silver-haired lady who shared her gummy worms with me.

I remember feeling so inferior against the lighthouse as if it was the biggest thing I had ever come across. At eight years old, it was. Now, I didn't feel so small—so scared—beside it.

The beacon wasn't as bright as I remember, but it still did its job; it guided people back to shore. I made it back to shore.

Absorbed by all that is Sawyer and my time spent with him, it was inching towards three in the morning. I felt like I was in my early years of med school with these insomniac behaviors. But after our second lap around the seaport, I felt ourselves simultaneously sober up and crash all within five minutes of each other.

"I think we should head on back, we have a whole weekend ahead of us," I said, hoarse with heavy eyes.

I slipped my hand into Sawyer's back pocket as we made a sharp U-turn back toward the shops. He placed a kiss on top of my head with a fleeting chuckle escaping his mouth to follow.

"Thank you for tonight," he said with a crack in his voice.

His stumbling had corrected itself over the thirty minutes of mindlessly walking, so I knew he wasn't buzzed anymore. But the need to *thank* me was still lost on me. He felt gratitude for the night we'd spent together when whatever I felt was indescribable.

We were inches from Sawyer's bike just as Carter came out the back door. I sucked a breath, one powerful enough to bring me back to reality. Shaking me from the daze of picturing many more dates like this one, possibly years from now. It was silly, truly. Wasn't it?

Eh, I was not drunk enough anymore to consider any of this.

"Hey, there you two are." His voice was like nails on a chalkboard at this hour.

Sawyer and I dragged our feet along the cobblestone. "Long night for you, I see," Sawyer mumbled out.

"Yeah, had a couple of idiots making out until last call, and then I had to do a large tip out to Gina." Sawyer cocked his head in Carter's direction. "Alright, that came out wrong. You just left a hefty credit card tip after tonight, didn't want her walking out with all that cash. Had to cut her a personal check."

I scoffed and nudged Sawyer in the side, and he shrugged.

"Alright," Carter huffed out, jingling his keys in his hands. "Let's go, you two." He walked over to Sawyer's bike and started pushing it toward his truck. He flipped the tailgate down and nodded to Sawyer, motioning for a hand. On the count of three, they lifted the bike into the bed of the truck. "Where're we heading?"

"The Hillside Cottages," Sawyer muttered.

We both climbed into the cab and drove back through Downtown Rider after a night I'll never forget.

We pulled in front of the cottage and I stumbled out of the truck. "Try and get some shut eye, okay? I'll see you in the morning." I nodded in response as Sawyer rubbed the side of my arm before placing a hoppy-tasting kiss on my lips.

Carter shut his headlights off as they backed out and down the driveway. Instantly, I felt agonizing emptiness inside of my chest being away from Sawyer.

Deep down, I knew that anything after this would never make sense. Falling for someone over a single weekend was too rom-com-esque for me. I didn't do romance. I did reality, predictability. And the reality of it all was that this would never work. But we were smushed side by side, and the tips of our knees brushed up against one another. I felt at peace for the first time this summer. Being beside him felt right.

Chapter 20

Lucy

I was too high off of the insanity. The wonderful, *sexy* insanity of the night. I had given up any hope I had of falling asleep, and instead, I dragged myself up out from under the covers.

I had another date with Sawyer to get ready for—an early morning date.

My hands shook with excitement as I filtered through the closet today. I was humming old Motown tunes as I flipped through my options. I was—without a doubt—giddy. I threw on a simple blue and white pinstripe maxi dress so I could match today's pickings of hydrangeas from my grandmother's garden.

> Good Morning, sleepy head. My vehicle has four wheels this time and I am a couple minutes away. No need to rush, just letting you know. I'll wait for you.

I locked my phone screen and slid it into my crossbody.

He climbed out of the truck as I was walking down the steps. "You look good when you're sleepy," I yelled out as I approached him. But he looked far from it. He was fresh-faced, wide awake. You'd never guess we re-lived early college-year antics last night.

"Hey, what do you think you're doing? I'm supposed to come and greet you at your door."

I shrugged and giggled. "Guess I'm too impatient."

He leaned down to kiss me as I approached him. Those damn butterflies that seemed to only visit when I'm around Sawyer, whirling around nonstop, had crashed our date.

Billy popped his head out the side of the passenger side door, wagging his whole body in anticipation. "I hope you don't mind a third wheel, he wouldn't stop begging as I was putting my shoes on."

"Of course not!" I walked over to the truck, rustling up Billy's ears. "Hey, bud!" his cold, wet nose gave me a little boop on my inner wrist.

"Ready to go?" he asked as he reached for the door handle.

"Yes, but before we go, I want to talk about something." Sawyer dropped his hand from the door and I slid in between him and the truck. I leaned my back against the frame. "Last night... I don't want you to get the wrong impression of me. You said you wanted to get to know me and I didn't want you to think I was someone that just throws myself at people. Because that is *not* what I do. I'm sorry for basically groping you, I will make it a point not to drink around you if that's how I end up acting."

He smiled and let out a curt laugh. "I promise you don't have to apologize for 'groping' me. We were making out and you were just being very touchy, nothing wrong with that. But if you want future make out sessions to be very PG, as PG as they can be, I will tie my hands behind my back if I have to."

"I don't know," my voice raised about twenty octaves, "that sounds pretty kinky to me."

He snorted out a laugh. "Get in the car!" He opened the door and I slid in beside Billy. Sawyer stuck his head in through the window after closing it and kissed my temple. "You're something else, you know that."

I reached for his hand and brought it over to rest on my thigh. Every so often, he'd remove his left hand from the steering wheel to shift gears.

I unlaced my fingers from his as I noticed. "Oh, gosh...I'm sorry. That's right, you need to drive." I felt a heat crawl up my neck, landing on my cheeks. "I didn't mean to—"

"Don't start with me." He grabbed my hand back, this time resting it on his leg. "As long as you let me, I'll hold onto you any chance I get. I can shift gears just fine, okay?"

I looked over his way as he stared straight out the windshield. His side profile was almost as perfect as his entire face. And the scruff was doing him *all* of the favors. With his grasp gripping tighter over my hand, he shifted once more. He truly had a handle on things.

"If you say so," I spoke softly into my lap, though I felt my chest getting tighter knowing he didn't want to let my hand go. He didn't want to let *me* go. And then I couldn't really imagine being that close to him without touching him either.

Even the slightest graze against an elbow, or a brush of a shoulder—Sawyer's touch sent shivers down my spine all while setting my body aflame. How did that work? I had yet to know.

I've always had an interesting relationship with physical touch, but all of a sudden, he makes it my favorite love language. That was something I never expected to get used to. But I noticed I was doing a lot of that lately when it came to Sawyer.

Passing Hummingbird Lake, we headed up the main street with the windows down and my hair blowing all around. Four storefronts down from Jitters, what was once the general store, now housed Bird's Nest, a farmers market.

The exterior looked like it belonged along the coast of Cape Cod Bay with its shingle siding and vibrant blue awning.

Consisting of homemade jams and freshly grown produce, the walls were lined with wooden crates used as shelving. Billy instantly ran up to the store workers, they started shoveling dog biscuits down his throat.

"Hey, Lionel, Rachel," Sawyer went in for a hug with the two who were wearing matching linen overalls. "This is Lucy Collins."

"Collins?" The couple asked in unison, almost taken aback. "You're Sunny's girl, aren't ya? Wow, you sure have grown up."

I recoiled at the mention of my mother. I had been in the clear so far since being back, anyone who knew me and my history, knew not to ask about her. Gus and Leanne had done a wonderful job of not bringing her up.

"We heard you were off in California becoming a nurse. She talks about you all of the time!"

"Arizona," I said bluntly. "I just received my MD at the end of May."

I shifted my posture and stood firm, but my insides were set to crumble any second and my knees turned weak. Sawyer's hand appeared on the small of my back to steady me. I started to fidget with my necklace.

"Are you okay?" he whispered over my shoulder.

I gave a single nod.

"I'm sorry, but how do you know my mother?" I cut into their side conversation with one another. I didn't remember them in the way they clearly remembered me.

"We spend tons of time together when the time allows it! She and I go on walks, Lionel helps her with taxes every spring, and we do 'paint and sip' parties once a month at our place. She comes to every one of them. It's sort of like a book club, but with—"

"With painting and wine," I finished Rachel's sentence.

The talk of my mom in general struck a chord as it was, but talking about her to people I never even met, let alone heard of? I was even more out of touch with her than I thought I was. She did paint and sip. She still painted. She made time for friends and clubs and herself. It was like I was hearing about a person I barely even knew.

But that's exactly what it was, she was someone I barely even knew.

"It was great seeing you two, but I'm going to show Lucy out back." Sawyer snapped his fingers at Billy, who was trying to get into the treat bag beside Rachel.

"Of course. Oh, and Lucy? Tell your mom we say hi."

"I'll tell her," I mumbled under my breath, though it seemed like they would hear from her before I ever did.

Out through the main store, there was an enclosed cemented patio that had weekend vendors scattered around. Farm fresh eggs on one table, and wildflower bouquets on another. People were chatting and laughing, everyone was admiring handmade accessories and sipping on samples of smoothies. And there was no mention of my mother out here.

My jaw unclenched itself somewhere between the table with the palm reading and the salt water taffy lady.

This is my version of heaven.

Billy pranced around from booth to booth, vacuuming up scraps of dropped food and getting back scratches along the way.

"I knew you would like it," Sawyer pulled me in towards him.

He knew what I was thinking, and how I felt without saying a single word. A rare moment where I could hold my emotions to myself, and not feel like I had to verbalize them. He just understood.

"Here, for you," Sawyer plucked a single flower and sniffed it before passing it over to me. "Thanks, Roger," he waved to the florist as we walked away.

"What's this?"

"A peony."

"No, I know what kind of flower. I mean—"

"Promise you won't run the other way, completely weirded out?"

"I make no promises, Banks."

"I was bummed that I had to leave in such a rush when you came into The Hideout, the second time that first day that you arrived. I wanted to sit there and talk to you for hours if I could. I was fully prepared to run through all of Leanne's baked goods in the dessert case if it meant we had a chance to talk longer."

My cheeks became warm.

"And, well... Mel caught wind I was sort of, just a little bit, kind of, crushin' and turned into an FBI agent. It was scary. She pulled you up in zero point two seconds. Anyway, I saw the recent photos you were tagged in from your graduation. And I know that these were the flowers on the dress you wore."

My heart was seconds away from falling out of my chest and onto the ground.

I bought my graduation dress at the beginning of med school. It sat in the back of my closet and I promised myself I would never wear it. Not until everything fell into place, and I was certain that I would walk across that stage.

When it was evident that I would graduate, and that all of my dreams were coming true, I moved it to the front of my closet. It stared back at me every time I opened the doors to get dressed for yet another long, draining day. And then I had it hanging there, front and center for at least five months before I was going to walk across the stage. I didn't care that I had to push it off to the side every day.

It was a form of motivation.

"So, what you're telling me is you're obsessed with me?" I smiled up at Sawyer and lifted the flower to my nose for a single sniff.

Of course, I could have been weirded out, feeling as if my space and identity were invaded. But then I'd be a hypocrite—that's what social media is all about.

Unfortunately, there wasn't much when I looked him up. At least nothing more beyond the tabloids and town magazines, declaring him to be an insensitive disappointment. From where I was standing, he was anything but.

I could have said thank you, I could have held onto the moment more. Acknowledged and appreciated that he took the time to learn bits about me. But instead, I deflected. I used humor to push away the slightest amount of feelings that I felt growing inside of me. *So what you're telling me is you're obsessed with me?*

"How could I not be?" he said through an ear-to-ear grin before placing a kiss on the side of my head.

We stepped off to the side and listened to the small bluegrass band, staying for a few songs of their set before the market got busy. Lionel and Rachel sure made the most of their space here, but it still felt too crowded.

"Want to get out of here?" Sawyer asked. I nodded before his full sentence left his lips. I was enjoying the day, but back-to-back, highly-populated outings had become over-whelming.

He whistled for Billy and we made our way out and back to his truck. He opened the door and I climbed on in.

Instead of turning on the road that took us to the cottages, he continued down a winding road. At the end sat the entrance to Sawyers's lake house. I had only seen the backside of it, but it was even more captivating from the front.

Rows and rows of sugar maple trees separated his property from the hillside. Whenever I had cut through the woods on my way to the lake, I had always seen the A-frame roof pop out over the trees, but the snippets of imagination never did it justice.

There was a small river that ran before the front yard. He stopped the car at the start of a wood plank bridge that crosses the river into his perfectly landscaped yard. Billy ran up ahead of us, his nails clanked along each of the panels.

"Here, let's go around this way."

We walked along the side of his house, he had to hold the low hanging branches that hovered over the stone walkway. The short trail wrapped around his house and led to the backyard.

The Hideout looked so small from this side of the lake.

"Thank you for today. I'm sorry if I seem uninteresting or dull today, though. I can't say I got much sleep last night."

"You don't seem uninteresting or dull," he repeated back to me. "You seem calm."

Calm wasn't a word I often used to describe myself.

Something changed in me once I crossed state lines. I left Arizona, and somehow, so did my usual avoidant disposition. I *did* feel calm. I felt safe. I felt open.

Sawyer had that effect on me.

Chapter 21

Sawyer

"You head on down there," I said, "and I'll get us something to drink." Lucy and I broke off from one another. She headed for the dock while I slipped inside the house.

The kitchen window was practically the entire wall's length, long enough for my mom, aunts, or whoever else wanted a break from the outdoors to line along the counters and watch out. It had the perfect view of the lake.

And of Lucy.

You could see everything from here. She sat gracefully at the edge of the dock with her hands in her lap. I found myself standing in the same stance my mother would: arms extended out on either side, planted against the sink's ledge. Life felt endless from this standpoint.

Over on the side of the fridge was the most recent postcard from my parents from their time in Rome. A simple photo on a four-by-six cardstock. We were countries apart, but no matter the distance, their snail mail kept me feeling closer to them than I did when they still lived in Connecticut.

There have been days where I've wondered if I should have left Europe. It was a life full of constant adventure. It was everything I believed I wanted. It was the first time I had broken away from the Banks legacy. And often, I'm left second guessing if I had fully let time run its course. I had years of freedom to make up for.

I had been conditioned for so long to live a certain way and have particular beliefs. I owed it to myself to spread my wings. But I couldn't ignore the itching aliveness coursing through me. I was free, I could do anything I wanted. I still had drive and self-discipline, except now I could decide how I distributed it through life.

I broke the news to my parents in the middle of the Louvre. Captivated by the beauty of The Astronomer, I couldn't ignore the feeling that my time was limited. I turned to them, knowing that if I waited any longer, it'd eat me alive. That I was sure of.

By the end of the day, I was on a flight back to the States. And the greatest thing of all, they never once made me feel guilty or shamed me for not following their way of life.

My parents; the blueprint for breaking generational practices.

A nomad life was meant for my parents. Not me. I liked the quietness, the stillness of Rider. A life around Hummingbird Lake was it for me. There was no question about it. I have spent the last six years making what was only once a summer house a home and truly know what it meant to say the word.

I plucked the postcard from underneath the *Viva Las Vegas* magnet and placed it on the counter as a reminder to email them soon.

As I rapidly made mental notes of all of the things I'd tell them, I grabbed a couple of glasses, the makings for an at-home mimosa, and whatever fruit and cheese I could find inside of the fridge. A makeshift brunch, if you will. I pinched the stems of the glasses in one hand, grasping onto the champagne in my fist, then huddled the rest into my arm by scooping it off of the counter.

"Come on, boy," I called out to Billy. His nails scratched along the wood floor as he followed behind me.

Strategically, I released everything from my hold and placed it beside Lucy on the dock. I snapped my fingers two times and motioned to Billy to leap into the lake. At the speed of light, he plopped in and splashed us, getting water all over the sad excuse for a charcuterie board and our legs.

"Sorry about that," I said, hidden behind a laugh.

I picked up Lucy's flower that was next to her on the dock and lightly shook off the water droplets then placed it back. While I found amusement in Billy's antics, Lucy started to cry but refused to let it escape her body. Shallow sobs were trapped in her throat, and her chest heaved in staggered movements.

She shot straight up and gradually started to pace. "Fuck!" she eventually shouted out.

The weeping had turned into full-on bawling. She crouched down, wrapping her arms around her legs. Her eyes continued to fill with tears, my heart broke at the sound of wails coming from that tiny body of hers.

I quickly replayed every second of the day within a millisecond, trying to pinpoint where it could have all gone wrong. Where *I* could have gone wrong. I wanted nothing more than to make this day special for her—help her put her mind to rest.

When her body started to tremble, exhausted and overwhelmed by its own emotions, I moved my hand over her shoulder. Before I made contact with her skin, she shrugged my hand away.

"I'm fine!" she snapped, shooting herself back to a standing position.

She adjusted her dress strap that slipped from her hurried movement.

"I just don't get it! What's wrong with me?" she continued.

I would never have imagined Lucy to get this loud. She was otherwise sweet-tempered.

"After tonight, I have to force myself to forget everything," she said quieter, more to herself than to me.

"You don't have to... Are you... Do you want to forget it all?" I said with knitted brows.

Did she want to forget about me?

"No, of course not. But this isn't real life. This," she waved my arms over the lake, "this isn't my life. Not anymore. I don't have anyone to take care of me anymore. I don't get to have this—where I frolic around and ignore all of my responsibilities—and I'm a fool to think otherwise. The real world is still out there and I have to deal with it, fix it. There's so much you don't know. That *I* don't know... My mom, the person Lionel and Rachel know and went on and on about, is not the same person that I know.

"I haven't talked to her in who knows how long. My mother has hated me for as long as I can remember. We had what I would classify as a close relationship when I was very young. But then I grew up. And, well...I don't know anymore."

I ached for her. I could feel her pain, and I wished I could take the hurt away from her. *Please, Universe, throw it all on me. Lucy Collins does not deserve to feel this way.*

She exhaled a large breath before pacing again.

"On top of everything, I haven't studied more than an hour at a time since being home. I'm pretty sure I'll fail out of my residency program before it even starts. And I tried to do a couple of tutoring sessions over video chat, but that went to absolute shit with a poor internet connection, so I will be responsible for a freshman failing out of summer courses. He's failing, I'm failing…" She let out a shallow breath, "Oh, my god. I'm failing."

Lucy cupped her face with her hands and began sobbing again. All the while, I could see the chip that she's held onto since she got here slowly crumble and fall off of her shoulder.

I threw my arms around her. With a bear hug, I was stabling knees that were about to buckle out from under her. Lucy attempted to break out of my embrace, but I wouldn't let her. I couldn't let her. All I wanted to do was hold her, help her. "Listen. Lucy, I'm here," I said, but her breathing started to pick back up, drowning out my words. "I'm right here," I said louder, firmer.

Her body went limp beneath my hold, all of her weight fell onto me.

"This wasn't how I wanted today to go," she sniffled into my chest.

"I know."

I tilted her face up at me, her eyes were puffy and tears were streaming down her cheekbones. I wanted to kiss her, hug her, and tell her that everything was going to be alright even when I, myself, didn't know that it would.

All I knew was that it would be okay if we worked through it together.

I wiped her tears away. "You can't do all these things on your own, Lucy. You shouldn't have to. Pouring from an empty cup never works."

After a quick scan of my eyes, she pressed her mouth onto mine.

"Thank you," she said, wiping away at her bottom lip.

"Hmm, I don't think I have ever been thanked for a kiss before. I'll take it."

She pushed at the center of my chest, "Oh, whatever!" she said with a smile. *There it was.* "Thank you for this weekend."

The both of us returned to our spots at the edge of the dock. She lifted the flower and moved it back into her lap. The subtle sloshing sounds of Hummingbird Lake and the whistling of trees surrounding it received the memo.

The magic of Hummingbird Lake—it was in full force.

Lucy shut her eyes, regulated her breathing, and allowed herself to listen to the sounds around her. In and out, in and out, each breath mimicked the sound of the branches waving in the wind. She let her hands fall on either side of her, running her fingertips along the wood planks to feel every ridge and crack that ran along them.

She leaned her head against my arm before she hazily opened up her eyes. We both watched as Billy jumped into the lake for the millionth time. One thing about that mutt is he will not let anyone stay sad or mad for too long. "Thank you for this weekend," she repeated.

"Would I be completely crazy and make all of this worse by asking you to spend *one* more day with me?" I rested my head on top of hers, squinting my eyes shut as tight as possible out of fear to hear her answer.

All she did was pull away to pour out a mimosa that was more champagne than orange juice, then handed it over to me. She made another and motioned to a cheer with her head shaking and a roll of the eyes. A smile formed across her face, "You're something else, Banks."

"Is that a yes?" I clinked my glass into hers.

She popped a single grape into her mouth, then burrowed it into the side of her cheek like a little chipmunk. "I am learning that it's getting harder to say no to you," she said before crunching down.

Chapter 22

Lucy

Pouring from an empty cup never works.

Sawyer had a way of making his words play on a loop inside my head.

Normally, I'd retreat at the first sign of interest. I'd run the other way once I learned he was making an impression on me. Now, I revel in it. I couldn't imagine not being grateful for knowing him.

He was supportive in how he carried out our conversations. No matter how minuscule or major. Yes, I have noticed that it is getting harder to say no to him. But I was also noticing just how intentional this man is. He doesn't say anything just to say it, his words hold power.

It was admirable.

All of the firecrackers that you could find in a hundred-mile radius of Rider were going off all night down by the schoolyard. I believe the town goes harder for the eve of every holiday, than they do for the actual day.

Late into the evening, hours after I had decompressed from my cry session at Sawyer's, I watched as Gus and Leanne danced in their yard. The sparklers in the sky were the soundtrack to their night.

The Fourth of July has always been their favorite holiday. Never for the meaning, never for what it stood for. But because it reminded them of their love—explosive and colorful.

They embraced one another, eyes closed, swaying back and forth. I don't even know why I bothered bringing a book out there with me, I could have stood out on the back patio and followed their movements endlessly. The words on paper were no competition to their love story.

When I eventually moved myself back inside, I began to digest it all. The emptiness and the silence of the cottage left me with no choice. My eyes were heavy, but so was my heart. I started to turn on myself, I became furious with myself. For why, I don't know.

I probably dragged my feet around every square inch of the house last night. I knew that this wasn't going to be an easy process. Love and life and grief will never be an easy process.

I normally wouldn't be singing praises to the insistent noise of the holiday, but it kept me from overthinking well into the night. Maybe it was the physical exhaustion of having plans consecutive days in a row or the mental exhaustion from bawling my eyes out and having an anxiety attack, but either way, I was knocked out the second my head hit the pillow.

Once I woke up, refreshed and revived, I took Sawyer's advice.

When I'm a little more level-headed and have released my pent up emotions, I'm not as stubborn.

I emailed the two underclassmen that I have been tutoring with some news I am sure they never thought they would hear coming from me: I was canceling Zoom meetings for the next two days.

One emailed back with a thumbs-up emoji. The other mocked me by asking if my laptop had been hijacked by someone who was actually cool.

Whenever there was potential for a student to work with me, I would make all of my ground rules clear so they knew what to expect. One of them was that we worked through holidays. Success didn't have days off. Most of them hated it, which I understood, but those are the students who didn't end up working with me. The ones that *do* reciprocate and understand my conditions, we have built a great relationship.

I never hound them, I never work them into the ground. But we have a mutual understanding that we want what's best for their academic career. It works.

After I hit send, I figured it was in my—and the house's—best interest to put in some work. I am so close to the finish line, and then I am free to enjoy the rest of the summer.

Once and for all.

I have put it off long enough and I am itching to make some real headway. In less than two months, Kai and I had agreed to put on an open house. Now was the time to use some elbow grease and get into the nitty gritty of everything, even when I felt like I might not want to.

But even when I touched a new box, I found something new that held meaning. Somehow the smallest of items found a way to hold meaning for me. I have a hundred open boxes and one blurry mind. For that very reason alone, I decided to take my efforts to the shed. I figured a fresh space, a small one at that, wouldn't create such an issue. A change of pace might just be what I've needed.

I wove through the sparse rows of boxes living in the hallway and trekked through the backyard. The early birds have already started on their grilling. The smell of pecan firewood moved through the hillside. The sky blazes a bright blue with full clouds floating about. I don't even care that my skin already has a sticky feeling before the sun has reached its highest point. The humidity has never been my cup of tea, and I'd do anything for the dry, desert heat of Arizona right about now.

Back in the shed, stacked to the ceiling, there were more boxes than I remembered. With just enough room for a walkway, I had a clear shot of an easel and some paints sitting in the far back.

"Need any help?" a raspy voice called out from behind me.

Gus and Leanne neared me. Her holding a pie, him holding a leaf blower.

I spun around on the balls of my feet and huffed out, "Ya know, I think I just might."

"I'll bring this on in," Leanne held up her glass pan. "Want any tea?"

"Yes, please!" Gus and I called out after.

He set the leaf blower down, resting it against the side of the shed.

"I haven't seen this door here open in ages," he poked his head through the threshold. The canvas resting on the easel received a long stare from him, as well.

There sat a painting in its early stages, displaying the creek that ran along the cottage.

I remember when my grandmother had started it. It was from one of her better weeks in between hospital visits. She was restless, eager to do something that wasn't watching reruns on the Turner Classic Movie channel.

She pulled me out onto the back patio and we sat in utter silence. She painted while I read. There'd be a brief break in our self-care and bonding time where she'd share all about the plans she had for the painting and when I told her about the major plot twist I had just reached in my book.

Not even a full thirty minutes later did she grow tired and turned in for the day. I moved the painting into the shed with the plan to pull it back out for her the next time we were out here. Instead, her body and her heart had other plans for us when she woke the next morning. She never made it back home and she never got to finish her work.

I walked to the back of the shed to get a closer look. The bottom of the canvas showed the very edge of our yard. A thick strip of bright green with an outline of a duck waddling across it. The detail was impeccable. Everything else was lightly stenciled out but was never touched again.

On her stool that was beside her painting, the book I read that day remained in its exact spot. The outline of years' worth of dust bordered the edges. *For Whom the Bell Tolls.* I brushed my fingers over the cover and a trail of dust slid underneath my fingertip.

"That reminds me, I have another book for you," Gus croaked out with a hand over his chest, his eyes swelling with tears.

"I haven't even started *A Moveable Feast* yet. Haven't had the time..."

"And that's fine. You'll have another one waiting for you when you do finish it. I'll drop it off tomorrow afternoon, sounds good?"

I nod. "Will I see you at Sawyer's tonight?"

"You know it."

"Oh, we can't wait! I have a cake waiting to be iced back home as we speak!" Leanne smiled, walking towards us with glasses and a pitcher of tea in her hands. Thin slices of lemon floated on the top surface.

"How much of this do you think we can knock out before then?"

Gus blew out a breath. "Well, if you can find a speaker and put on some Willie, I think we can get through this in no time."

Hours upon hours had passed and sweat started to build up on the top of my lip. All but two boxes and the easel had made it inside before Gus and Leanne called it quits. Leanne had gone between our cottages all day. Alternating between the two, she checked on her baked goods and then on us. Listening to their bickering and teasing followed by slaps on both of their butts and kisses on the cheek in passing made the whole day worthwhile. Being around them made everything better.

The aroma of vanilla frosting oozed off of her. I wanted to eat whatever she was making now, but she scolded me and insisted that I had to wait until later tonight.

"Thank you guys, truly. I will see you guys soon, okay?" I swiped my brow bone where a layer of sweat transferred onto my hand. I watched as the two of them walked down the drive, Leanne's arm threaded through Gus'.

I wasn't playing any games tonight. I ran upstairs, knowing that tonight's look needed a little more attention. Bright red cowboy boots, a short enough white dress with a tiny bow in the center of the neckline, and a dark blue bandana wrapped around my ponytail. I did not want a smudge of mascara under my eyes or a hair out of place.

Sawyer wanted one more night of "Fun Lucy" and that was exactly what he was going to get. Even if it meant I had to play dress up as someone else for the night. Because for whatever it's worth, I like the version Sawyer sees of me. He makes me seem so much more collected than I actually am. Perhaps, it's the person I want to be, too. Against my better judgment and my allegiance to feminism, I will alter myself for a guy—just this once.

The rumbling of Sawyer's truck and Billy's noticeable bark got closer and closer as I finished applying lotion to my legs, leaving a gold, glittery sheen over the surface. I skipped down the stairs in all of my girlish-excitement glory.

Here goes nothing, I thought to myself as I have before. But this time it held a different meaning. The statement wasn't filled with trepidation, or an attempt to calm myself down. Now, I said it with pure joy, ready to see what the night held.

It was a strange feeling to be at such a crossroads. One where I constantly feel guilty if I am making the right decision. I couldn't even place my hand on the doorknob, out of fear that the moment that I do, it's some sort of symbol that I'm dismissing my feelings, pushing them down and away like I have time and time again.

But I inched closer, knowing that it was time to say "yes" to a life that's worth living sometimes.

I went to open the door and there he was standing with his hand curled in a fist at eye level. His arm fell to his side, and he flashed me a grin. Any doubts that I had vanished.

I took a step back, startled.

He bent to kiss my cheek. "How did you know I was here?"

"I think I have a sixth sense when it comes to you."

That made his lips curl up and his head bow bashfully.

"I'm kidding." I pointed at the still-running truck and Billy's excitement. "It's kind of hard *not* to hear those two."

I threaded my hand into his and we made our way down to the truck.

We were all but two strides down the walkway and there was Gracie at a standstill. Her golden blond locks were in their familiar, perfect waves that framed her face. She stood in her predictable pastel color palette. But her demeanor was all but colorful. Black, watered-down lines stained her cheeks.

"Hi," she let out a broken cry, clutching onto her designer duffle bag.

My heart sank and I ran straight towards her. She let her bag fall from her grip and onto the gravel. "Asher and I broke up and I didn't want to be alone," she said into my neck.

The news of their breakup didn't confuse me as much as the statement about being "alone" did. She had all her girlfriends, and her parents, and up until now, she had Asher. When she and I weren't together, she was with at least one of them. She always had someone. Gracie never had to experience being alone.

"I am going to kick his ass," I snarled. "When did this happen? What happened?" My mind was going a mile a minute. "Why didn't you call me? I would have come home." I scanned her eyes, holding her head in my hands.

She pulled away, "Please, I was not going to make you come home for this. It happened yesterday and—" She swiped a tear off her perfect, contoured cheekbone, "I needed my L.C. I hope that's okay."

I wiped another rolling tear away and touched my forehead to hers. "Of course, that's okay. I sure am happy to see you." I threaded my hand in hers. "Alright, let's go."

Sawyer reached down to lift her bag off the ground and slung it over his shoulder. He threw it into the back of the truck and motioned to Billy to climb back there along with it.

"W-what? Where are we going?"

"A party," Sawyer interjected.

"A party?" She looked over at me. "Who is that?" she mouthed to me quickly before Sawyer turned back around. I shook my head, dismissing her and she rolled her eyes.

I don't know why I haven't told her about Sawyer during our weekly Tuesday phone calls. And if she hadn't shown up, I'm not sure I would have. She is a hopeless romantic, and any mention of a boy would turn on some sort of switch I was not ready to figure out how to dismantle.

Sawyer is different, he's not your typical summer fling, and I didn't want her to classify him as just that.

"Let me get this straight... You, Lucy Collins, are willingly going to a party?" Gracie's feet shuffled fast behind me as we moved toward the truck.

"I'm sorry, did you forget that one we went to a couple of years back? I had to beg *you* to come with me!"

"You only went because it was a costume party. You can't pass up a costume party. And I only went because I didn't want to deal with long lines and expensive drinks at the bars."

Gracie let out a cracked laugh, and I could tell that the trip down memory lane danced through her head. I had dressed up as Maleficent that year, but at some point in the night, I had lost my cape, I broke the headpiece, and my tights had ripped. I had turned into Frank-N-Furter, and there was no convincing anyone otherwise.

The sound of her happiness returned. Even if for a fleeting moment, I had my golden girl here with me. She knew it before I did, but I needed her, too.

"You better have something you can change into when we get to his house, G. We are partying tonight and I would hate to see your loafers get messy."

I pushed her into the middle seat and slammed the door shut.

Sawyer peered his head around Gracie. "So, you get any work done today, my little busy bee?"

Gracie let out a snort. *Busy bee?* She mouthed over at me.

"Y-yeah," I said, awkwardly. "Gus and Leanne actually stopped by and helped me out. Well, Gus did. Most of the shed is cleared out. I'll get to the last two boxes tomorrow. Oh, Sawyer, Gracie. Gracie? This is Sawyer."

Sawyer nodded, Gracie gave a half-wave before reaching over and placing her hand on my leg, giving me a little tap on the knee and a raise of the brow. I held back a smile that I felt was pushing its way through.

"Look at you guys, that's so great. Just remember to take your time. You don't need to rush."

Gracie tapped my leg again, this time twice. It was our little signal for whenever we wanted to talk about something later when we were alone.

The three of us stared out the windshield in complete silence for the remainder of our drive. Those five minutes felt like five hours. It certainly felt weird merging my two worlds—but it didn't mean I hated it.

Sawyer bobbed his head to the music that played through his cassette, Gracie looked out at every person and tree and dog that we passed on the way, and I sat in my seat fending off all of the thoughts that were trying to ruin this day.

Tonight, I could be whoever I wanted to be.

I had my guy and I had my Gracie. But at the strike of midnight, Type A Lucy would be back because I didn't actually have all of the time in the world. I'd have to turn in the dress and shoes for a mop and bucket once more.

Chapter 23

Sawyer

The sun had dipped behind the trees and beneath the horizon.

And right on cue, the fireflies emerged from the woods for the younger kids to chase after, giggling and sprinting, seeing who could catch more than the other. Anyone and everyone who didn't have plans of their own tonight migrated to the Banks residence.

In my honest opinion, this was what the lake house was always meant for.

Hits from the early 2000s blared over the stereos, but all I could hear was Lucy's laugh from down by the fire pit. She had become more playful, more flighty. And even in the middle of dancing up a storm and catching up with people she hadn't seen in years, she managed to check in with Gracie. All she had to do was place a hand on her elbow or raise an eyebrow to show that she was there. Despite her efforts, Gracie shooed her away, reassuring her with laughter and smiles as she flirted the night away.

I couldn't help but laugh into my drink at the thought that Lucy still tried to multitask at a party.

Half of our little town flooded in and out over the course of the evening, I almost couldn't keep track of who all was here. Jet and his buddies kept to themselves over at The Hideout, where I am certain they were feeding Billy scraps of brisket. When he retreated to my whistle, he came running back smelling like a Texas barbecue. Mel, Kai, and Cherry played corn-hole down near the water—I could hear Cherry's screeching laughter from a mile away every time she scored a point. Lionel and Rachel made their rounds with their all-out red, white, and blue accessories flashing vigorously. And Gus and Leanne sat up near the house watching over us all like the proud parents they are.

Even with all of the commotion, the intermittent firecrackers and loud cheers, Lucy and I made it a point to find each other through the crowd. Like we were the only ones here, like a single glance from one another could make the world feel at a standstill.

I tried to pretend that I wasn't getting closer to her, that I wasn't nearing her, but inch by inch, I approached her. I didn't want her to feel pressured to have one more person to entertain, but I made sure I kept her in my proximity. You know, in case she needed me.

I slung the log tote that was resting beside the equipment shed over my shoulder and paraded myself down to the fire pit. I could feel Lucy following my every stride. I plopped the bag down and started loading additional logs into the pit and added lighter fluid.

Those huddled around cheered in their drunken state for the split second that the fire grew. But that was not the force of nature I was interested in. I looked over at Lucy, hoping to find her eyes meeting mine, but instead, she was immersed in a new conversation.

I met her down by the water, placing my hand on the small of her back. She let her body fall into my touch while I greeted the rest of the group. Mrs. Tidewater, the principal from

Hillside High, and Franklin, the karate instructor down at the rec. center, said their hello's and thank you's for inviting them tonight.

"That fire sure is growing, nice job!" Franklin commented.

"Yeah," Lucy smirked, "You got some nice wood, Sawyer." She flashed me a wink, and I squeezed her side. She muffled a yelp over her shoulder while Franklin and Mrs. Tidewater awkwardly stood across from us.

"Thanks, Franklin. Gus and I cut that batch up over there," I nodded to the pit, "last winter. But Lucy and I just gathered a new collection a few days ago for the colder months." I pulled her in closer to me.

"Ahh." He stretched out and started rubbing at the top of his shoulder. "I've been meaning to sharpen that axe and get on out there, but you know," he shrugged, "life."

I said nothing, while Mrs. Tidewater nodded her head in agreement. They started their own conversation that I had no interest in being a part of. All I wanted was to take Lucy away and have her all to myself.

"Come with me," I whispered into her ear.

We wave our goodbye's to the two of them.

We walked along the water and placed ourselves down in some old, weathered Adirondack chairs away from everyone.

"Hi, Pretty Girl," I said, pulling her into my lap, halting her from sitting in her own seat.

She snickered into my shoulder. *I see she's opted for the giggly drunk persona tonight.*

"This is cozy," she spoke softly.

The early moonlight was starting to dance on top of the water. The reflection was bright enough to cast off of Lucy's face, exposing her flushed skin and heavy but happy eyes.

I looked over at the empty chair beside us and couldn't help but picture her sitting there at the start of every day with her too-strong coffee made by Mel, or covered up in layers of my jackets that were a few sizes too big on her while she read well into the night.

My mind turned into static at the thought. I am completely, one hundred percent falling for this girl. And it pained me to know that in a matter of weeks, she was going to forget all about me.

Girls like her don't fall for guys like me.

"Hey, Lucy?" My words were in a stranglehold.

"Mmhm?" she hummed out.

I opened my mouth but nothing would come out. She pulled her feet up towards her chest and balled herself into my lap. I wrapped my arms around her, never wanting to let go. The sound of the boat rocking at the end of the dock, people singing at the top of their lungs, and the rustling of the wildlife scurrying around in the trees were loud. But they were nowhere near as loud as the thoughts inside my head.

I've never had an issue with saying what I need to say, so what the hell is wrong with me now? She had this hold over me. One that made me afraid to look like an obsessed fool in her eyes. I hated the idea that I could scare her away by simply sharing how I felt.

"Have you ever been skinny dipping?" I broke the silence with a question that I had no intention of asking. At least not now? I want to know everything about her, but god, this was not what I wanted to know right now. I really wanted to know how she felt, where her head was at. Were we on the same page? Maybe she's in a completely different book.

She snorted, then lifted her head to study me. The way her eyes tried to narrow themselves, I could tell she was wondering if I really just asked her that.

"Uh, yeah. Once. It was in my junior year of med school. Gracie and I had made some friends during winter break up in the mountains. This girl that I was flirting with on our first night had dared me to jump into the lake. Completely juvenile, I know. But I did it anyway. I had to prove that I wasn't a little bitch. And sort of as a solidarity thing, she jumped in, too. Then we made out. Naked. In the freezing water. When I tell you my nipples could cut glass, I mean it!"

"That sounds like a wild ni—"

"Luce, Luce!" Gracie hurdled towards us, her drink sloshing over the edge of her cup.

"I'm sorry," Lucy winced, crinkling her entire face.

Gracie was buzzed to say the least. I'd say full-on drunk was more like it. She pulled Lucy up to her feet, dragging her behind.

Just like that, they were swallowed by the group of guys that had been surrounding Gracie for most of the night. They immediately encouraged the girls to play drinking games. Squeals and shouts came from everyone that was near as Lucy and Gracie shifted to the corn-hole area. If they missed, they had to take a shot, and already, they were terrible at the game. I leaned against the kayak rack off to the side as I witnessed the excitement stir through everyone.

Before attempting another round of their mess of a game, Gracie stopped in her tracks as an upbeat country song trickled its first few chords through the speakers. "Stop! We have to do it!" she claimed with slurred words.

Lucy playfully rolled her eyes as she assumed her position next to Gracie. Gracie slanted herself into Lucy's shoulder and they both let out a squeal. They threw themselves into a full-on, choreographed line-dancing routine. Lucy looked so free.

When they shifted directions, she would embellish the toss of her ponytail over her shoulder. Those around joined in, some knew the moves, while others stood off and mimicked the steps from behind.

Once the song ended, the girls touched their foreheads like they had earlier in the evening and giggled between themselves. Lucy's infectious laugh struck a chord, I could hear it from here, and it traveled through every fiber of my body. As they broke away from one another, Lucy was intercepted by a yank of the wrist by a guy with shitty hair.

"Hey!" I shouted. I threw my drink off to the side and marched over to them. To her. My strides had become larger, and stronger, but it did not feel like they were fast enough. The heels of my boots pressed into the damp lawn as I pushed through multiple conversations, not caring who was in my way. All I cared about was getting to Lucy.

We were only a few feet away and it felt like it was taking an eternity to get to her.

"Sawyer!" Lionel and Gus yelled. They both stalked after me as I made my way to Lucy. Gus grabbed at my shoulder once he reached my heels, but I shook him off.

Her body was forced against his, his hand found its way to her ass. Aaron had Lucy locked beneath his arm. She squirmed to break out, but he wouldn't budge. Her face was filled with disgust at the stench of the distillery living in his mouth that even I could smell from where I once stood.

"You were real sexy out there. I saw you looking at me. Were you dancing out there like that for me?" he slurred his words, dragging his fingers along her face.

"You fucking wish!" she snapped back at him, pulling away from him. But his tight grip cinched her waist, making it impossible for her to break free.

I yanked at his shoulder. Caught off guard, his grip on her loosened and she managed to squirm away. In a matter of seconds, my knuckles met his face and the sound of a cracking cheekbone rang from the contact.

"Sawyer!" Lucy shrieked, her voice breaking over the outcry from people rushing towards us.

For being as lanky as he is, he could shockingly hold his own. He jumped up from the ground. Besides adjusting his neck, he didn't seem to be too messed up. I guess I could thank the drunkenness for that. All of his limbs were too loose and he was so relaxed that he couldn't even process what was going on until it happened.

Aaron swung back up at me, only for me to stop his arm from reaching. I released his fist from being entrapped under mine, threw his arm down, and swung at him again. He fell back down on the ground, except this time he was unable to get back up. His hand twitched, but other than that, nothing. Frankly, I didn't care if he cried out for help or if he was dead.

All I knew was that, after all these years, Aaron Nelson was officially dead to me.

I crouched down beside him on the ground and whispered in his ear, "Don't you ever think about touching my girl again, got it?" I pushed up off of my knees to stand up.

I looked at Lucy. Her eyes were wider than ever, wider than usual.

Lionel placed a hand on my shoulder again, but I shrugged him away. Again.

Stone-faced, I made it my mission to get inside the house. I could hear Lucy run up behind me before catching up. "Let's get you cleaned up," she said with a gentle touch on my elbow.

Chapter 24

Sawyer

My hand was covered in blood. Mine, Aaron's—a mixture coated my knuckles. The vibrations of the speakers outside followed us through the screen door and everyone slowly shifted back into party mode.

"Where is your first aid kit?" she asked, tightening the ponytail high up on her head. I pointed at the cupboards above the fridge and scooted myself onto the kitchen counter. She walked back over to me, pulling my hand into hers. "What were you thinking? Nevermind. You weren't. *Clearly.* You're too drunk to be thinking."

She tore open the antiseptic wipes and immediately the stench of any pure alcohol wafted through the air. It made the liquor that's been passed around tonight smell like fruit juice.

"I'm not drunk."

"Yeah, well neither am I anymore. Talk about sobering up," she huffed out. "I had it handled, you know," she wiped at the broken skin on my hand.

I flinched at the stinging sensation. "I am sure you did. But I'm not sorry that I hit him. I didn't like how he was touching you. He ruined everything," I said as I hopped off of the counter.

I planted myself in front of her, she stumbled back just a step. I watched as her chest heaved up and down with every deep breath that she took. The overhead light shined down on us, on her, making the sweat look more like a sparkle across her collarbones.

"You were glowing down there," I said in a lower tone than before. "Lucy, you should have seen yourself from my point of view. But then that scumbag put his hands on you and took that shine away. Even for a second, I hated it."

The rage that I felt only minutes before started to filter through my body again. But then she looked at me in a way only she knows how.

She let out a heavy sigh as she searched my eyes, neither of us were able to find the next words to say. She pressed her head into the center of my chest and started to rub the side of my arm. She dragged her hand down to mine, holding the bloody fingers in hers. Aaron's hard head hurt, it's all cement up there, but the pain hurt a lot less in her hold.

The pain hurt a lot less in her hold.

"Lucy, I could watch you dance and smile and laugh forever. Oh, you have no idea how bad that I want to."

She dropped my hand.

"Sawyer—"

"No. I want you to listen to me." I took her head in between my hands. Her cheeks squished up under my grip, we couldn't help but snicker a bit. "I want to be with you. And I know what you're going to say. You have to go back to Arizona. You have to be the badass woman that you are, I'm not going to ask you not to be just that. But I also need to ask you to be with me. You don't get it, it's a *need*. I need you, Lucy. We can figure the rest out at a later time."

She pulled herself out from my hold and walked a few steps away, turning to face away from me. "I don't know if you noticed, but I'm not the type that can just *figure it out*," she muttered into the ground. "Things need to be structured. I can't afford them not to be. I have to know how things will work before I jump in."

"I know that you're that type, and I lo—ike, I like that you're like that," I said to her back. *I wish she would just look at me, let me look into those beautiful green eyes.* "I like everything about you, what about that don't you get? I will go at your pace, I will fly to you every weekend if you'd let me. If you want to drop me the second your plane touches down, then that's okay, too."

I paused.

Her shoulders raised with a heavy sigh, then she brought both arms to the center of her chest. I could see the chain of her necklace move against her neck. It's how I knew she was fully concentrating on my words, processing them completely. She only fiddled with her necklace when something really struck her.

"I'll be heartbroken, but I would rather go through the pain if it meant I had the chance to give my heart to you. For what it's worth, though, it's already yours. I don't want to go another day where I don't get to call you mine, Lucy—"

She whipped her head around at me and ran straight into my arms. The reminisce of Lucy's IPA melted off her lips and onto mine. Our tongues danced along to the beats of the far-off music, and our breathing mirrored one another.

It was heavy, it was loud, and the sounds of our panting and lips smacking drowned out the singing and screeching of those *thankfully* still down by the lake. But before I knew it, there was inaudible chatter filling my ears; I tried to ignore it. Louder and closer, we were interrupted by two voices crossing the threshold into the kitchen.

Gracie and Mel entered the room linked together laughing, faces turned in towards each other. "Oh, I—We'll leave you two. Sorry," Mel interjected. They turned away, mumbling little nothings under their breath like little school girls.

I'm still getting interrupted by employees when trying to kiss Lucy, and I'm not even at work. But I don't think I have seen Mel that animated, ever. Unless it was to be a smart ass. Those were some genuine expressions coming from my little grump of a best friend. For that alone, I wasn't as pissed off. Only barely.

I tugged at my already tight jeans and adjusted myself while Lucy wiped at her bottom lip and tamed her ponytail. I turned to wrap my hand up with an ace bandage.

I spoke into the counter, "You tell me what you want, and I'll give it to you. I'll give you everything."

She pulled out the bar stool that was tucked under the counter and perched herself up on it. I didn't need x-ray vision to see the gears cranking inside her head, they were so loud that I could hear them. Lucy's face scrunched up in a deep thought, a bunch of hemming and hawing was muttered under her breath. I wanted nothing more than to climb into that head of hers and know what she was thinking.

The only time she would lift her head from the array of first aid supplies was when a premature was lit off from the other end of the lake. Other than that, she focused on crumpling up the used band-aid wrappers and sanitizing wipe packets.

As she shifted in her seat, a whiff of her perfume and the mutual, lingering arousal hit me like a ton of bricks. *Thump... Thump... Thump...* My heart was beating inside of my head. If Mel and Gracie never walked in, I could still be tasting her.

"What do you think of me staying with you tonight?"
She's joking.
"You're joking."

She shook her head. "You're right, Sawyer. I need to take each day as it comes. And I want to spend my days with you. Of course, I do," she said right above a whisper.

I spun her around on the stool and swooped her up in my arms. My mouth consumed hers, pressing my body as close to her as I possibly could. And she did the same.

I spoke into her mouth, "Follow me." I placed her feet back on the ground and started ahead of her with my hand extended behind me. She intertwined her fingers into mine and followed afterward. I wanted to kiss her over and over and over. But I didn't want to risk anyone walking in and ruining this moment... *again.*

Through the kitchen and off the dining room, I led us into the sunroom. Not much besides a couple of rocking chairs and a day bed that faced the water filled the space. The golden hue from the outside lights cast a glow, leaving a silhouette of Lucy's body on the wall behind her.

She stepped towards the window and watched as everyone danced and gathered together in crowds. She let out a small laugh beneath her smile as she observed each person, but all I could do was stand back and look at her. Her happiness from earlier was back.

Her shoulder, the crook of her neck. They exposed themselves in a way I believed they were made just for me. Like her skin was meant to be kissed by only me.

I came up from behind her and I trailed my fingers slowly up along her arm, landing my hand atop her collarbones. She tilted her head welcoming me with a faint moan, only for it to get trapped in her throat. I felt her tremble slightly beneath my touch.

"You smell amazing, Lucy," I said into her hair.

I moved onto her other side, brushing her skin the same way, and her arm filled with goosebumps. I placed myself between her and the window, she let out a small whimper as I hoisted her back in my arms.

She giggled, "Hi."

"Hello," I growled out.

Her legs wrapped around my waist and her arms locked behind my back, I could feel her breasts press hard into my chest. I moved my hands beneath her ass, then gave it one hard slap. She let out another whimper, this time louder and right into my ear. My body filled with warmth and my heart started to beat faster.

I walked us backward, falling onto the daybed. Straddling my waist, Lucy slowly gyrated her hips into mine. My pants became tighter, I was certain that I was going to break right out of my zipper. I pulled back at her hair, exposing, elongating her neck to me.

I sat up and took a bite out of the side like she was the sweetest apple I had ever seen.

"You taste even better," I said as I ran my fingers over the individual indentations.

I had the honor of making my mark on Lucy Collins.

"You haven't tasted anything yet." She pushed me back down on the bed and started to leave small pecks down my chest.

I've had the luxury of getting to know the kept-to-herself girl that sat along that damn lake for the last month. She turned out to be the beautiful and strong, yet perfectly complicated woman that I can't imagine my life without now.

The way she moved, hovering over me, she made me believe I could do anything. Like I could write poetry or ballroom dance if I wanted to. She was dainty, elegant—and sexy. She's undoubtedly the sexiest person I've ever laid my eyes on and I felt my entire body become electric under her touch. She shimmied her way down my torso, unzipping my pants as she reached my waist.

I watched as her gaze locked itself on my dick as it sprung out of my jeans. She flashed me a devilish grin before moving her warm mouth down over me. I let out a hushed gasp and threw my head back. She looked up at me through her eyelashes while I was still inside of her, then let out a muffled laugh that sent vibrations up my entire body.

I threaded my fingers through her hair and started moving her head up and down on me. Faster, stronger with every tug. She didn't balk. She took it all, all while spit was dripping down both sides of her mouth. The tip of her tiny nose bobbed against my groin.

Lucy pushed herself up off of me and stood at the edge of the bed. She kicked off her boots and moved onto lifting the hem of her dress.

"Wait, wait, wait," I pushed up on my shoulders. Shallowed breathed as ever. I covered her hand with mine, stopping her as she reached her hip bones. I had let my insistent need for her cloud my decisions. "I don't want you to think that this is the reason I said what I did. *This* isn't what I am looking for with you. I want *everything* with you."

She slid the rest of her dress up above her head, "I know," she said, smiling down before climbing back on top of me. "You said you wanted to give me everything. So give me everything you got, Banks."

She pulled at my shirt, convincing me to pull it off in solidarity. Though there wasn't much convincing needed. Lace underwear was the only thing that acted as a barrier between us, her nipples played peek-a-boo beneath a bubblegum pink, satin bralette. I couldn't help myself but lean forward to take a nibble.

She yelped and tugged at the top of my hair, pulling my head slightly back. She stared into my eyes like she could see every part of my life that I had ever lived. And I wanted to share all of it with her.

"Okay, okay. I like where your mind is at, but don't start any hair pulling *just* yet." I leaned off the side of the bed, Lucy still pooled in my lap. I held onto her with everything that I had. She let out a roaring laughter right into my ear, I couldn't help but laugh over the awkwardness that was occurring. I felt like I was in my early twenties again, giddy and excited—and completely ungraceful.

But that's how she made me feel. Like a young'n, and not like I was thirty-eight.

I scrambled for my jeans that we threw on the floor and pulled out my wallet. I went to pull out a condom, but she stopped it from even leaving its slot.

"No need," she said as she pointed to the patch on her lower back.

I ran my fingers over the thin square. Almost too thin, I wouldn't have realized it was there otherwise.

"That's fine and dandy, sweet thing, but I am well aware that these little guys," I said, tapping the outside of my wallet, "do a lot more than act as birth control."

She bit her bottom lip before kissing me. Tenderly, softly.

"You're truly amazing, you know that. But I will say, I'm cleared. And I don't know about you, but—"

"I am, too."

"So," she kissed me again, "give me *everything* you got, Banks," she whispered into my ear.

The eye contact that we shared was constant. Neither of us looked away for even a sliver of a second. Our touches were natural—as if we had memorized the feel of each other's bodies in another lifetime. Her glow was back. I was certain of that. And the utmost passion and love radiated off of her.

Lucy lowered herself onto me right as another round of fireworks began to blare in the distance. Her eyes rolled back, and I started to thrust into her. Striking displays of red, white, and blue, then all of the colors of the rainbow ran through my body the same way that they filled the sky. On their own, and then all at once.

I did not only have Lucy, but she had me. All of me, for as long as she wanted. My mind, body, and soul belonged to her.

The sparks had ignited and flew through the sky tonight, and I was scared to ever know a day that I didn't feel exactly how I felt at that moment.

Chapter 25

Lucy

The mid-summer heat had arrived, even early in the morning.

I kicked off the blanket that Sawyer tossed over me somewhere in between round three and downing an entire glass of ice water in the middle of the night. He kept the sunroom cozy with neutral colors, the paneling was a deep, espresso stain. I could lay on this daybed for an eternity with him. And that's when it hit me... I could get used to the idea of waking up next to him.

I wanted what he wanted.

For the last six weeks, he has always been there. Even when I didn't expect him to be, he was there before I even knew I wanted him there. And now everything has changed. We crossed a line, more like several. Now they're all blurry.

Today, I learned that he was a stomach sleeper. Rolling over onto my side, I draped my leg over his bare body. I tucked my foot under his leg as I intertwined myself with him. I traced letters on his back muscles over the brightest of red scratch marks that remained as prominent as ever from the night before.

"What are you doing back there? Putting a hex on me, or something?" he said with his face muffled into the pillow, wiggling underneath my touch.

"Don't hate me, but I think I gotta get going," I said, pressing my chin into his shoulder.

He angled his head around before he did his body, then shot up in a seated position. He fixed a straggly hair that hung over my eyes. "I could never hate you," he grumbled. "But I am bummed, I wanted to make you breakfast." Soft, subtle kisses trailed up my arm, ending on the tip of my shoulder.

"That is very tempting... How about you make me dinner, instead? Besides, I have to figure out what's going on with Gracie. I should be there for her. I feel terrible that I neglected her after everything."

"You're too good for this world, Lucy Collins. Dinner it is."

I shut my eyes at the sound of my name on his lips. It does something to me as it courses through my veins.

"Anyway," he laid back down, resting his hands behind his head. "Something tells me that Gracie is just fine."

"What do you mean?"

"She was laughing and smiling all night."

"Yeah," I looked out the windows, envisioning where she stood last night. Every guy under the age of forty was captivated by her last night. She danced, she sang, she drank... She made friends in a town she'd never been to. Maybe she was fine. "She always starts out that way. But then it slowly hits her. I want to be there when that happens."

Sawyer pointed to his jeans bunched up on the floor, falling his head back onto the mattress, he rasped out, "Take my truck."

I slithered out of the bed and gathered my clothes. I was itching to see him again and I hadn't even left yet.

At the door frame, his voice stopped me in my tracks. "You look gorgeous in the morning, by the way," he said with closed eyes, drifting back to sleep.

I plucked the keys from his jean pockets and spun them around my finger a couple of times, stopping the movement in the palm of my hand before I walked out of the sunroom.

He kept up with his house, it was far from a cliché bachelor pad. He had paintings scattered around his walls, decorative bins for throw blankets, and top-of-the-line cookware hung above the kitchen island. And that's only from what I could tell from here. The opened rooms had people scattered across the beds and chairs, and there wasn't a surface in the living room untouched by limbs.

Gracie was cuddled up and asleep in Mel's arms on the chaise lounge in the corner. The leather squeaked underneath her when she shifted.

I crouched down so that I was level with her. "Morning, G. Wakey, wakey."

She grumbled, wiping the sleep from her eyes. "What time is it? Oh, jeez, I'm sorry. I tried to find you, but I guess I fell asleep at some point during my search."

"That's fine," I whispered. "Look, there's a bunch I have to do today. I'm sort of on an adrenaline rush if you will." I shook Sawyer's keys in front of her face. "You coming?"

She rotated her head around, found Mel beside her, and then looked back at me. "I–I'll catch up with you later."

I found comfort in knowing that Gracie could hold her own in a house full of people she barely knew. That's where her sweet, outgoing personality always came in clutch.

Whenever she and Asher got into their numerous fights, I always made it a point to be there for her for as long as she needed. I had never experienced a friend going through a breakup, though. I was nervous, I hurt for her. But she did seem okay, so I decided to bask in my bliss and left her there. At least until the sun had fully risen.

My favorite part of the day was right now; the sky was still a blueish-gray hue from civil dawn, cascading over Hummingbird Lake.

I cranked open the driver-side door to Sawyer's truck, smokey notes of vanilla and chestnut were intoxicating as I climbed inside. I settled into my seat, I wanted the aroma to bleed onto my skin so I could bring his scent home with me.

I admired the vintage feel of the truck. Never did I think when Gus taught me how to drive on stick shift that I'd ever truly need to know—but now the talent was coming in handy. I pushed in the cassette sticking out of the radio system and played whatever he was last listening to. I hum songs I never knew before now and dance as much as I can in my seat the whole drive home.

A stupid little grin wouldn't leave my face even if I took a chisel tool to it.

Once I reached the cottage, I practically leapt out of the truck and skipped into the house. I threw open the door and placed Sawyer's keys down. Another piece of him finding its place in my world.

Straight ahead, I stared down the hall at the backdoor. On the other side, I knew I'd be met with the unfinished work of yesterday, but I wasn't scared anymore. I was done hiding from the mess of reality.

***

I didn't have time to think about the maybe's and what if's when it came to Sawyer. For that, I was grateful. If left alone for long enough, I knew my thoughts had the power to make me believe that I've been hit by a blow dart. Completely immobilized as I fall into a never-ending cycle where I'd find a reason to stray. But right now, I want to live on this pink cloud for a little while longer.

In the resonance of my steps against the hardwood, my life memories play out in front of me. I am reminded why I left, why I never came back. It wasn't for the sole reason that my grandmother wasn't here anymore, it was because she was *everywhere*.

The floorboards were flooded with memories of her chasing me up and down the stairs, and playing board games on snowy days on the living room floor. The baseboards bled out every scent that has ever passed through this house—I smelled the fresh sourdough bread in the oven and the homemade apple cider in the fall months.

Everything was her.

Walking through the front doors today, it felt like I was finally coming home for the first time. There was a sense of passion, a feeling of devotion. It broke me that I didn't initially fall back into place like I'd imagined I would. I thought I could come home after all this time and it would feel the same—like seeing an old friend as if no time had passed.

But that just wasn't the case.

For the last six weeks, I have felt like a zombie walking around parts of a town I've known every nook and cranny of for my entire life. It felt like I knew nothing at all.

Now? Now, I was home.

Tugging at the backdoor, the humidity making the frame all that much more stubborn, I paraded myself through the backyard. Whatever will be, will be. Leaving the cottage didn't mean I had to leave Rider for good. Because of my grandmother Tiffany, Rider will always be home.

I swung open the age-worn wood door to the shed and thin slivers of paint chipped off with contact with the siding.

There it still sat in the same spot, the painting. The stool, the book, the painting. They've made themselves a home back here without even intending to.

Two remaining boxes are stacked behind the easel with un-washed paint brushes stuck to the top. As I moved the stool into the back corner of the shed, the dust stuck to the palms of my hands. The unoiled hardware of the easel cracked as I dismantled the stand. I tucked it under my arm and stacked the canvas and book on top of the boxes.

Back inside, I removed the standard painting you could find at any department store on the wall that separated the living room from the kitchen. I observed the space on the wall and exhaled as I prepared to mount my grandmother's unfinished painting in its place. I sat on the ground with crossed legs and stared up at it.

I flipped through the pages of the book, it still had the old book smell that I love so much. The edges were faded only a tad from the sunlight that would sneak in through the windows. Other than that, it was in perfect shape. I held it tight against my chest.

I dragged the last boxes standing over my way—it finally felt like there was light at the end of the tunnel. More notes, more photos. What looks to be a dozen love letters to Tuck, *from* Tuck. Tiffany's merlot lipstick stained most of the envelopes tucked away in the old cigar box.

You had my attention from the first time I laid my eyes on you.

As I read through the rest, my heart danced a melodic con-temporary number—I always knew their love was timeless and poetic.

Except *these* didn't belong to my grandmother.

I fanned through it faster. Double, triple-checking.

There wasn't a single thing that could have prepared me.

My heart now lives in my throat.

Signed, With Love, Christian Parker.

I spread everything out in front of me and scanned the top of every piece of paper. They were all addressed to Sunny. *My mom.*

What was once hidden at the bottom of a flimsy box now canvassed the floor in front of me. There were some photos of my mom standing on her own in front of Highway 57, or outside of Hillside High. I saw a few of my grandmother with my mom and a handful of my mom from when she was pregnant... It was a secret shrine of Sunny Collins at my fingertips. This was yet another version of her I didn't know. Another lifetime.

And then I came across one of her with a guy. His hair was a soft brown, slicked back, and had caramel eyes. A smile was drawn across her face, something that was rare. I had never seen her smile, especially not like that. She did once, though it was in a very passive-aggressive manner.

I'm sorry... It doesn't have to be like this... We can work something out...She's my daughter, too. I ran my fingers over the indent the pen made on the paper.

My chest heaved. I grabbed onto it, trying to manage it, control it, wrangle it—anything. But nothing worked. Nothing was going to cure this feeling. I felt myself removed from my body, like I was hovering over a body, a person, a life that was not mine and could never be me. That had to be the case.

This wasn't happening. It couldn't be.

The walls closed in on me and I sunk into the floor beneath me. The light that I was so close to touching, vanished. Everything went black before it turned a blinding white.

My dad. My fucking *dad.*

No one had the nerve to tell me, not in all of the years that my mother had been absent from my life. I didn't expect her to tell me, I learned to stop expecting much from my mother long ago. Fuck, honestly, I didn't know what I wanted in this moment.

I kicked away at all that sat in front of me or my lap and I chucked the empty cardboard boxes down the hall. The echo of them slapping against the hardwood rang through the whole house.

I couldn't have it near me. None of it.

Though, what lingered closer to me than the rest, was one more letter. Just my luck. This one was the only one in a sealed envelope with faint writing on the front that read *For Lucy when she turns 18.* This one was written in my grandmother's handwriting.

She wasn't around to see me turn eighteen. Did she not expect to see me turn eighteen? Did she plan to not tell me, but rather read all of this for myself when I turned eighteen?

Those were just two more questions added to the many I already had.

Growing up, I asked about my dad. I was curious to know all about who he was or where he was, of course I did. But I learned at an early age to not ask more than once.

When I was five, after my first day of kindergarten, I came home with all sorts of information—and many, many questions. I waited on the blacktop while kids in my class were picked up by their parents, both parents, and that was the first time it hit me that my life looked different.

All I knew was my mom and my grandmother, Gus and Leanne. They were the only family that I knew.

I asked my grandmother on our way home from school. She looked at me in my booster seat through the rearview mirror. With a look of endearment and a touch of fear, she told me to talk to my mom about it.

So, I did.

At dinner, I shared with her all about my day. I talked about how awesome it was to play all day long at school, but that I was ready to come home by lunchtime. That I missed the two of them. I talked about seeing my new friends "mommies" and "daddies" and I asked where my daddy was. For only a beat of a second, she looked up from her phone, stone cold as usual, and stared me down.

You could hear a pin drop. I tensed up in my seat.

How, at five years old, did I say something so wrong?

She clicked her tongue before parting her lips. She said I didn't have one, and to *never* ask her again.

So, I didn't.

Over twenty years later, I never thought about it, or him, again. Why is that? The world is at my fingertips thanks to the internet, thanks to advancements in science. I could have done some research of my own. But in true Sunny Collins fashion, she still had a hold on me. Even out of her vicinity, I was stuck under her thumb. I'm afraid I always will be, and though she has no problem hurting me, I could never imagine doing the same to her.

The door knob twists and I shoot up straight as an arrow in my spot.

Shit.

I looked down at my phone and it was already eight in the morning. I had meant to call Gracie over a half hour ago.

Gracie zipped through the threshold, giddy as ever. "Oh, my L.C., I am *sooo* over Asher."

I wiped away a tear that managed to escape. "That's great, G."

"What's wrong, what is it?" she slid herself onto the ground beside me, her knees almost leaving track marks behind her.

I handed her the single letter but struggled to let go of it. I could hang onto it and never tell a soul that I found these. The only other living people that know would be, of course, my mom. Then there's Gus and Leanne—but they wouldn't say anything until I say something first. They weren't the type to air out other people's dirty laundry. *They know, they have to know.*

I didn't have to share this with Gracie, I could've pulled it back and acted as if it were nothing. Instead, she won the fight with my gorilla grip and a small piece of paper ripped off the side as she took it in her hands.

Nothing, she says nothing.

Instead, she took me in her arms and I was fighting back all the urge to let it all out, to finally cry. Up until an hour ago, I didn't have a dad. That's what I was told, that's what I was made to believe. I didn't have a dad.

But now I had a dad and he had a name. My dad was, *is*, Christian Parker.

"I can't be here, I can't do this," I said, muffled over Gracie's shoulders.

"Luce, Luce... Breathe... Do you want to go back to Sawyer's?"

I broke loose from Gracie's hold and scrambled to find his keys, but I couldn't remember where I put them. I can barely remember my own name right now. I stop, my hands perched on my hips. My chest heaved in and out once again, but I fought back the tears with all that I had.

Gracie stared at me waiting for my next plan of action, but I didn't have one. "I—Uh," I sucked in a breath. "I'm supposed to go back there tonight. A date, we have a date. But—"

Right when I allowed myself to fall, straight into Sawyer's arms, I felt the need to crawl right back up the bumpy hill that had a barricade between the two of us. This was too much for me, this was too much for anyone—there's no way I could start a relationship like this.

"A *date?* Lucy, how long has this been going on? Why haven't I heard of him before?"

Maybe because if I spoke it into existence, it made my feelings all that much more real. That wasn't something I was ready for.

"I actually met him on my first day here. Man, it was a wreck. A car wreck, that is. Like one you couldn't look away from. I'll tell you about that another time. But, I don't know, he's sort of been around. Everywhere I turn, there he is. And he's been nice..."

"It looks a little more than nice, if you ask me. I saw the way he looked at you in the truck last night."

My skin burned at the thought. His eyes, they do something to me. He has a way of making me feel like I'm the only girl in the world. It's insane.

"Yeah, but that doesn't matter right now. And anyway, I can't go like this."

"Well, yeah. Not like *that*." Gracie took a step back and evaluated my current state. Smudged mascara and all, tears were seeping through my dress. I was a mess. "We'll go shopping!"

"What? No. No way. I have to figure all of this out." I waved my hands over the disarray of stationary under my feet.

"All of that is still going to be there when you get home. It's been there for twenty-six years, it can hold off for another twenty-six hours."

I looked back at Gracie, then down to the floor again. There was a truth within her words. It's been there for ages, if I never found it, I'd be dancing around the living room right now counting down the hours until I saw Sawyer again.

"Ah, okay. I'll go change."

"Oh, this is going to be so much fun!" Gracie started to jump up and down. "I need a distraction and a reminder that love still exists!"

"No one said anything about love."

I dropped my head and focused on the way the light reflected onto the floorboards. The sunrays waved back and forth, and the shadow of the trees in the backyard filtered through and painted the floor in front of me. Try as I might, I couldn't join in her excitement for all of this. Not when everything that just unveiled itself is staring up at me.

"I better get upstairs," I choked out.

She stopped me as I reached the bottom step and pulled me in closer again. This time tighter. And that's where it all comes out and I can't find a way to make it stop. The aching, piercing sobs escaped my mouth and I began crumbling to the ground.

Chapter 26

Lucy

"What about this?" I held up a smock dress that fell right beneath my knees.

"Do you want him to think you're there to bake him bread and tend to his chicken coop? You're not wearing that on your first date with Sawyer."

"It's not our first," I mumbled under my breath.

"Lucy!"

"What about this?" I held up another knee-length dress, it being more form fitted.

"Better, but not quite what we are looking for."

"*We?*"

"Mmhm! Here." Gracie handed over a stack of four dresses. "Try these on."

The first boutique we stopped at was a total fail. The second had some good contenders, but I wasn't feeling it—and most of the ones I liked were sold out in my size. This is the only boutique on Main St. that I've felt remotely hopeful at. I dreamed of the day when I walked along the store fronts that I could come into these shops and mosey around for hours on end. I'd stand outside and look up at the window displays and imagine playing dress up in outfits just like these.

I hung up the options that Gracie handed off to me on the wall opposite of the mirror, and drew the curtain close to the changing room.

"Hey, Grace?" I called out.

"Yes?"

I poked my head out from the curtain. She sat crossed-legged on an ottoman a few feet away. "Are you sure you didn't hand me *your* options?"

"This isn't about me, this is about you. Don't knock 'em till you try 'em, come on, I bet they'll look great!"

I closed the curtain back up and evaluated the dresses once more. And just like that, I knew I didn't have to try on the rest. With a tight midsection that had buttons trailing along it, the sleeves of the dress fluttered out and there was a plunging neckline. But it was a sleek black color, a dress that fit like a glove. And you can't go wrong with a Little Black Dress.

I stepped out and did a predictable twirl. Gracie gasped and I felt myself getting misty eyed. This is exactly what Little Lucy dreamed of. Dress shopping before a big date with her best girl friend. The bookworm, school nerd that kept to herself when she was last in Rider would have never imagined this coming true.

"What do you think?" I smoothed my hands over the skirt of the dress.

"First, I want to see something." Gracie turned me to face the mirror beside the changing rooms. She stood behind me and pulled my hair back at my temples. She clipped a silky, black bow into my hair, then pushed the bottom portion over my shoulders. "What do you think? I found this on the stands over there while you were trying this on."

"I love it."

"Then let's get it."

I turned back around and hugged her before returning to the changing room. I gave myself one last look with an ear to ear grin to dress the look up, then switched back into my clothes.

For a single moment, it felt like everything else could actually wait to be dealt with and the world wasn't going to blow up into flames.

Chapter 27

Sawyer

Mood lighting, check. Background music, double check. Nerves flying through the roof, check, check, check.

I placed my mother's candle holders in the center of the table and lit the wick. The best part about dinner on the deck during summer is that the air was still; the wind flow was almost nonexistent, even at night.

I angled our glasses just a smidge and tugged at the tablecloth, evening it out around the edges. I stepped back to observe what was in front of me. You would have never guessed that there was an overpopulated party here last night. I figured out that I am the master at panic cleaning today.

In a matter of seconds, Lucy was going to have dinner with me. She actually said yes, and was willing to let her guard down.

I didn't take this lightly, knowing that I had the chance to hold her heart in my hands. Her trust, her patience, her willingness. It's an honor and a privilege, and I don't know what I did to deserve it.

When the doorbell rang, I had to force myself not to rush the front door. I pulled back and steadied my footsteps. One foot in front of the other, not taking strides two steps at a time. I exhaled deeply before opening the door.

"Wow. C-come in, hi," I stammered out. She slipped in beside me, but I stopped her, and spun her to face me. "I missed you today," I said through a kiss upon her cheek.

She flashed me a grin, but kept her attention at our hands that found each other. She rubs her thumb over mine.

"You okay, Pretty Girl?"

"Yes, yeah. Of course. I'm here with you." Her words caused an electrifying jolt within my ribcage.

She dangled my truck keys in front of my face. "I almost don't want to give it back."

"You can drive the truck anytime you want, just say the word."

"Ooh, I might hold you to that."

"Here, let's go out this way." I motioned toward the side door that leads out to the deck. She walked off ahead of me, her heels clicking along the planks and her hips swaying with each step.

I pulled the chair out in front of her as we reached the table.

"Oh, Sawyer. They're beautiful..." She reached down for the bouquet of peonies that I had placed on her seat earlier in the evening. She brought them to her nose and took a sniff, then placed them beside her on the table.

"I can get these out of the way if you want?" I started to grab for them when she placed her hand over mine.

"No, keep them. They're too pretty, you almost don't want to look away."

I know what that felt like.

I gave her a wink, then a kiss on the top of her head before pushing in her chair.

"Wine?" I held up both a red and a white.

"Dealer's choice."

I poured the Riesling in hers, the Pinot in mine, and motioned for a cheers.

"It smells amazing in there," she admitted as she finished her sip. She licked at the thin layer that lingered on her upper lip.

"Oh, shit!"

I rushed inside, and the excitement riled Billy up, leading him to follow in after me from the furthest part of the backyard. He barked as I made my way to the oven. I pulled out the cooking sheet and slid it on top of the stove. *Just in the nick of time.* I plated the salmon and roasted squash and balanced them in each hand.

"Do you need any help?" Lucy called out, though I was already headed back outside.

"No, no. I don't want you to move a muscle. I'm here to cater to you tonight."

I pushed the plate in front of her, then mine at my place setting. "Go on, boy, inside." I snapped my fingers to send Billy off on his way.

"Sawyer, this is—" she let out a sigh, then tilted her head at me. "Thank you."

I held my glass up for another cheers before we dug in. There was a sense of relief that rushed over me, this night truly turned out exactly how I imagined it.

Here she was across from me, smelling like a field of wildflowers and looking the way that she does—man, she looked out of this world—and I didn't burn dinner. This night is *better* than I had imagined it to be.

***

With no food left to spare, we pushed our plates away into the center of the table and sunk into the backs of our seats.

"I could eat that every day for the rest of my life," she blew out an exhausted breath as she placed her napkin on her plate.

I propped my elbows onto the table and leaned forward. "I could eat *you* ev—"

"*Sawyer!*" She picked her napkin up and tossed it across the table toward me.

"Sorry," I chuckled out. *I'm really not.*

The silence between us grew, the sloshing of the lake water down below filled the space instead. I focused on how her mouth twitched as she stared back at me, trying to hold back a smile. I could tell when she chewed on the inside of her cheek.

"So," I started, "tell me something, Ms. Lucy Collins."

"Always." She took another sip of her wine.

"How do you always seem to have everything so planned out?"

She scoffed at my statement and placed her glass back on the table.

"No, really. I'm serious. Look at you. You are one of the most structured people that I know. I wish I could be more like you."

She paused before she spoke.

"I can't tell if you're joking," she said with narrowed eyes.

"One-hundred percent honest. Scout's honor." I held up three fingers. "Do you, like, schedule everything you do? Know exactly what you're going to be doing a year from now?"

She nodded.

"I figured. I bet you even have a five-year plan."

"In a perfect world? I'll be done with my residency by then, getting ready to start at a private practice. *My* private practice. It will be in a quiet neighborhood, and I'll offer affordable care for low-income families and adaptable care for neurodivergent kids. There will always be something captivating and thrilling about the big hospitals, but they've never felt personal to me. I want to build meaningful and impactful relationships with my patients and give kids the health care they deserve. There's not always one right answer when it comes to how to go about things."

I bit back my emotions that were rising to the surface and reached my hand across the table. She placed hers inside of mine. "You're going to save the world, Lucy Collins."

I am undoubtedly so in love with this girl. I couldn't help it.

"If I'm lucky," she finally said.

"Come on, let's head inside." I started to stack our plates on one another, while she blew out the candles.

Billy followed in after us but galloped over to the sunroom. He jumped onto the unmade bed.

"He likes it in there, too, I see," Lucy chuckled.

"He's been in there since everyone left early this morning. I think he hated not having you here. He liked the idea of having you in this house, I think."

"Oh, whatever," she snorted out. She shot her head up at me, embarrassed. "Oh, not that again."

"It's cute, stop it." I quickly placed my hand on her upper arm, but then pulled it away. Just touching her, I didn't want to stop. Even if it lasted a second. I coughed into my opposite hand and backed away. I grabbed the other wine glass on the counter. "Nightcap?" I asked.

"Yes," she smiled up at me. We plopped ourselves down on the couch, she pulled her legs up to the side and her knee brushed against me. She flinched slightly. "Sorry," she said, as she adjusted herself into her seat.

"Don't be." I rested my hand on her knee and traced my thumb over the tip of her bent leg. "But hey, look at this." I reached to pull a DVD from the coffee table. "I picked this up, maybe we could watch it."

I handed her a copy of Mary Poppins.

The apples of her cheeks grew in size as she nodded in excitement. "I still can't believe you've never watched it, it's a classic!"

"So I'm told."

I walked up to the DVD player and then returned to my spot beside her. My fingers, with a mind of their own, started to move over her legs again. I could feel the goosebumps that formed on her skin. She followed the movement before completely dissociating.

"Lucy?" A beat passed, and then she brought her attention up to me. Her eyes were even with mine, but it felt like there was nothing behind them. I paused the movie. "Are you okay? Where'd you go just now?"

She started to sniffle. "Sorry," she said, her eyes were lined with water.

She shed a single tear, though her face never faltered.

"I almost didn't come tonight," she started. I furrowed my brows, but she continued before I could say anything. "And not because I didn't want to. I wanted to. I mean, I want to be here. I'm happy I'm here." She leaned forward and rested her untouched wineglass on the coffee table. "But when I went back home today, to finish up all the packing and get it ready to bring to the donation center or storage or whatever, I found one last box that's been in the back of the shed."

She shared all about her mom and letters that she found, new information regarding her father. She started to shake as she uttered his name. I held her tight, letting her talk when, and how, she wanted to. There were long moments where neither of us said a single word, she just fiddled with the knots in the throw blanket.

The only sound was faint humming from the music I had forgotten to turn off from earlier, and her rapid heartbeat.

I was unsure if I wanted to ask her what she wanted to do or if she even knew herself. All I wanted to do was hold her and let her know I was there for her. Oh, how I hoped she knew that I was there for you.

"I know that I shouldn't even worry about it. It's been ages since he wrote her those letters. Who knows if he even wants a relationship with me anymore."

"Don't say that. He would be lucky to know you. Anyone that knows you, knows just how true that is."

"Hmm, maybe." She stood from her seat and walked back over to the kitchen counter. "It's not gonna change anything. Finding him, knowing him, having a relationship with him... And it sure as hell is *not* going to fix the relationship I have with my mom."

"Maybe not, but what if—" I stopped myself. I was not going to be the person who pushed unsolicited advice on her. I'm sure she has always thought of all of the what-ifs already. "Look, is there anything that I can help you with?"

She stood on her tiptoes and kissed me. She planted her feet back down and studied my eyes. They shifted from one to the other, her mouth drew into a thin line.

"I just... Oh, god, I can't believe I'm about to say this."

My heartbeat quickened its pace and I'm preparing for my world to come tumbling down. And just like that, in the blink of an eye, the sound of shattering glass filled my ears.

"I want to give you everything that you want, I want everything that you want." I shut my eyes tight, I thought they would rip at the seams. "But I think I do need to figure all of this out before we start anything up. I want to do this right."

I couldn't argue that. Could I?

All my body allowed me to do was nod, and hold her in my embrace one last time. *Please don't let this be the last time.*

"Okay," I finally said above a whisper.

She kissed me again, and there was a sadness behind it. Like this was hard for her, too. *I have no idea what's going on right now.* She turned away and walked back out the side door.

I couldn't watch her leave—I looked back out over the lake, the table still partially set. She left her flowers on the back patio but took my heart with her. It was a trade I was willing to accept, because for whatever it's worth, I knew this was not a goodbye.

This can't be goodbye.

Chapter 28

Sawyer

"You look like death." Ah, yes. My favorite way to be greeted in the morning.

"And you look ravishing as ever, Mel," I said with a stale expression as the screen door to The Hideout slammed shut behind me, making the bell above rattle crazier than ever.

"Thanks, it's my new haircut, isn't it?" She pursed her lips and feathered her fingers through her bangs.

Fixated on pure isolation, I book it around the bar counter and head straight down to my office. I had no interest in playing my "customer service" cards today. Mel marched vigorously behind me.

"Excuse me. You're going to have to talk to me at some point. It's been a month."

Denial.

I stopped in my tracks, and Mel crashed right into my back. I spun on my heels to face her. Her deep brown eyes stared back at me inquisitively. Admittedly, there wasn't a single thing about me that Mel didn't know. And at no fault but my own, I made my emotions accessible to her. She knows how I'm feeling before I do most of the time.

I parted my lips and she perked up, excited to finally get me to talk, but I promptly drew my mouth in a thin line.

I turned back around and sauntered away from her. It felt like ages before I reached my office. My feet dragged beneath me. The reminder that I have been avoiding any talk about Lucy since she left my place a month ago was slicing right through me.

Mel showed up at my house on the days I refused to come in to work on payroll or check on inventory. It was all work that she was trained and certified to take care of, but she's convinced I'd be "so annoyed" with her lingering around that I'd end up doing it myself and it'd distract me. She brought paperwork for me to sign once she realized I wouldn't leave the confines of my couch and wine cellar. I'm stubborn when I need to be and was set on leaving it all for her to do it. But, doing work of a smaller magnitude was our compromise; Mel was nothing if not persistent.

I told her I was fine every time she asked when we both knew I was lying. I was taking some well-deserved time off. I deserved to do that, right? I had been wracking my brain to the point where I wanted to hit my head against a wall, wondering how I felt so strongly over a girl I barely even knew. I suppose that made me more captivated and intrigued than ever. That happened almost never.

Mel was right when she called me a lovesick puppy, I was one when it came to Lucy. I saw this place in a new kind of way thanks to her. I felt calm and exhilarated all at once when I was around her. Within a matter of weeks, I was wrapped around her finger.

Today was the first time in over a week that I made it into the restaurant. I shut the door behind me and I left Mel standing in the hallway. I couldn't tell if she didn't want to pry for the time being or if she was conjuring up new ways to get me to talk. All I know is she didn't try to barge in and it was nice to have a barrier between me and my newly acquired shadow in the shape of my five-foot-one best friend.

I stared into my office that now felt like it was closing in on me.

I could still see Lucy spinning in the chair and our almost-kiss.

It felt like an eternity ago.

I started to spiral and played the game of "what ifs" in every aspect.

What if I had stuck with my grandfather's plan? I'd be in New Haven and I'd be mayor… Hours away from Rider. I would have never called it home. Rider was always supposed to be a summer house. Never the place that held my heart in its hands.

What if I never let her walk out my front door that day? I'd be there to work through whatever was going on alongside her. She wouldn't have to feel like she's going through this alone. *I hoped that she wasn't going through it alone.*

I didn't know what I should have done, but all I knew was Lucy held my heart in her hands. But she walked away. I hate that I let her walk away.

Anger.

As I pulled myself away from the office door, it slowly creaked open behind me. "Hey… please don't bite my head off," Mel squeaked out as she slid in through the door.

I made it to my desk—I knew that if I could just sit down in my office, I could manipulate myself into being productive. Unless it's work-related, I don't have time for Mel's bullshit. But like a Great White shark, she cuts across the floor softly and silently before attacking.

"Get up," she demands. I am her wounded prey, and she can't leave well enough alone.

I'm here, aren't I? Isn't that what she wanted?

"I'm *sorry*?"

"No apologies needed. But this isn't the Sawyer I know, and that is something you should be sorry about."

That was a good two minutes and thirty-seven seconds without her meddling.

But I remember that I've made it a habit to follow her lead, I respected her too much. So as bad as I didn't want to play into her games, I do as I'm told. Mel is a petite girl, but when she means business, she means business and I don't question her. Her eye twitched slightly as she got ready to speak, but I cut her off before she could say anything.

"You don't get it," I huffed out, crossing my arms across my chest. The lack of showers diffused off of me, so I placed my arms back down, tight against my side.

"*I don't get it.* Huh, okay. Do you hear yourself? Of course, I do! And I know that you know that. You picked up all the pieces when Jamie and I broke up last spring. She ghosted me after we signed a lease together, then went downtown to party. *You* were there when she pretended like I didn't exist. Just because you are in a hetero-normative relationship, it doesn't mean it's any harder for you. Relationships are complicated no matter what. I know how girls are, I sort of am one, so I know there has to be some reason why you haven't heard from her."

"From my point of view, it looks like you were getting pretty cozy with Gracie that night. That's her best friend, she must've said something to you."

"We met that same night, then she went back to Lucy's cottage. I know nothing." She threw her hands up as if she was being interrogated.

Silence passed between us.

"You know something, don't you!" I slammed my hands onto the desk, definitely interrogating her now.

Mel tried to hold a stiff face, but her lips curled at the corners. "I might have gotten Gracie's number before she left your house, but that's *it*! And that has nothing to do with you. I promise she's tight-lipped. Like you said, best friends and all."

I softened my stance. "Find something out for me?" My voice cracked. I was claiming defeat, I was admittedly desperate at this point. "Maybe if you sneak in my name, it will spark something. I will do anything. I just need her to talk to me, I need... something. I need her."

Bargaining.

She stood and walked over to me. "What exactly happened between you two?"

I looked to the ground, tears welled in my eyes. She wrapped her arms around my waist and fell into my chest.

"Forget I said anything. Talk when you're ready."

I tried today, I did, but I wasn't ready to be in a setting in which I had to appease people. Or was expected to plaster on my customer service smile.

I grabbed the keys to my bike from my pocket and cut out early. I haven't been able to touch my truck since that night I picked her up at the cottage.

I don't want to taint the memories.

I zipped through the main road, but the drive that I am so familiar with felt daunting. I pulled the throttle back to its full potential, the bike vibrated as my speed increased and the engine drowned out all else. *I wanted nothing more than to get home.*

I skirted into the driveway and a cloud of dust hit the side of my truck. I aggressively struck the kickstand out and marched inside.

Billy met me at the door with loud barks and body wiggles. I kicked off my boots and gave him a single pat on the head. I hated that I'd been less than attentive to him as of late. But in true Billy fashion, he was always there to keep me company and tried his damndest to keep my spirits high.

I walked past him and straight into the kitchen.

I ripped the freezer door open and yanked out a chilled bottle of bourbon. I flicked the cap off and drank straight from the bottle. I hadn't done that since college.

I pulled out my phone, contemplating if I should text her. However, I had yet to get any response back from previous messages I'd sent. In the beginning, I'd send a quick good morning text or tell her I was thinking of her. I had sworn I saw text bubbles pop up one day, but it must've been my imagination. I slipped my phone back in my pocket and strolled around while the bottle hung from my hand.

Depression.

There was an absence around the lake since she left. I threw a couple more shots back at the thought. The sun didn't shine as bright, the birds didn't sing as loud. She brought life and love to Rider. To Hummingbird Lake.

The sunroom remained in its same state. The imprint of her body was left sketched into the sheets. I dreaded the day that it all faded. The blankets and pillows were scattered around, everything was left a mess. A perfect, beautiful mess with a smell of gardenia and citrus.

Billy still scratched at the door to go in on the days he could sense it was harder for me.

I moved her flowers inside, into a vase, but when I hadn't heard from her after a week, I figured they were staying put in my kitchen. They were wilted and dried out, barely any petals were attached to the buds, and the water had a filmy layer on top—but even then, I couldn't bring myself to get rid of them.

All that was left was distraction. I just wanted to be distracted from it all. I shut the curtains and kept the lights turned off in the main part of the house. I threw myself into the recliner and turned on the TV.

News channel, news channel, daytime talk show, another news channel. Another swig of alcohol as I clicked through them all.

"...Banks is here to make a public service announcement in just a few short minutes," the newscaster said into the camera.

What the actual fuck.

"Hello, New Haven!" My grandfather stood behind the podium in his cold, gray suit that was perfectly pressed and steamed. His eyebrows arched in a way that even when his face fell flat, he still looked as if he were scowling at you.

The audience cheered and whistled as he took his place on stage. There was no escaping him, he was on every local news station. It was exhausting. Normally, I'd turn the volume down until he left the screen, but I felt compelled to have the TV on its max volume setting. It was like adding salt to an open wound.

"You're all looking beautiful today!" he said, waving to his admirers. *What a smug son of a bitch.* "I will make this quick, though please note this was not an easy decision to make." He took a pause, only to add a dramatic flare and nothing else. He's the type to go on and on, talking to anyone who would listen, as long as the cameras were on him.

"I will be retiring," he declared. I practically flung out of my seat. "And my grandson, Sawyer Banks," he looked straight at the camera as if he was looking right at me, "will be campaigning to be your next mayor. I endorse him, and I encourage you all to keep the Banks legacy alive."

The out-of-view crowd fell silent right alongside me. I dropped my now empty bottle to the ground, glass shattered everywhere making Billy whimper. He wove himself between my legs as if he knew something was wrong. And something was very, very wrong.

"Mr. Mayor, Mr. Mayor... Lewis Banks..." the reporters behind the cameras chirped out, but I cut the TV mute. I couldn't take it anymore. There was a ringing in my ear. I unplugged the TV from the wall and rushed to the kitchen once more. I cracked the cap of a bottle of vodka.

I was taught never to mix my liquor, but here I live another day where I have to share the same blood and name with a man I never want to be. It's justified.

Chapter 29

Sawyer

Bright and early, I am face to face with a hangover—something I hadn't experienced in years. By the time I turned twenty-seven, I learned to manage my alcohol so I wasn't the tool that was regretting it all the next morning and relying on sports drinks and dark sunglasses to get through the day.

I fought with all that was inside of me as I sped into the city.

The sun danced behind the New Haven skyline coming into view and I was reminded of the last time I made this drive. It was the last summer I had spent here in Rider before college and I was hungry for my new beginning. I was ready to fall into line so easily back then. Now, I made the same drive with the same initiative of a new beginning, but it's a story that is written by me and me alone.

Slicing through the fresh, summer air, I was able to fully come to. Just the way my grandfather taught me, I had a motive for being here today. *Never insert yourself in someone else's day unless you have intent and motive.* I had both of those things.

There was no avoiding it, there was no other way to go about this. As usual, I had to be the bigger person when it came to Lewis Banks because he would never admit he was wrong, let alone realize he did wrong on his own.

I clenched my hands into tight, white-knuckled fists at my side. No more than twenty feet away from the entrance, I stood there staring up at the City Hall building. But I couldn't bring myself to walk in. The adrenaline, the angst—it's doing nothing for my momentum right now. Turned to stone, I was becoming one with the cement.

"Long time, no see," a familiar voice struck behind.

"I didn't expect to see you here," I said before turning to face my freckled, curly-haired cousin standing across from me.

"You didn't expect to see me in the place that I work? Good one, Sawyer."

I had tried to convince Holland to "jump ship" with me, but he didn't take the bait. Granted, the so-called "bait" was just me going on a rant about how awful our grandfather was and that we didn't need him. It was a nice attempt, but he enjoyed politics too much. Had he left with me, he would have never become the Director of Communications. I'm too proud of him to be upset.

I was convinced I almost had him in the middle of my rampage when he nodded to the absurdities I reminded him of from our childhood. He and I had always been so similar. We could smell our family's bullshit from a mile away and hated that our dads fought over this life constantly.

We are like brothers ourselves, and while that's a bond I knew we are forever grateful for as only children, that wasn't enough. Being as close as we are also meant we drank the same juice and were both raised and conditioned to fall into this lifestyle.

"Lewis has been asking about you, man. Told him we haven't spoken much."

"No need to lie, Hol."

Holland and I made sure to stay close and make it a point to talk semi-regularly. I would like to see him more often than I do, but I know that our grandfather has him on a short leash and I never wanted to risk running into him, even if we agreed to meet on the other side of town. With my luck, he'd find a way to be there.

For now, texting and the occasional comment on Facebook would suffice.

"Yeah, well… You know him," he shrugged. "It would somehow become my problem that I couldn't convince you to—"

"Convince me to what?" I snapped at him. I hated that I was letting the annoyance I felt towards our grandfather out on him.

Holland held his hand up over his eyes, blocking the sun as he squinted up at me. I always had a couple of inches on him. He hated it.

He stayed silent, but I heard him loud and clear. He scanned the vicinity before leaning in to whisper, "What was I supposed to say?"

I huffed out a low sigh. "I don't know. Something, anything. He respects you."

Holland rolled his eyes, "You're still his favorite, you know this. That's *your* name that he mentioned in his speech." He spoke hushed over his shoulder, "Even after everything, you're still his favorite."

The chatter of business people zipping by swallowed us.

I patted Holland on the back and we went our separate ways. I felt his eyes burning a hole in the center of my back as I headed inside.

Even after everything.

The inside of City Hall still had that musty, old wood smell that hits you the moment you walk through the metal detectors. Growing up, when I'd run down these halls and my light up shoes would reflect off the tiles, I dreamt of the days I would walk these very floors. Instead, I'd wear expensive Italian loafers that complete an iron-pressed suit and the heels would click against the glossy flooring.

Lewis' assistant caught me in the hallway, grabbing me eagerly by the arm. "While I live and breathe, Sawyer? Is that you?"

I turned slowly, dreading the greeting I knew I couldn't get out of. "Hi Cindy," I said curtly, "I'm here to see my grandfather," then left her there in shock.

Cindy was the type that would corner you and by the time your conversation was over, it had already been twenty minutes. It was unnecessary—especially when it started at the ripe age of fourteen. What the hell are you going to talk about with a fourteen-year-old, Cindy?

I walked in as he was finishing up computer work. He was wearing the same style suit that he did for his press conference yesterday, except in a deep, blue shade.

His door cranked closed behind me, and the hinges squeaked just the way I remembered them to. All of the color disappeared from his face, for the smallest second, he was scared. But almost immediately, a smirk appeared. I had never seen it before. He was genuinely intimated—until he wasn't. Lewis Banks doesn't get intimidated, he doesn't feel remorse. He knew he fucked up. But he's ready to go to bat and doesn't regret a thing.

I could see it in the Banks Scowl.

"What the fuck was that?"

He pushed away from his desk and stood at the edge of his chair. He rounded it and leaned up against the tabletop. He unbuttoned his sleeves and rolled them up. That infuriating grin never once faded. He was enjoying this.

"I don't know what you're talking about," he crossed his arms, falling into himself.

"Bull-fucking-shit, Lewis."

"Language," he said sternly, looking behind me and out his office doors.

I bet he's regretting having wrap-around glass walls now.

"Language, my ass. This is dirty, this is vindictive. This is exactly why I didn't want to work for you, to do any of this." I waved my arms around. "You play dirty to get what you want." Then his smugness vanished. "What exactly is it that you do want? What was the purpose of all of that last night?"

"When are you going to give up your little endless summer vacation dreams and get serious? I'm getting older. There's no need for me to be in this game anymore." He took a step towards me, a pleading look in his eyes. "This was supposed to be you, this was supposed to be all of yours."

"I don't want any of this, I never did!"

"You used to."

I did, I wanted it more than anything. "Not anymore," I said as I took a step back.

The entire office gawked at us through the glass walls—I felt them watch our every movement, our every gesture. I whipped myself around and they fumbled their papers and folders as they scurried off, as if they weren't all just eavesdropping.

My blood was boiling, but then I realized I wasn't just mad at him.

I mean, I was. I was furious. My anger that had built up over decades towards him was finally coming out, I was laying it all on the table. But the repressed anger and guilt and regret I held for myself was rising to the surface, too—that I was certain of.

No matter how content I was in Rider, I couldn't help but beat myself up.

When will it end? When will I stop feeling bad for letting people down who couldn't care less about my feelings?

"Not anymore," I said again, softer this time.

He pinched the bridge of his nose as he made eye contact with the ground. Four lines on his phone rang at the same time, and I could hear the fax machine down the hall. I'd become aware of all of my senses as silence filled the room.

"I should have handled this a different way."

"I'd say so."

"I'm sorry," he said, loosening his tie.

I choked on the air. *I'm sorry.* He's sorry?

"You're just giving up?" I strengthened my stance. There's no way he's just *giving up.*

"What do you mean?"

"You went through all of that just to concede after a few minutes alone with me? That's not the grandfather that I remember. You once held a three hour long debate with Dad over what Chopard watch to get Mom for Valentine's Day one year... You wouldn't settle until he got the one that *you* suggested." The memory got a snicker out of him. "And that was over a damn watch. And now you're saying sorry and giving up on this dream you have for me just like that? You hate it when people don't do what you want." I threaded my brows together, I truly was taken aback.

He exhaled sharply out of his nose as he rubbed the back of his neck. "And that hasn't really been helping my case with all of you, has it? Like I said, I'm retiring. I can't do this anymore. It's exhausting. I'll be honest, it started as a power play back many, many years ago when I entered the scene. You know, Sawyer, I was a party boy back in my day. This life was pushed on me, the same way I ended up doing to your father, to you. But you didn't go off and rebel, you did what was expected. At least that's how it was for my generation.

"Everyone knew about me from the tabloids, the Mayor's "Wild Boy" at a new bar or "Banks Boy Has Bad Blood" with a picture of me yelling at a valet attendant. Acting cold, and on a power trip, was my redemption story, I suppose. I had to prove myself. Eventually, it became my skin. A layer that I couldn't shake. But look, it's torn us all apart. And I'm to blame."

Wow... He's honestly apologetic, and I'm afraid that I believe him.

"I planned on ripping you a new one, hyped myself up—the whole nine yards—on my way in," I said as I walked over to his office window that looked down into the courtyard.

I spent many lunches, working away, in here beside him. We bonded over paperwork and the plans we envisioned for the city. He walked over to me and placed a hand on my shoulder.

"I don't know if *ripping a new one* is an appropriate thing for grandsons to do, but hey, I probably would have deserved it." He handed me back my phone, then paused as he looked out the window. "I definitely would have deserved it," he corrected himself.

I ran my hand over the scruff built up on my jaw. "I can't come back, you know this."

"I know, I just miss ya, my boy."

I turned towards him. "You know where I live. I'll cook you dinner. A real one, not one that you find in a styrofoam container. You and Grandmother need to be better about that." He nodded and laughed. It was unfamiliar, but it sure was comforting.

He sat back down at his desk and flipped through his stacks of paperwork. "What am I supposed to do now? I just made a public declaration not even twenty-four hours ago," he sunk into his chair, folding his hand in his lap.

"Holland."

"Excuse me?"

"Holland. Endorse Holland. He's ready."

"You're okay letting a political science degree from Yale go to waste like that?"

"I've been okay with it for a while," I scoffed. "I think that's something for you to come to terms with now."

He brought the tips of his fingers to a point and perched them under his chin. "I guess I just don't get it."

I never considered the fact that he was simply blind to any type of life that wasn't the one he'd known since he was in diapers. It's generational, I know that well. He is in his own bubble and forgets that people can be successful outside of their suits and tall buildings. At least that's what I tell myself so he can keep a human status in my mind.

"You know, you never showed up to my opening."

His mouth opened, but he quickly became tight lipped again.

"You didn't show up," I repeated myself. "I wanted you to be there." I took a seat in the chair across from his desk. It was easily two feet wide, but I had never felt closer to him. I was talking, and he was listening. "I named it, I fixed it up. It's looking nice over there. I got a few workers, they're amazing. I know you don't understand it, or you don't want to understand it. Maybe that's something *I* have to come to terms with. But I would love to have you be a part of it, even if it's to tell me you're proud of me."

I choked back the lump in my throat and all of the tears I felt forming.

"I am proud of you, boy." He crossed his arms and rested them on the desk. He leaned forward, looking straight into my eyes. I could see that we have the same shade, and they crease in the same spots. "You have no idea how proud of you I am."

He reached into his desk and pulled out a rolled-up news-paper. Across the top in bold letters was the news about my ownership. There was a picture of me and Gus, his arm around me, sat off to the left side of the page. He spun the paper around where I could see.

My heart twinged. It didn't make sense. For a split second, I felt myself understanding it all. Whatever grudge I have been hanging onto was starting to wash away, until I threw a dam up real fast. It didn't change anything. At least it didn't feel like it did.

"So, why didn't you respond to my RSVP or call me back? You didn't even call me back..." I stood up, hovering over him now. Looking down at him, there was a softness to his face. His eyes were droopy and his brows arched down.

"I wish I had answers," he said into the desk below him, bowing his head.

I didn't bother challenging him anymore. I knew that there was this standard that he had to uphold. Some things were just the way that they were. I wanted to leave, walk out, and leave our conversation where he felt bad. A part of me wanted him to feel terrible, to feel responsible for tearing our family apart. But that's just it—he didn't. And I can't blame him for having a different outlook on life than the one I ended up developing.

"I guess all we can do is go up from here."

He lifted his gaze to me, smiling at me, and shook his head in agreement.

The fifty-ton weight felt lighter and the dust began to settle. I went to walk out of his office, knowing that everything was on the up and up, but then he stopped me.

"Holland, eh?"

It was nice to see that the idea didn't seem so foolish as the moment passed. The gears started to turn and it seemed like I might be able to have my family back.

Now I just had to work on getting my Lucy back.

***

I rushed back to Rider, I never wanted to get somewhere quicker than I did at this moment. Instead of the lake house, or even The Hideout, I went straight to the cottages.

I knock on the door that belongs to the fourth cottage on the left. My palms are sweaty, I feel as nervous as I did the first day I showed up here. I could hear footsteps near the door, but imagine my surprise when it was a stocky old man who answered.

"Gus?" I said, disgruntled.

"Nice to see you, too," he chuckled out.

"But it's not Sunday, what are you doing here?"

"Eh, Lucy asked me to look after the place while she's been gone."

"G-gone? What do you mean? Where is she?"

"No clue. She called me a few weeks ago, and asked for me to look after the place until further notice."

"Until further notice," I repeated after him. "Heh, okay, thanks."

I turned on my heel and started back down the walkway when he stopped me. "Check with Mel," he yelled out. I faced him, and he nodded in the direction of their cottage. "She's home."

I didn't know how much help that was going to be when just yesterday she said she knew nothing. But desperate beyond belief, I headed on over.

Mel opened the door by the third knock and stepped onto the porch step.

"Hey, bud. What's up."

"Do you know anything else? Any new information?" I blurted out. She crossed her arms across her chest and knitted her brows. "Mel, please."

She sighed.

"Mel," I repeated, more desperate than before.

"Okay, okay," she surrendered and pulled out her phone. "I don't know *anything*, but I do know where they're at. And because you're borderline pathetic, and my best friend, my loyalty to you trumps girl code."

"Girl code? How is this—"

She held her hand to my face. "Shush, it just makes sense, okay? Here," she held up her phone screen. A search of a hotel... One state over.

"Where the fuck is Knightwood?" I tried to grab her phone to get a better look, but she pulled it away.

"Look it up, but that's all I'm giving you. I'm not sending any screenshots or anything, to have this betrayal trace back to me, or whatever."

I did a quick search of my own and saw that it's a four-hour car ride away. But only an hour flight. Without a second thought, I purchased the next flight out for tonight.

"Perfect, thanks!" I started to run down their walkway and back over to my bike in Lucy's drive.

"Get some sleep sometime soon, will ya?" Mel yelled out after me. "Maybe shave while you're at it!"

I threw a middle finger up over my head, before a thumbs up. "Love you," I yelled over my shoulder with hopes she could hear me.

I was going to get Lucy back, I had to.

Chapter 30

Lucy

"Alright, I'm heading downstairs to the gym. You sure you don't want to come?" Gracie raised her brows at me.

"Uh, yeah. I'm fine right here." I reassured her by pressing my ass further into the window seat cushion.

I had only been to Knightwood once growing up, I think we drove through it to get to Maine, but never spent any time here.

"Okay, suit yourself!" She placed her headphones over her ears, but stopped before the doorframe. Distracted by whatever was on her phone.

"What, can't find the right song to listen to?"

"Huh?" she mumbled out but kept her attention on her phone. "Oh, ha, yeah."

"What's going on? Are you and Asher back together?"

She snapped her head up at me. "Oh, fuck no!"

I waited for her to continue, as she is not one to shy away from gossip hour, but nothing. Whatever it was—*whoever* it was—surely held her attention in a way I'd never seen before. Her head hovered over her phone screen. I walked over and waved my hand in between her and the screen. "Just the other day you were crying over everything with Asher. Don't tell me you already started dating someone else."

"If you must know, I am texting Mel."

"Mel. Mel? Sawyer's Mel?"

Her mouth was agape. "That is the first time you have said his name in almost a month."

My face burned as I let my subconscious thoughts surface. Despite everything on my plate, all that is "Sawyer Banks" managed to flood my brain at the worst of times. As much as I tried not to talk about him, he still rented a space in my head despite my best efforts. Biting my lip, I looked away. His name left a familiar taste on my lips, one I'd been craving—a craving I was fighting.

"That is so not true," I spoke into my next bite of food, then sat up straight, ignoring her moment of deflection. "Don't do that, don't make it about me and what I don't want to talk about. Let's talk about what *you* aren't talking about. Mel. How are you talking to her?"

"We exchanged numbers at Sawyer's Fourth of July party while you were off doing whatever you two were doing. It's no big deal, we sort of became friends."

"Friends."

"Yes, *friends*."

"I don't see friends texting like that. I don't think I have ever seen you that giddy while texting me. Seriously, who are you texting?"

A distraction over Gracie's new beau was exactly what I needed. I wanted to get excited over love and something new and shiny.

"How would you know? I'm texting *you*, which implies you're not around. For all you know, I kick my feet and twirl my hair."

Gracie has spent a lot of the time that I've known her in tears over Asher, years that were once Instagram captioned as "some of their best years" before she archived them all.

I never understood it. She always brought happiness to those around her, but now it seemed like she was finally allowing herself to feel that same happiness. I didn't want to push it anymore. Whoever, whatever was going on between her and the person on the other side of the screen, I didn't mind all that much. As long as she was smiling again.

"I gotta get going," she said, letting the door slam behind her.

I've always hated that habit of hers, letting the door slam shut behind her. She always seemed to have earlier days whenever I had the chance to sleep in, and she would let the door become my new alarm clock. It's safe to say that is one thing I hadn't missed about being away from her this summer.

I closed the laptop from my completed video call with one of my students; it felt great getting back into the swing of things, scheduling more tutoring sessions than I had been this summer. A lot of them were spent over my phone as I rode shotgun—Gracie and I have spent the last three weeks road trippin' through New England—but it still felt like I had a purpose again.

I sunk into the couch this time and became familiar with the ridges and paint strokes of the ceiling as I waited for my food delivery to arrive. Falling into a deep haze over whether it was marshmallow white or off-white was the most tranquil thing I've done in weeks.

Sometimes I mourned my summer, the idea of what it could've been. I meant it when I said I wanted everything with Sawyer. But I'm thinking that that's all that it was—an idea. It didn't mean that I don't still daydream about the possibilities that could have come with staying the remaining seven weeks.

Would we have had more farmer's market dates? Would Leanne and I have been able to make pies and pastries? Would Sawyer have taught me how to make a Manhattan? Would I have fallen in love with him?

I guess I'll never know.

Chapter 31

Sawyer

They say that acceptance is the last and most healing stage of the grieving process. But a life without Lucy was one that I did not want to accept.

I pressed the elevator button to the top floor, the entire time spent wondering what I'd say. I walked down seven doors from the elevator and knocked on the Kingsley Suite room. The door swung open and her arms fell to her side, she stiffened. The shock that hit her body siphoned blood from the face I'd been dying to see.

"What are you doing here?" She crossed her arms over her chest while she assessed me.

And my gaze fell to the mole above her lip, and back up to her eyes. The sparkle that's been there in the past was duller.

Here I was, once again, standing frozen in front of Lucy at her door. A shiver shot down my spine at the recollection of history repeating itself.

"You're not excited to see me?" I croaked out.

"That's not it. Just not the person I was expecting to see."

I took a step back. "Oh." My response was of a pained tolerance. The idea that Lucy already moved on made me ill.

"No, it's not like that." She moved off to the side and welcomed me in. "I have frozen yogurt being delivered soon."

The hotel room smelled like fresh limes and coconut, it was as if she managed to bring the scents on Rider with her wherever she went.

I picked up my pace and grabbed her from behind like no time had passed at all. I rested my head in the crook of her neck. I could feel the pulsating of her veins against my cheek. I felt the movement of her breathing against me, it turned shallow.

"Sawyer..." Her voice was fragile.

"Not right now. Let me hold you first?"

She exhaled softly. "I've missed you."

"I've missed you, too, Lucy." I spun her around. This was real life, her in front of me. I longed to be this close to Lucy after an agonizing month without her. I had a crumb of what it was like to have someone like her in my life, and I didn't want to re-accustom myself to a world she was not a part of.

She pulled away from me and returned to her reserved posture. "What are you doing here, Sawyer?"

Just like that, a cold breeze filled the space between us again.

"I wanted to see you."

"How did you even figure out where I was?" She cocked her head.

"Gracie," I began. Lucy shifted her weight all onto one side. She pressed her fingers to the bridge of her nose. I corrected myself, "It was Mel, technically. She got it from Gracie and then she told me. And then—"

That got a faint laugh out of her. "Mel does it again, providing you with more intel on me." Her eyes went soft for a split second until she drew her brows together. "But I don't get it." She stopped in the center of the living area and turned back around toward me.

"What's not to get?" I sat on the arm of the couch, pulling her between my legs. "I wanted to see you, so I came to see you," I said, looking up at her.

She pushed my hair out of my face. "You look exhausted." She weaved her fingers between mine, moving them in and out of my hold. She jumped at the knock at the door. "I'm sorry. I'll be right back."

She pranced over to the door. "Hi, thanks!" she perked up as she grabbed the bag. She faced me and held it up. Guppy's Creamery, it's a New England delicacy. "If I knew you were coming, I would have ordered you some," she said, snippy.

"Chocolate chip, that's my favorite. Just in case you need to know for future reference."

She rolled her eyes, "Black coffee... Chocolate chip ice cream... You're so basic!"

I hold my hands up. "What can I say?"

Her phone started to ring. "Agh, hold on." She pulled up the screen and a scrawny frat boy with amber-colored curls stared back. I walked up from behind Lucy, and his eyes widened. "Hey, Griffin. I'm sorry to do this, but I'm gonna have to reschedule."

"Yeah, she's a little busy. Sorry, man." Lucy threw an elbow into my stomach. "She and I have a chemistry assignment we have to get through," I teased, my mouth twitching with amusement.

"I'll email you tomorrow morning and cut the session fee in half, I promise." The kid slowly nodded, then disconnected the call. Lucy turned to me, "You're terrible, you know that?"

"Ooh, my bad, teacher. I think you'll have to discipline me."

"I'll have to do something to you, you're right."

I walked backward towards the main living area until she took the lead down the hallway. "Oh, no, not the principal's office," I said sarcastically.

"Oh, shut up!" she squealed.

Lucy shut the door behind us and pushed me back onto the bed. I looked up at her, bare-faced, loungewear, and all. She will always be the most beautiful person I have ever had the privilege of laying my eyes on. She looked down grinning like a devil as she straddled me and my heart turned over in response.

"*Wow.*"

"What?" she covered her face with her hands, hiding in herself.

"You. Just, you. You're everything." I ran my hand down the side of her arms. "You're perfect."

She leaned down and placed her lips softly onto mine. Kissing her felt right, kissing her felt like I had never gone a day without. Everything about it was slow and tender, meaningful and passionate. Reclaiming her lips, our undeniable attraction was renewed. Her body molded into mine, her nearness made my senses spiral.

"I am really happy that you're here," she spoke quietly into my ear.

Hours had passed, but our lips never grew tired. The humming of the AC unit drowned us out, so we didn't hear it when Gracie had gotten back. The door flung open and she stood in the doorway.

"What. The. Actual.."

Lucy and I sprung up, acting as if we were teenagers who had just been caught by their parents.

"I didn't hear you come in," Lucy stammered as she reached for her shirt which somehow came off in the last hour or so.

"I can see that. It's nice to see you, Sawyer," she nodded, holding back a smile.

I nodded back, hiding a laugh that tried to break out.

Lucy slipped back into her top and moved herself down to the edge of the bed while smoothing out her hair.

"We are going to have to talk about this, you know."

"It doesn't look like you're *that* mad," Gracie shrugged.

"Not the point!" Lucy exclaimed as she threw a decorative pillow towards Gracie.

Gracie gasped and giggled simultaneously, throwing her hands up in surrender. "Okay. Well, look, I'm tired. I'll be across the hall in my room...remember that."

Moments later, her door slammed shut and Taylor Swift started playing noticeably loud. Lucy got up from the bed and closed her door with an embarrassed look on her face.

"I am so sorry. I didn't think she would be back until—*Oh, my god*," she threw a hand over her mouth as she looked at the clock beside her vanity. "It's already nine."

I shrugged. "Yeah, what about it?" I stood up and met her. I pinned her tight between me and the door.

Awkwardly, she cleared her throat. "We still have a lot to talk about."

I walked back over to the bed and I sunk into myself. Shame and guilt were the first two emotions that rushed my body. I wish I was here for the sole reason being that I *wanted* to see her. But parts of me felt like I *had* to see her to deal with everything that's been going on.

"Some shit went down with my grandfather and frankly, you were the first person I wanted to talk to about it. I don't know how much you already know. Honestly, it feels like everyone on this planet knows. There wasn't one person at the airport who wasn't giving me some type of look. I lost count of how many people looked between me and the front cover of their magazines. It's been a hard couple of days."

Lewis retracted his statement and endorsed Holland earlier this afternoon. Only an hour after I had left his office, he called an emergency press conference. The camera panned over to where Holland was standing, a quick smile filled his face until he noticed he was on display. The expected scowl made an appearance as if he had to hide his joy. It pained me.

The crowd reacted a lot less frantic with the change; they were cheerful. He passed it off like it was a mishap when calling out my name instead of his. He took all of the blame. Even if it meant it made him look bad. What he explained to those on his staff and to Holland himself? I had no idea.

I looked forward to Holland's mayoral term, but I hope he learns he doesn't have to be our grandfather to be successful.

She sat beside me. "I feel like a complete asshole by saying this, but I don't know what you're talking about. I have... made it a point to not give myself much free time, so I haven't been on my phone all that much."

I let out a moan of distress as I fell back onto the mattress. I held my hands on the center of my chest while she wrapped her arm over me. We both looked up at the ceiling fan and watched it spin around while silence filled the room. It was nice to have a calm atmosphere—and mind—for the first time in what felt like forever.

I eventually filled her in on everything that has gone down in the last couple of days. Starting from the television appearance, and finishing up the possibility of me making him dinner at the lake house.

"Are you happy that you walked away from everything? From your family, from the possibilities and all of what could have been?"

I propped myself on my elbow and faced her. I waited a beat before answering, then I fell back down beside her. "I think you're the first person to ask me." She wrapped her leg back over me while I yammered on. "I think initially, I was in the whole 'I'll show them' stage of life. I wanted to do everything on my own. But then, I fell into regret. I was terrified and thought I completely screwed up. It wasn't until The Hideout and everything Gus and Leanne had done for me that I truly felt secure in my decision. It was hard. There was only one life that I had ever envisioned for the longest time. Until I created a new one. This is the kind of life that I have always wanted, so yeah, I am happy. More than."

She shut her eyes and nuzzled herself into me.

"That makes me happy," she said into my chest.

Chapter 32

Lucy

We spent hours that felt like mere minutes talking about all of the little happenings of Rider since I'd been gone. However, it also felt like we were both beating around the bush of what we genuinely wanted to say, to ask. All of it.

Sawyer was that old friend you could fall back into place with as if no time had passed. I was comfortable with him the moment he stepped through the threshold. But there was still that ghost of awkwardness that crept around the corner, fighting its way in, making itself known.

I snuck out to grab some water, but a moment later, I heard scuffs of slippers along the floor enticing me to peek my head around the hall. Gracie shuffled down the hall with a blanket wrapped around her. "Is he asleep?" she asked in a whisper. She grabbed my glass from the counter and took a sip.

I shook my head.

"Sooooo,"

"*Sooooo,* nothing."

"You're telling me that this man flies to another state for you and you don't rip his clothes off and bang one out?"

"You're making me sound like I just give it up."

"And that's okay if you do." Gracie raised her brows and shrugged.

I started to chew on the inside of my bottom lip.

She moved my glass off to the side and lifted herself on the counter. "Oh, my god. It's more than that, isn't it?!"

"Will you keep it down?! He is still awake... only fifteen feet down the hall."

"This reminds me of last fall. We went out for my birthday and you were making eyes with the waitress all night. It was nauseating, really, with how fast you two started hanging out. You were linked at the hip, and—okay this isn't the time to repeat just how annoying it was that you spent more time with her than me... But the second she voiced she wanted something more serious, you friend zoned her so hard. You better not friend zone Sawyer," she scolded me.

How could I when no one has even been able to light a wildfire inside my heart the way that he has, but still, I said nothing. Samantha was nothing more than a fling. I made that clear from the start, the same way I had with Sawyer. The difference is I rode that wave with her. And the moment I started to get swallowed by the current, I fought my way back to shore. Feelings were never supposed to be involved.

But Sawyer... Even when I tried to keep my walls up, he came crashing in like a five-ton wrecking ball.

"You got it bad, don't you? What am I saying? Of course you do. I've never seen you like this."

I lifted my glass to my mouth to buy myself some time from answering—either way, I knew that I was going to counter argue her claim. Because she had no idea what she was saying. At least that's what I told myself. But my silence spoke volumes, and at this moment, I knew there was no convincing her—or myself—otherwise.

She jumped off the counter and the blanket fell to our feet. Gracie had a knack for reading me like the back of her hand, so when her eyes widened, and they were almost misty with pride, we both knew that she didn't have to say anything else. I already knew what she was about to ask. And she already knew my answer.

"Shut up."

"Lucy!"

"*Gracie!*"

She started to whisper, "Do you love him?"

"I have to get back in there."

I walked past her and back into the room, my face warm to the touch.

"I thought you were getting water?" Sawyer asked.

"Right..." I brought my hand to my cheek. "Gracie came out there and totally snatched it from me."

He sat up straight. "What's wrong?"

I shook off my conversation with Gracie and painted a smile across my face. I wasn't going to let anything ruin this night. I had Sawyer with me tonight, and if tonight was all I had left, I was going to make the most of it.

"Nothing! I'm going to get ready for bed. You should, too." I walked into the bathroom and started my night routine.

He stared back at me, his mouth agape. "Y-you want me to stay the night?"

"Well, yeah."

A smile crept across his face. "I'll cancel my hotel reservation right away."

There was a sense of comfort that came with knowing he didn't assume he'd stay the night. In the reflection of the mirror, I saw Sawyer climb up out of bed. He lifted his shirt over his head, then slipped out of his jeans. This isn't my first time seeing Sawyer near to naked, yet I'm drawn to memorize every inch of his body. My gaze dropped from his toned shoulders to his chest to his briefs.

They hugged him in all the right places.

A stream of toothpaste-filled drool dripped into the sink as I watched him undress. I coughed out the excess that gathered during the trance that I had been in for far too long.

Sawyer rushed into the bathroom and shut off the water that was still running. "Are you okay?" he asked, holding back a laugh.

He stood behind me in just his underwear, they hung low on his hips. I spit out the toothpaste into the sink and held out a thumbs-up. I stood up and observed us in the mirror. Something so mundane felt oh, so normal. Getting ready for bed with him felt right.

"I'm so sorry you had to witness that," I said wiping away at my mouth.

The corner of his mouth lifted as he spun me around. I missed his smile. I missed being the person that made him smile. There was so much I wanted to say, but none that I could even form into sentences. I felt our breathing become one and I am reminded of how easy that happens when we are together. Everything else that occupies my brain disappears when I am around Sawyer.

He twisted the loose hairs at the nape of my neck, the ones that can never quite reach my hair tie, around his index finger. The slight graze of his touch on my skin sent shivers all down my back. My whole body shuddered, so I wiggled the feeling away. He smiled, proudly, as if he achieved some sort of goal.

"Fuck it," I muttered under my breath. I pressed my mouth into his, showering his lips with kisses and along his cheek and jaw. I nibbled my way up to his earlobe and I let out a weak moan. Our kisses were that of urgency like we had been waiting forever to kiss each other again. That's exactly what it felt like.

"God, you have no idea how much I hated being away from you," he cried out a shaky breath.

Sawyer pressed himself into me and I could feel *everything*. His briefs got tighter if that was even possible. His thighs already filled them out. I let my hand drift down in between us, stopping at his very present erection. From my slightest touch, he let out a quiet moan into my neck.

I pulled at his underwear. Quickly, they pooled at his feet and he kicked them off to the side. He lifted my bralette off, my breasts bounced as the fabric moved over them. He cupped them in both of his hands and gave them a little squeeze.

"Fuck, you're perfect," he said as he trailed his hands down my bare torso. He pushed my shorts off next, leaving us both standing here naked on the cold tiled floors. "Your ass looks amazing in the mirror, too." He gave one cheek a nice, hard slap before hoisting me up on the counter. I yelped at the coolness beneath me, and he gave me a devilish grin.

I wrapped my legs around his waist before reaching down again. Only a few strokes in, and I could feel him pulsating. I rested my forehead in the center of his chest and looked down between us. I watched as my hand went up and down, letting my grip tighten with each squirm that he made. Witnessing him edge himself already was satisfaction in itself.

I hopped down off the counter and led him to the shower. I leaned in to turn the water on. A mischievous grin formed on my face, saying all that I needed to say without once opening my mouth.

"Only if you join me," he nibbled at my shoulder.

I pulled at my hair tie, letting my hair fall over my shoulders. "Let's go." I let my hand lead the way, testing the water temperature before getting in.

Being near him was overwhelming in all of the best ways. He brushed a kiss across the top of my head. My pulse leaped with anticipation.

I swallowed tightly as I looked up at him through my lashes as I started to crouch down. Kissing along his torso, down to the peaks of his hip bones, I reached his crotch.

With a few soft kisses on the tip, I covered my whole mouth over his dick, letting it hit the back of my throat while I cupped his balls. I glanced up at him right as his eyes rolled back and his head dropped. He tightened the grip on my hair.

With each thrust, he only grew bigger, harder, and my mouth widened to accommodate. The tingling in my stomach grew with every heavy breath of his that traveled down to me. I reached down between my legs, I'd grown too impatient. Moving my fingers in circles, my skin prickled with heat from my own touch. A moan of ecstasy escaped my mouth only to make his whole body tremble.

I slipped my mouth off of his dick, still stroking him. "God, look at you," I said looking up at him. His jaw tense and the veins of his neck popping out. "You're such a good boy, so close to coming for me, aren't you?"

He bent over, picking me up by my arms. "That's enough," he growled into my ear as he spun me on my toes. He faced me against the shower wall and bent me at my hips. He leaned forward, making his chest press against my back, and whispered, "You better be real quiet. There's no need to disrupt your friend in the other room."

He cupped his hand over my mouth and thrust into me. I bit at the top of his hand, holding back my desperate need to scream out with every slam into my body. I gasped in sweet agony. This was much, much more than a sexual desire. This was a type of hunger, and I was starved.

The sound of the splashing water between us suffocated my inability to keep quiet, though I tried. I cried out into the palm of his hand as he pressed it tighter against my mouth.

"Now do me a favor. I want you to come for me like you did the night before you left. Do you think you can do that for me, my pretty girl?" And just like that, I was done for. I surrendered myself to Sawyer Banks completely.

***

We were naked under the sheets, we grew comfortable with our faces pressed against dampened pillowcases. We had gone a couple more rounds once we made it back to the bed, each one better than the last. Sawyer pulled me near him, his hair in a shaggy disarray and his eyes tired. My weak limbs clung to him, I'll never grow tired of his touch.

"Lucy, you right now, laying beside me with messy hair and soft eyes, is the absolute best." He started to trace various lines down the side of my arm.

"Now you're the one putting hexes on *me*."

"Tell me something," he shifted onto his side to face me, completely changing the subject. When I tried to make the moment light, I had a feeling he was taking it down the more serious path. "Why did you leave Rider? Why not –"

A familiar knot formed in my chest. *The real world is still out there.*

"You knew I'd have to leave."

"I thought we had more time. I thought you needed space. But not *physical* space." He tucked a strand of hair behind my ear.

"I didn't mean to leave, at least not like that. It's just…" My voice was shakier than I would have liked. All of the air had left my body, I didn't know what to say.

I was afraid I'd run into him at Jitters, and I knew I'd see him at the lake—I was certain he would look at me with those eyes of his or kiss me the way only he knows how to and I'd fold. I needed this time away.

It wasn't fair to leave the way that I did, but I still believed that it wouldn't have been fair to make him deal with someone who was emotionally closed off. Sawyer has so much love to give, that is something that I have learned this summer. And I was ready to match him with that energy. But I couldn't give him what he deserved and I tried to preserve his heartbreak by apparently creating a whole different kind.

"You know, I never traveled much. And what's 'much' when I'm talking to someone who has probably seen the whole world? But this last month, I drove up and down the coast of New England with my best friend and I felt free. I wasn't tied down to anything, I didn't take care of anything I didn't want to. I knew I wasn't going to be reminded of the secrets kept from me for my entire life everywhere I looked. "

He kissed the side of my head. "How do you feel now?"

"When it comes to all of that? No clue. When it comes to you? Better."

He sucked in a breath. "And what's your plan when it comes to Rider? Are you going to finish out the sale?"

"I mean, yeah. I have to. I have to see it through and go from there."

"So you are coming back to Rider?"

"I feel like I have done so much work virtually with Kai thus far, I don't need to go back," I said, facing away from him.

And that was that. I heard him exhale, then turn over to face the other side. But I couldn't fall asleep if I tried.

***

The beacon light always guided me back toward Rider. Now, I felt like a sinking ship lost at sea. I racked my brain trying to conjure up the pros of returning. I'd want to visit Gus and Leanne, but that could be figured out down the line. Nothing else came to mind at the moment. Nothing except for one thing, one person: Sawyer.

I'm aware that I made thought-out decisions. So when I considered jumping all in with Sawyer, that scared me. It was so out of character. But because I *am* the type to make such thought-out decisions, I knew I wasn't getting in over my head. Being with Sawyer would never be the wrong decision.

All of the world's tornadoes and hurricanes filled my stomach when I figured out that I was ready to tell him I'd go back with him. And I was able to find peace with my next move.

When I flipped over to nuzzle into his side, ready to start the day with the news, his side of the bed felt empty and cold. The room felt empty and cold. I frantically rushed out into the living room.

"G, where's Sawyer? I mean, he's gone. I know that much." I clutched my chest. "I told him why I left Connecticut, he asked me to come back, I said there was no point, but—"

"Sit down." She motioned to the couch, but I slid down the hallway wall instead as a hot tear rolled down my cheek.

"I am so fucking dumb. I do this every time."

She sat down next to me and I moved my head into her lap. She started to rub my hair as my breathing returned to normal.

Gracie placed a small piece of paper in front of my face and shot up straight.

"W-what is this?"

"I ran into him about thirty minutes ago, I told him you'd be up soon, but he said he had a plane to catch. He left that with me—and this." The next thing she handed to me was a plane ticket. With my name on it.

"Nothing says you can't go back to Rider."

"What, now? And leave you here? No way. Besides, I don't know if I'm ready to go back. And we have to get back to Arizona soon."

I wanted to reassure him, let him know that I would work on it with him. Regardless of what would happen with us, going back to Rider was a whole other story in itself.

"Lucille Collins, you are not going to let your profession keep you from love. And anyway, I gotta get back like *now*. He had a ticket for me, too, but I told him that I spoke to my dad this morning. I think I will start interning a few weeks early if they'll let me. You, though, have a hot ass man waiting for you at the airport."

All I had ever known was to focus on school and work and my success. Family and love and life outside of that didn't matter. Heck, I didn't matter. She chose her career over me, a family.

It was easy to hide behind the studies and the schedules. I never had to feel anything deeper than academic stress. Sure, I was taking time off from schooling at this very moment, but I was still working towards what I wanted, what I always dreamed of.

Every experience, job, internship—it all enhanced my resumé.

"But, work comes first, love comes after," I said, wiping away a tear as I sat up against the wall.

"Fuck that. Being happy comes first, and worrying comes later. Focus on what you want right now. What do you want right now?"

I reached for the note that Sawyer had left and opened it up.

I'LL BE READY WHEN YOU ARE.

XO. BANKS.

I shrieked, I groaned, but then I smiled. I now had my answer for Gracie.

I wanted Sawyer.

Chapter 33

Sawyer

There was a lot I'm not sure of in this world. I'm not sure why a woman like Lucy would give me a second of her time. And I'm definitely not sure why I could never make love work out the way I want it to. What I was sure of, though, was Rider will not be the same until the day Lucy returned.

In my senior year of high school, I believed that I was all in with a girl that I had dated all four years. We made it into our freshmen year of college before we broke things off. Our love was nowhere near as passionate and thrilling as the love I have for Lucy. And that's okay—it was young love, a kind I was thankful for.

We never had any bad blood, we simply fizzled out. *Fizzled out.* Almost five years together and all I could do is compare the relationship to a flat soda. It wasn't far from it, though. Our love became tasteless.

She would stand beside me at press conferences, clap when my grandfather completed his speeches, or nod when he suggested new concepts at family dinners. I knew how life with her was going to look before it even started, it became predictable with her.

She was a dream girl. For someone else.

A month after we broke up, she started dating none other than Aaron Nelson. They got married and then divorced by the age of twenty-two.

I never wanted a love like that again. I wanted electricity to surge through my veins at the simplest thought of my significant other. And I found that with Lucy.

I knew she never had plans to stay from the get-go. But I wasn't going to let the opportunity pass without experiencing a love like this. Lucy is the kind of person who searches for more out of life while simultaneously making the most of what she already has.

The smell of sunscreen and early morning airport brew wafted back and forth with every terminal that I passed. There was officially one month left of summer, with families and bachelorette parties in full vacation mode and all I got were these summertime blues. Pizza was already in the oven at one of the corner restaurants. I stopped to grab a slice and a beer before bothering to find my terminal.

A dark green duffle bag with fairies and flowers all over slammed down in the seat beside me, nudging into my elbow and almost spilling my very much-needed drink. I picked it up with the overflow spilling off the sides.

"Need a napkin?"

"Yeah, tha—"

I dropped my drink to the ground, stunned.

I'm sorry to the custodian for this mess, I promise it was an accident and completely worth it...

"You came."

"That's what she said."

And suddenly we were back at The Hideout, walking the loop around the lake.

I remember feeling incredibly shocked that she showed up. Sure enough, the ego balloon deflated when I remembered she knew other people there that night. But it still felt like she was there for me, and me alone.

It was the beginning of everything.

I have a feeling this is just another one of those beginnings.

"Oh, my Lucy," I cried out and leaned over for a kiss. It was a drug-like kiss and I was getting my fix.

"I'm ready to come home," she spoke into my mouth.

I pulled away and widened my already enormous smile. "Home. I love the sound of that." She was ready to go home, and I was ready for my home to be her. I pulled her bar stool over, the legs making a heinous screeching noise that made those around us turn quickly.

Steadying herself, she stared at me as if she could see all of me. I couldn't wait to share all of me with all of her.

The reflection of myself in the lightest shade of green told me all that I needed to know—that I could see forever with her.

As we settled ourselves, I closed out my tab and moved us to our terminal. I flung my backpack over my shoulder, took her bag in one hand, and used my free hand to hold her tight against me. She took her ticket in between both of her hands and gripped the edges. The glow of her smile warmed me by just standing beside her.

"I don't want you to think that I am coming home for you. I–I mean, well... Let me start over. I'm not coming home for you," she said in a serious tone that pulled a chuckle out of me. "Man, I'm messing this up."

She shook her words off and sat herself up straight, placing her arms on either armrests.

"Being back at Hummingbird Lake, I found myself again. The person who used to look forward to her future. And for a fraction of a time, I was granted peace of mind this summer. Even when it didn't feel like it, even when I did everything in my power to push it away, the salt air somehow cleansed my soul and I felt like me again. I realize that now. The soft dirt and dark moss that belong to Hummingbird Lake belonged to me again. You helped make that happen, ya know." She softened her voice and took my hand in her lap. Her thumb traced over mine. "I don't want to push you away. I don't want to push anything away anymore."

Hummingbird Lake always had a way of making your life change for the better. It held answers in the rings of the trees and gave you purpose whenever the sun glistened on top of the water.

"I'm just scared of—" she paused and started to blush.

"I got you. It's okay..."

"I think I have the potential of really falling in love with you, Sawyer Banks. And that scares me."

I inherited a grin that the Cheshire Cat would be envious of.

"I think you made it known you were falling for me from the first day that I met you."

She looked at me, stunned. It took her a second to register. She then pushed at my chest and snickered.

"That was more like falling *into* you, not the same thing."

"Oh, sorry, my bad." I pulled her in for a hug, a laugh broke from my chest and vibrated against her head. "It felt all the same to me. But maybe that's because I started to fall for you the second I laid my eyes on you."

A tender kiss was placed on my cheek after she broke from my hold.

"I still can't help but feel like this is crazy, like *we* are crazy... Like I am crazy for going against the grain," she said quietly into her lap.

Everything has always been unspoken between the two of us. Right from the beginning. We fell into step with each other and I cannot wait to walk through life with her to the ends of the earth. And I am here to reassure her that she is the most sane person I have ever met.

"Alright, say that you are. Say that we are crazy," I finally said. "Are you going to say it's a coincidence that the universe has pulled us together, needing and wanting each other, all summer long?"

"I guess not..."

"We were meant to meet in this lifetime, Lucy. And I am so lucky and privileged to admit that I am madly, deeply in love with you."

And now, the knot inside my chest had undone itself. The words I've wanted to say from the moment I realized I felt them were out in the world. I could breathe again.

***

I had no idea when I'd have the nerve to drive the truck again, but considering it was raining when it was time to head to the airport, I opted out of using my bike. A promise I had made to my mother was I would never drive in wet weather. It was a good call, and I believe it worked in my favor. A good lucky charm of sorts.

Lucy had fallen asleep on the way back from the airport. Her muffled and barely there snoring filled the cab.

"Hey, baby. We're here," I kissed the top of her head that was snuggled into my neck.

She slowly pulled herself up straight and looked out the passenger side window. "Ah, yes. *Coffee*." She perked up, already with her hand on the seat buckle, and bolted for the door of Jitters.

I strolled in behind her as she was quick to start ordering from Kai. They leaned over the counter to hug her, spewing out all sorts of things they had to do to prepare for their open house.

"Let the girl get her caffeine, will you?" I came up behind Lucy, placing my hand on her lower back as I slid my card across the counter.

Kai tapped away on the tablet, entering our order. "I'll call you later, okay?"

"Sounds good," Lucy gave Kai a gentle smile as they handed us our drinks.

We hadn't even made it two steps from the counter before it plunged to the ground. Vanilla-scented coffee and ice splattered on our feet.

"*Mom?!*"

"Hello, dear." A woman who looked like Lucy, they could be twins if only Lucy had frown lines and a permanent look of disgust, stood inches before us. She reached her hand out to me, her nails perfectly manicured a devilish red color. "Hi, I'm Sunny. Lucy's mother."

"Sunny, is it? You don't look very *sunny* to me. Let's go, Luce." I pulled her in close to me, covering her whole body with mine. Knowing what I now know, I was not going to let Lucy spend a second on her and I wanted to shield her from that walking hurricane.

We had made it to the door when the screeching sound of her voice brought us to a standstill. "Wait! A word with my daughter please?" She demanded.

I looked down at Lucy. Her face was a ghostly shade of white before it turned green. She looked over at her mom, at me, and then out the front door. She was assessing her options.

The presence of her mother dulled the sparkle in Lucy's eyes. The darkness alluded to her wanting nothing more than to book it out the front door. And I'd run out right alongside her. Instead, she pulled away from me and clenched her jaw.

"I'll only take a few minutes. Wait for me?"

I pushed the door open and stood in the entryway, "Always. I love you."

She perched up on her highest of tiptoes and planted a kiss on my cheek. She marched away, switching to an identical scowl, the same one her mother was sporting.

Chapter 34

Lucy

The last time that I saw Sunny, I was fourteen. It was Christmas time, and we had run into each other at the General Store. A bottle of Cabernet was clutched in one hand and a stack of fashion magazines were in another. The true delicacies of Sunny Collins.

My mother scanned me from head to toe, I could feel the judgment seep out of her practically non-existent pores as she zeroed on into the scarf I was wearing. My grandmother had knitted it for me. It was the same winter that I learned how to knit thanks to her. But to my mother, if it wasn't designer, garments were meant to live in the trash.

I admire her for all her hard work. She has what she has in life because she worked day and night for them—trust me, I know that firsthand. But the materialistic lifestyle with the money and the houses and the kind of clothes she wore or the cars she drove was more meaningful to her. I never understood it considering it wasn't always like that for her, for us.

She wouldn't know what it was like to be humble if it hit her in her botched Botox face. There were nights of pulling everything from the pantry to create dinner or calling friends to see if they had hand-me-downs so I had something to wear when the weather changed. A way of life that she associates with shame, is a life I am lucky to have lived.

You can work hard for your future while remaining grateful for where you came from. That was a concept she never grasped and she was willing to hurt anyone in the crossfire. Point blank period, I am living proof of that.

"Upstairs, now," I demand. I was not going to let her intimidate me. I wasn't the avoidant little girl she once knew, always afraid of upsetting mommy dearest.

With a sly grin, she walked ahead of me. Her Jimmy Choo pointy-toe pumps clicked with every step she took up the stairs. Her footsteps were a siren—a warning signal. A packed coffeehouse and of course, she had to be the loudest one in the room.

I waited while she punched in the door code to her condo. I used to think it was the coolest thing living up above a coffee shop. I saw people do it all the time in my favorite TV shows and movies. Once I reached my teenage years, I was hopeful that with *Jitters* becoming my favorite coffee shop to study at, I'd get to see my mom around. She'd have a reason to see me. But that's when I learned she no longer resided here—at least not full-time.

She kicked off her velvet pumps and unbuttoned her blazer. "Would you—" she started out.

I held my hand up, stopping the bullshit that was bound to come out of her mouth before it even began. "No, no. I'll start. California. You've been telling people I am in California?"

She shrugged her shoulders. There was a smugness about her action.

"Arizona, Mother!"

"Alright, whatever. How was I to know? I'm rarely here. I spend more time in the city, anyway. This is merely a tax write-off. For all I knew, you were back here. But, hey, it seems like you are."

At least she didn't pretend to be an active part of my life. She admitted that she didn't know where I'd been or what I'd been doing. I'd give that to her.

"You're unbelievable," I said under my breath. Not hushed enough, but I didn't care anymore.

"*Excuse* me?"

"Yeah. You. You're unbelievable. I am here to sell the cottage. I haven't been here since Grandma passed. I couldn't bring myself to," my voice cracked on the last bit. "If you must know, I didn't want to risk running into you and tainting every feeling I had towards this town."

She walked away, avoiding eye contact with me as she made her way into her room. I followed after her in a huff. She fanned through the clothes in her closet. The top shelves were lined with an overstock of designer bags, all with original tags still attached. She and I share looks, but that's where the resemblance stops. I am nothing like my mother.

"That makes two of us," she said into her row of Lululemon shirts hanging up. "Why do you even care?" She spun around. "This town is a dead end. Everyone is always in everyone's business, they care way too much."

Oh, the fucking horror to have someone care.

I was paralyzed in the doorframe of her closet, watching her act as if this were normal. Act as if I wasn't even here. But she wasn't acting, that's just it.

"I found the boxes that Grandma had hidden away," I finally said. Her hands froze before they fell to her side. She stared off into her clothes in front of her as her face turned red.

"What are you talking about?" she said flatly.

Sunny Collins pretending something doesn't exist when she doesn't want to deal with it? I expected nothing less.

I walked up beside her, inches from her side profile, and whispered into her ear. "You know exactly what I'm talking about." I could see the hairs on the back of her neck standing at attention.

She angled herself toward me now, her breathing on the side of my face sent shivers down my spine. I had entered a sparring match and there was no telling who would win. It was like there wasn't even a person behind the mask that was her face. It was a cold, heartless body that stared back at me. But then she said, "I'm not sorry," and then pushed past me and headed back for the kitchen. She pulled out all sorts of vegetables, a knife, and a cutting board, and started chopping away.

The blade of her knife struck the cutting board and she continued as if this was a conversation we have had time and time before. I watched as she prepared her food. I might as well be invisible. At this moment, I wish that I was. I had an awful taste in my mouth as I fought back tears. This was who she was, who I'd always known her to be. Why is this all of a sudden so hard for me to process?

She slammed the knife down and shot her head towards me. "What do you want me to say? Like I said, I'm not sorry. I never liked that she kept those photos, I didn't want you to know. You want to be mad at someone?" She jutted her chin out. "Be mad at your grandmother. Oh wait, you can't. She's dead."

"Fuck you!"

"Fuck *you!*" She waved her hands above her head. "I never even wanted you. Is that what you wanted to hear? That's why you don't know about your father. He knocked me up the summer before college, but I never wanted a kid." She was on a roll, now. "I did want him, though. He promised me the world, that just meant you had to be a part of it. I guess he caught on." She picked back up her knife and chopped away at her cucumbers. "He told me I was miserable to be around, whatever that means, and he broke it off with me. But he still wanted *you*." She pointed the knife towards me. "I wasn't going to let that happen." She resumed her cooking with an emotionless grin across her face. "I couldn't have who I loved, so neither could he. He knows you exist and hasn't even come looking for you. So, what does that say about him?"

I walked very slowly over to her, though it felt like my knees could buckle at any moment. A force of anger, hurt—something took over me. I never truly wish ill on anyone, and would never want to physically hurt someone, but next thing I know I am grabbing her face in my hand, pinching her chin between my thumb and finger. I stared deep into her eyes while the skin beneath my grip turned whiter than her already fair complexion.

But I didn't care that I could be hurting her, I knew that vampires could heal themselves quickly. "I want nothing to do with you. You are not my mother. I am not your daughter. You got your wish, you no longer have a kid." I released her face from my grip, whipping her head back straight, and walked away from her.

Once the door shut behind me, I felt my chest close in and my legs turn numb, but I knew I had to get as far away as possible from her. I don't care what she wanted to say to me. I just knew that I had a million and one things that I *needed* to say to her.

I dragged my hands along the wall, my eyes blurry, and managed to find the top of the stairs. I centered myself in the doorframe. The music inside my mother's apartment turned on and I could hear her singing at the top of her lungs.

She felt no remorse. No shame. She now had a reason to celebrate. Her life's biggest secret had been revealed and she didn't even have to lift a finger or utter a word. That hard part was already done for her the moment I found that box. Just my luck, right?

I don't regret finding out the truth. I regret thinking I'd ever get a different version of my mother once I spoke to her about it. But I couldn't help but wonder if she would have ever been honest with me. Would she have come clean about not wanting me had I not run into her? Doubtful.

I always knew I was a thorn in her side by simply existing. But I factored in the stress of starting at a new law firm or trying to be a single mother. It was always more than that, though. And now I know. I'm glad that I know.

I ran down the stairs and out towards Sawyer who was leaning against the bed of his truck waiting for me. I fell into his arms, never wanting to leave him. The looming blanket that my mother has had me under for all these years disintegrated the second I walked out the doors and into his arms.

Chapter 35

Lucy

I thought that that was going to be a lot more difficult for me. Not only to have seen my mother for the first time in years but to finally close that door on our relationship for good. Fittingly, I've never felt more free and have shed very little tears since seeing her a week ago.

Kai sprinted around the cottage in a pantsuit, looking the polar opposite of their usual bootcut jeans and rolled-up sleeve tee shirts. No one was safe from their consistent bossiness all morning.

"Jet, can you please not track your muddy boots in here?" Kai rolled their eyes. Jet grumbled.

I walked over to Cherry and Mel. "What's with Kai fixating all of their stress on Jet today?" I whispered between the three of us.

From the moment everyone showed up to help today, the two of them have been neck in neck with one another. I couldn't tell if it was from the expected stress of the day, if Jet was pushing buttons just for the hell of it, or what... but it was killing the mood. I was supposed to be pumped and hyped up. This was a big-girl type of day, the cottage is up for sale, and I needed everyone to act their age.

"Because Jet probably deserves it," Cherry pursed her lips.

"It's nothing. They tried to date last year and it got too complicated, so there's always been this awkwardness about them. You get used to it. Sometimes it's funny to see how long Jet will put up with it before he bites back," Mel explains.

The three of us laughed, then dispersed to our stations and responsibilities delegated by none other than Kai. I stopped in the hallway at my grandmother's unfinished painting. This painting belonged in the house even if I felt like I didn't any longer.

I felt a soft graze to my lower back with a hard growl to accompany it. "Hello, my Pretty Girl."

"I *am* yours, aren't I?"

I'm getting ready to say goodbye to a very big part of my life just to enter *another* different part of life. And I get to do it with a group of amazing people. I thought I'd be sad today, I suppose there is a dose of ache in my heart, but I'm also happy. I'm so fucking happy.

He spun me around and picked me up, my legs molding around his body.

"You can if you want to be?" he said as he slowly released me.

I looked around to make sure no one was around before I threw my arms around his neck to kiss him. It wasn't that I didn't want people to know about us, I just wanted it to remain "ours" for a little while longer.

"Alright, everybody!" Kai yelled out from the living room. We huddled around them. "I've never been able to get a sale on the same day of an open house, so please... be on your best behavior, and let's sell Lucy's cottage!" Kai walked over to the front door and opened it up, welcoming in the few people already waiting outside for the viewing.

Their words stung me more than I would have expected.

Selling the cottage has always been the plan. But now this seemed like yet *another* plan of mine with lines that are blurring.

"I have fresh cookies!" was sung from the front door. Standing at the threshold was Leanne and Gus with a tray of chocolate chip cookies, the smell filled the house immediately.

As they were finishing up shaking hands and hugging some of the staff from Bird's Nest, I was already skipping down the hallway to meet them.

"Well, we can't have an open house without fresh cookies! They look delicious," I said.

"Yeah, they do," Mel says as she hikes up the front steps behind them. She reaches for one, but they slap her hand away with a laugh. "Ow," she winced, dramatically shaking her hand.

"We left some for you back at the house, these are for prospective buyers," Gus let out a playful snarl, then kissed her on the cheek.

Mel squeezed by us with a couple of people trailing behind. Leanne followed after holding the tray of cookies but cut off into the kitchen.

Gus and I stepped off to the side as more people filtered in and out. We found our footing in a corner of the living room where a chaise lounge used to live. My mind burned with the memory of when I had fallen asleep on it on one of our game nights. That is until I woke to a roaring laugh from Gus.

My grandmother, Leanne, and Gus had put reruns of *Freaks and Geeks* on the TV after a grueling game of Yahtzee and they couldn't stop comparing their high school years to what was portrayed on the screen. I had dozed off—sometimes being the only kid around wasn't all it was cracked up to be when I had no clue what they were talking about.

"How are you doing, kiddo?"

I wish I could give him a straight answer.

What if I give the wrong response? I'll say I'm fine, but what if I'm not? Maybe I'll tell him I'm a mess, but I'm just trapped inside of my head. He'd know, either way, the truth.

I didn't know how to feel right now and I wish that someone could tell me. I needed Gus to tell me what to do, Sawyer, Leanne—I needed Tiffany. My grandmother always knew exactly what to say.

For the better part of the morning, I gnawed at my fingernails while people strolled through the rooms. They talked about how they liked the flooring or hated the wall colors and couldn't wait to change it once it was theirs. I had to hear it being talked about as if it was no longer mine.

"Excuse me," I said with a crack in my voice.

You will always do what you think is best, bud.

Gus' words from earlier in the summer rang through my ears. Man, what a lifetime ago that was. What if I don't know what's best? What if there was no one way to go about this?

Thankfully, everyone had migrated into the kitchen where the desserts stole the show so I could be in the backyard alone. I sat in Tuck's chair, faced Tiffany's, and thought about everything I wished I could say to her.

"I'm sorry if this isn't what you would have wanted," I started while biting back tears. The ripples of the creek off to the side are grounding. "I've always wanted to do right by you. I wish I'd spent more time over the last eight years talking to you. I still have your number in my phone, I should have called to talk to you on the phone. You wouldn't answer, but I know you'd be there, you'd listen. I should have never stopped sharing my feelings with you just because you decided to dance with the stars. Missing you comes in waves, but I need my grandma all the same. That will never change."

Then I realized I wasn't just asking for guidance on what to do today. This was a talk I needed to have with her, as someone who depended on the constant force of security and comfort she always brought to my life.

After she passed, the only consistency I knew of was knowing she wouldn't come back home and finish her painting, make me another cup of coffee, play her favorite vinyl, or knit me a new scarf. After she passed, any guidance I had in life was purely instinctual.

And this summer has taught me just how scrambled everything has gotten. My mind turned to mush and I've grown the most uncertain about what I'm getting out of life than I ever have before.

"I hope you turned a blind eye when I was out of contact with Gus and Leanne. I feel terrible about that. I saw you in her eyes and felt you in his hugs. It became too hard. But they've been my rock this summer. Then, of course, there's Sawyer. I'm sure you've seen him around the lake on your morning visits. Please tell me you still visit the lake even now. I don't even have to tell you about Sawyer, though. I know that you *know*."

I closed my eyes as the knot inside my stomach untied itself a little looser.

"And those letters. I want you to know that I'm not mad."

I barely got the last word out before I was clutching my chest. A hummingbird fluttered right in front of me. Inches away from the porch, it hovered at eye level.

I shot up from my seat and rushed to the door. I had to tug at it, it wouldn't budge. I tell myself I'll sand it down, that I'll replace the door in its entirety, but I knew that I wouldn't.

I swung it open and shouted down the hall, "I can't do this." Everyone shot their attention my way. They gripped their bottled waters and flyers, startled by my announcement.

These people, these extremely nice people that mean well, were walking the floors that I learned to walk on and in the kitchen where I baked pies with my grandmother and Leanne. They were making plans to make my home their home.

But the truth of the matter is the fourth cottage on the left will always be my home. All I've ever needed out of life could be found right here living along Hummingbird Lake.

"The house is no longer on the market, I apologize for any inconvenience this creates. I hope you all have a wonderful rest of your day."

I found Kai in the crowd, their mouth agape. Their cheeks were flushed. I felt terrible. I am not only making a fool out of myself, but I am connecting their name to this disaster.

I'm sorry, I mouthed in their direction before turning back on my heels. The most cathartic sob broke free from my chest, one I've been holding in since I returned in June, and I headed straight into the hillside.

Chapter 36

Sawyer

I was met with deafening chatter as I walked through the front door.

"What just happened?" I asked Mel as she frantically charged me, plummeting down the stairs.

"Where the hell have you been?" she said, a little hushed.

"And why do you have a hammer?" Cherry joined us a second later.

"I was fixing the mailbox, it was wobbly."

Mel took the hammer from my grip and placed it on the entry table. "Not the point," she said in a stern voice now. "Lucy backed out of the sale. She's gone. What I mean is she—"

I didn't let her finish her sentence before I pushed past the girls and down the hall. I swiveled my head back for a split second once I reached the back door and that's when I saw Gus giving me a single nod and a thumbs up.

I stomped down the porch steps, the wood paneling creaking under my boots as I moved down them. There's only one place she could be. I follow the imprinted footsteps that begin where the grass ends. My jog turned into a full-blown sprint as I hurried through the hillside—I wanted nothing more than to be beside Lucy.

My heavy soles are forced into the dampened soil, but the light at the end of the tunnel is reaching Lucy.

I came to a quick halt as I saw her perched up on the picnic table. The path of trees dispersed as I reached the hill beneath The Hideout. I had a clear shot of her. Lucy's knees were pulled to her chest and her face was buried into them. I slowly approached her, I observed her. Her body was still, so I don't think she was crying.

She's kicked off her white slip-on shoes—they're covered in leaves and dirt under the bench. Her toes wiggled, dancing to whatever beat she was humming to herself.

"Can I join?" I croaked out.

She turned her head toward me at the speed of light, and kicked her feet down in front of her, letting them hang off the edge.

She wiped away lingering tears on her cheeks and gave me a half smile.

"What were you singing just now?" I said as I climbed up on the picnic table.

"Oh, uh..." she spoke softly, "*Bad Reputation* by Joan Jett."

"Interesting. Didn't take you for a rock music fan."

The corners of her mouth creased and a faint smile crept across her face. Weaving her fingers into mine, she took my hand that I'd placed on her thigh. She rested her head against my upper shoulder.

"I'm here," I spoke into the top of her head before placing a kiss on the crown of her head.

"I know." Looking straight ahead, she focuses on the lake. "Kai must hate me right now," she said flatly.

"No one knows how to hate you."

She jumped down off the table with a sigh, slipped her shoes on, and enveloped her hand with mine. "Let's walk."

"I can't believe that on this very lake, I spent summers acting a fool. And you were over here, assumingly with your nose in a book. And we never crossed paths. But now I couldn't imagine a world that you were not a part of."

She looked up at the hillside, then pointed ahead at the cottage. "That's my home."

"I know, baby."

"I can't sell."

"I know, baby," I said again through a kiss on the side of her head.

"You added purpose to my life, Sawyer Banks." She stopped to face me, her back was parallel with the water. "I slowed down for the first time in years. You showed me the importance of stopping, of taking a break."

I narrowed my eyes on her. My heart ached for her. It took her twenty-six years to finally breathe, and while I am forever honored that I played a small part in making that happen, I wish it hadn't taken this long. She deserved more, she deserved everything she wanted.

"I'm scared that by pushing my residency aside, I won't have a plan for the first time in life."

"Maybe the new plan is to not have one?"

"Yeah, maybe," she said into the ground.

I pushed her hair behind her ear, she raised her attention back at me. I rubbed my thumb along her cheekbone. "What is it that you want right now, Lucy Collins? At this very moment? I will make it happen."

"First, I want you to kiss me."

I devoured her words with my kiss and did as I was told, pulling her firm against my body.

She pulled away in a haze. "Second, I want you to tell me you love me. Because I can confidently say, without a shadow of a doubt, that I love you so fucking much."

Her declaration made my head spin and my heart sink. All in the best way possible.

"I love you, I love you." I broke my praise up with kisses spread all around her face. She squirmed and squealed. "I love you, Lucy."

"Wait, wait. One more."

"What is the third thing I can give to you?"

The corners of her eyes creased and her nose crinkled. "I just really, really want..."

I raised my brows in anticipation. She curled her finger towards herself, enticing me closer. I dropped my ear to her mouth and she whispered, "I want a nice slice of key lime pie."

I barked out a laugh and flung her over my shoulder. I ran us back towards the cottage, dropping her on the steps of the porch once we reached the backyard.

All of the potential buyers had left, and Mel, Kai, Cherry, and Jet were in a half-circle under the overhang. They offered us a plastic cup of iced tea and I could see the tension leave Lucy's shoulders.

She furrowed her brows and pouted in Kai's direction, never once saying a word. Kai stood and took Lucy in their arms. Kai wasn't the type to hold grudges, and we were all aware of what this cottage meant to her. Even if it took her a little while longer to figure it out for herself.

I clapped my hands. "Alright, let's go."

The rest of the group stood.

"Where're we going?" Gus and Leanne emerged from the house.

Lucy skipped up the stairs to them and squealed as she threw herself in their arms.

Lucy wiggled in place and I led us back through the hillside. I took her under my arm and we all walked together toward The Hideout.

I was once told that Rider was a place for nobodies. But the people I loved lived here and they were somebodies to me.

Chapter 37

Lucy

Two Months Later

Spiced cider was now served at Jitters and Leanne had baked apple fritters and pumpkin muffins to keep in the dessert stands at The Hideout. I sure do love New England in the summer, but fall in Rider was a close second. The leaves were their vibrant red, orange, and yellow hues and they crunched under your foot. You couldn't beat it.

I couldn't believe it, but this has been the longest Gracie and I have gone without seeing each other since we met. We texted constantly and FaceTimed each other while we got ready for the day, but it wasn't the same. The last time I saw her, we were bawling our eyes out as I was climbing into a U-HAUL with Sawyer.

She flies in next week and I have already started planning a whole itinerary of all of the things we can do and places to see.

I thought she'd be a lot more pissed with me for leaving, considering she was going through a breakup—and has never lived alone—but she was jumping up and down when I broke the news.

She's a sucker for a good love story, and wouldn't shut up about how happy she was for me. Her parents were at our place to help pack up and send me on my way. I hugged them and thanked them across the board for all they had done for me.

"Sheesh, slow your roll. It's a small town," Sawyer exclaimed as he plucked the paper out from in front of me.

I swiped it from his hands, "I know. But the last time she was on the East Coast, she didn't get the chance to spend much time here. I want to make sure she gets the whole 'Rider' experience."

"She will. She'll be with you."

"*Aw,*" I said mockingly.

It's been an adjustment to share my days with someone else. Dating Sawyer, I was constantly reminded to also date myself. I became conscious about leaving space in my day to spend time alone. It took a while to find something I liked doing that didn't involve benefiting someone else, but I managed eventually.

"So," he said right above a whisper. His cheeks turned pink and his eyes widened.

"You're scaring me."

"No, no. It's nothing like that." He handed the paper back to me, but then walked over to the fridge. "Have you given it any thought about Christian's letters?"

We came to an understanding to not classify him as my dad. At least not yet. I wasn't ready for that.

I went back to writing, more like doodling, in the margins of my paper. Circle after circle, I was buying myself time.

He walked over to the counter and leaned against it. "I'm not trying to put pressure on you, by any means. I want you to do what you're comfortable with. But I also don't want you to feel like you can't do this if you think you might. I guess what I'm trying to say is I want you to know that I'm here for you. Whatever you need. Always."

I swung my legs to the side and faced him. They hung over the edge, and I kicked them against the siding of the bench like I used to when I was a kid.

I exhaled. "I know," I reassured him with a faint smile. "I think I'm going to wait. At least for right now. I don't want to jump into anything."

And that was that.

He flashed me a wink, then started to make some coffee while I went back to my list.

There was no shortage of changes, even when I thought I finally had my head screwed on straight. Something I couldn't quite change yet was my need to help people.

Old habits die young, and all of that.

I'm the newest member of the volunteer program at Hillside General, and shockingly, I'm loving it. I didn't think I'd be able to step foot in there again. But it's become a full circle moment. I put my residency off for a year, but only because I'm that much more passionate about my career, my future.

I wanted to make sure I was going to do it right. Whatever was going to happen next, I knew I didn't want to push Rider away to figure it out. I still get to help people here. If all goes well, I'll get an official placement for my internship.

I learned to enjoy the slower parts and smaller acts of life these days.

Weekly, Gus and I get together at our bench at the lake and we exchange books, give suggestions on new books to read, or simply read beside each other in silence. I go down to Jitters around the time Kai is getting off of work and chat over coffee. And when I'm up for it, I go into The Hideout and help Mel and Cherry out during a lunch rush.

I have yet to feel comfortable learning how to sling drinks behind the bar with Jet. One, because I am afraid to upset him if I make a mistake. And two, Sawyer promised to teach me himself. A fantasy of being taken right then and there on the bar, alcoholic paraphilia coming into play, was a fantasy that only he could fulfill.

"So, what are you up to today?" Sawyer slid in beside me in the breakfast nook, breaking my daydream of pouring tequila down his torso.

He passed a cup of coffee across the table before leaning over me to open the curtains. The curtain rings clanked as the panels were pushed to the side. The kitchen was instantly illuminated; the streams of sunshine reminded me why I loved this house so much. It felt warm, even when the heater was off.

"I gotta get through the last few chapters of the book Gus gave me. He's hounding me about this big action scene and I think he's upset I'm not there yet."

"You're not talking about the one he just gave you last week, are you?"

"I know, I'm moving at a snail speed. I don't know what's wrong with me."

He clicked his tongue at me. "You're ridiculous."

"What about you, Banks? Got any plans today?"

"Thinking about heading into the city. Holland is stressed over his speech on Monday, figured I could recite it back to him so he can listen to how it sounds from a different perspective."

"Smart tactic," I blew at the steam coming from my coffee and took a sip.

"But I could cut out early and put *you* on my schedule for the day."

I let out a snort. "You are such a guy," I said, then winked at him. "But you're my guy."

Sawyer hoisted me into his lap, and my butt knocks into the table, making our coffee overspill by the movement. Thankfully, it missed the handmade doilies that belonged to my grandmother that I sewn together to become a table runner.

I squealed as he positioned me in the perfect straddle. Our mouths laced into each other and the hazelnut creamer I have convinced him to start putting in his *boring*, black coffee stained his lips. We have kissed over a million times in the last couple of months, but this one was the softest of them all, the sweetest.

I could taste him, kiss him, and love him forever.

He grasped my hair and ever so slightly pulled my head off to the side. He began trailing a row of pecks down my neck that led into the center of my chest.

"I can hear your heart beating." He left another peck, this time over my heart. "I can feel it, too."

Sawyer removed his mouth from my chest and placed his hand over my heart instead. He locked eyes with me, and my cheeks became a sweltering temperature. What only lasted thirty seconds felt like an eternity.

The intensity of our eye contact was easily the most intimate exchange I have ever had wit another human.

I squeezed my eyes shut, tears form in the corners of my eyes. A few slipped out despite my best efforts to prevent them from escaping.

Sawyer wipes away a tear and cups my face in both of his hands, "Oh, baby. What's the matter?" he asks frantically.

I laugh through a faint sob, "Nothing."

"But you're crying."

"You've never cried from happiness before?"

He studied my face. "You are a form of art, a kind I could stare at forever."

"Do you remember the first night we spent together?" I ask with a shaky voice.

"I don't think I'll ever be able to forget it."

I playfully roll my eyes. "Psh, no. I mean, do you remember when I was tracing my fingers along you? Your back?"

He nodded.

"I wrote a single word."

He nodded again, a faint hum accompanied it.

"Love."

"I know."

"You know?" I perked up. "Why didn't you say anything?"

"I knew before you even wrote anything, I knew by the way you looked at me right before we fell asleep. I knew from the way my body burned with every touch of yours. I knew."

"I think it's so wild that my heart knew what it felt like to love you before my mind really did. Like I was taken over by a strong force of some sort. Now look at us..."

"Well, love is a pretty powerful force, my dear."

"Oh, sheesh. You are such a softie!"

He shrugged his shoulders. "What can I say?"

"Say that you'll marry me?" I blurted out in response.

His face went blank. He scanned my eyes, started laughing, then went back to an unreadable deadpan.

He lifted me off his lap and walked back over to the fridge. He pulled down an empty vase, reached his hand through the narrow opening, and pulled out a small, velvet box.

His devilish grin that I love so much appeared on his face as he pulled the lid back. "I had a whole day planned," he said into the ground as he walked towards me. "I was going to fill that vase with flowers, bring you down to the lake... I've been working on it for about a month now, but if I'm being honest I've been planning on marrying you since the first time you came into The Hideout and broke my jukebox almost six months ago." He lifted his gaze at me, I was a blubbering mess.

Tears, snot, puffiness all around—it was the least sexy thing ever. I let out a chuckle as he bent his knee.

"And don't think you're getting out of it now, either. It just means I'll have to propose to you for a second time." He knelt to the ground and held out the ring. Sawyer took my hand in his. "So, to answer your question my Pretty Girl, yes. I will marry you. A hundred times over. But I need to know...will you marry me? All you have to do is say that you will, say yes."

"Always."

He placed the emerald cut ring over my finger. We kissed and cried and laughed, and kissed some more. Billy ran into the kitchen at the sound of excitement. His dog tags jingled against his collar and he barked, adding to the commotion. The both of us crouched down to Billy's level but ultimately end up lying on the kitchen floor.

Rider was starting to feel at home again, and for once, I'm not itching for what could happen next.

All I know is I love this life for exactly how it is right now. It's the best.

About the Author

Elaine Richards resides on the east coast, but she will always be a California Girl at heart. Writing has always been a passion of hers and she hopes to do it for as long as life will let her. When she is not buried in a book or typing away at a new story, she enjoys sipping on an iced coffee while frolicking around a farmers market. Follow along on her author journey over on Instagram @authorelainerichards

Acknowledgements

To seven year old Elaine, thank you for deciding this is what you've wanted to do with your life. The love that I have always had for writing is out of this world.

To my son and daughter, thank you for showing me the importance of living out childhood dreams. I can't wait to watch you both grow up and find yours.

To my husband Chris, my biggest supporter, I wouldn't have been able to do this life without you. You're the most understanding and selfless person that I know and I am so lucky to love and be loved by you. You believe in me and my dreams, and I couldn't ask for anything better. You are my real life book boyfriend. You are my always!!!

To my aunt who raised me as her own, thank you contributing to my notebook hoarding addiction. Those dollar store spirals and composition notebooks were the start of it all. But most importantly thank you for being my first ever sounding board, being the first person I shared my writing with all those years ago. You always told me it's going to take a lot of work to become an author. And you were right. (Look, you have it in black and white proof that I said you were right!)

To the connections I've made on Instagram, thank you for being some of my favorite people ever.

To Cindy, I am so grateful to know you and have you be the "aunt" to all my book babies. You are always there to listen (and hype up!!) my ever changing ideas. You'll always have a spot in my book acknowledgments!

To Marina, Marja, Madison, my story grew to its full potential because of your suggestions in the early stages, and I appreciate the love and attention you've given my manuscript.

And to whoever decided to pick up this book written by an indie, debut author, thank you times infinity. You're making my dreams come true.

Coming Soon

Hummingbird Lake Series Book 2
(Mel & Gracie's story!)

Hummingbird Lake Series Book 3

Want an early look at Mel & Gracie's story?
Keep reading...

Chapter 1 — Mel

My ass sunk into the chair for the first time today. But straightaway, the door swung open. Relaxation, never heard of it.

"Oh, shit. I'm sorry," Jet, the night-only bartender, mumbled as he barged in. "I wasn't expecting for you to still be here."

Even though Jet refused to take any days off, and was very particular about how the bar runs, he often forgot that he did indeed need help during the lull between the day shift and nighttime. Making sure all systems go and there's nothing he would have to worry about while he's on shift alone was just my little way of showing him I was there if he needed me.

Jet would never admit it, and neither would I, but I was certain he knew that I lingered just to "keep an eye on everything." The way he had his quirks, I had mine, and I had the same need to be in charge.

"You're all good, I should be getting out of here anyway." I sprung up out of the chair almost as fast as I sat down. I squeezed beside him as he moved to the desk and the filing cabinets that were behind it. But the slapping down and vigorous flipping through of folders on the desk caught my attention enough to stay back.

I hesitantly retrieved my coat and bag from hanging behind the office door. "Everything okay over there?" But I wasn't too sure I wanted to know... There was a difference between "Work Stress Jet" and "Personal Life Stress Jet" and right now, the lines looked a little blurry.

His brows furrowed. "I think Beau gave us a couple extra cases of stouts..." He flipped open the folder that housed our invoices from our alcohol distributor and pulled out the one on top.

I slid my arms into my leather jacket and cuffed the sleeves only a quarter of a way up. I scoffed as I let his revelation hit me. "Wait, you're kidding? They're disgusting, for starters..." I seriously couldn't help but laugh. They were the worst drink ever—and that's saying something since I haven't tasted one in almost ten years. "Does anyone even order them?"

"My thoughts exactly." He pulled his phone out from his front pocket and started to tap away. He brought his device to his ear. "I'll see what's up."

"You're good, we will figure it out. We always do. It's probably just an honest mistake." I tried to reassure him; I hated it when Jet started to spiral, worried that he couldn't fix everything in front of him.

"No, it's my fault. I should have been there for delivery. It won't happen again."

"Jet," I grabbed his free hand. "I promise, it's okay. Just text or call me when you have any news. Or you can let me know when I see you tomorrow. Up to you. But hey, I really gotta get going. I'd stay and help, but I am just—"

"Go on, get. You've done more than enough, Mel Bells." He let out a sigh and started to twist his cuff bracelet around his wrist. The room was drop-dead silent, but I could hear his heart beating a mile a minute from the threshold where I stood.

I think he could feel me staring at him, doing that one last sweep of a check-in with him before I left because he lifted his head for only a moment and gave me a half smile and a nod.

It's been an adjustment, to say the least, with Sawyer and his fiancée, Lucy, doing all of their traveling or spending most of their weekends in New Haven. I am over the moon thrilled that he has reconciled with his grandfather, I just miss having him around.

And I miss having the extra set of hands.

It's been three years now since Sawyer Banks took over my grandparents' no-name restaurant and turned it into The Hideout, and only a little over a year since he made his big "debut" that he was the official owner.

Since then, it's been go, go, go.

It's a vast difference from when I was sixteen when I helped around whenever I came down for visits. Not only because that was almost fifteen years ago, but because of the polar opposite clientele that's been showing face.

With every month that has passed since the grand opening, I have seen more dyed hair, handlebar mustaches, and vintage motorcycles than I ever have in my life.

With just Cherry, our daytime server, Jet, and I working front of house most days... Well, I somehow feel responsible for when we all feel spent. But we love the game, the never-ending need to keep going.

I mean, that's what the service industry is for, right? For the people pleasers who get burnt out by repetitive schedules and day-to-day expectations.

It's because The Hideout is *our* hideout; the place we go when nowhere else is sufficient in letting us escape from the outside world.

"Hey, Mel?" Jet stopped me as I was about to shut the office door. I peeked my head back into the room and he flashed me a sympathetic look and curved up his mouth, attempting a smile when I knew it had to be forced. "We are going to get through this, you know..."

I let out a sigh. "I know."

And I did know that. Or I had to at least pretend to, right?

Even if I showed up early before a shift, or stayed late before Jet took over, I still felt like nothing would carry us out of the hole we had seemingly fallen into. But what was I to do? Convince myself, and the others, that it might be time to hire another person? Hire someone who was basically "replacing" Sawyer?

We have a system, a particular dynamic that works. Or I should say, *worked*.

My grandpa Gus was adamant about insisting he could travel down the short road from his cottage to help out on the days Sawyer was out of town, but that defeated the purpose of him retiring. I wanted him and my grandma, Leanne, to finally relax, and enjoy the family time they oh-so-deserved.

Granted, I was their only family here besides one another—the rest of the Dennings' have stayed put at the homestead up in Northern Connecticut since the nineties.

"Family is family" only when it was convenient for them. As for me, family was the one you created in your twenties. And that's what I've done here down in Rider, here at The Hideout, here amongst my fellow people pleasers.

So it's only understandable that adding a new person to the roster and bringing in a new hire was something I needed to sit on. Surely we could make this work, we could get through this. Jet said so.

***

Want to keep reading? Mel and Gracie's story is in the works! Can't wait to share more soon. <3